PROLOGUE

He did not look like a dying man. Dr. Theodore Elias made a dispassionate examination. Excellent muscle tone for a male, age fifty-three. Normal pulse, blood pressure in the low-normal range. Hands steady, no sign of tremor. Eyes clear, intelligent, penetrating. A near-perfect specimen of the middle-aged adult male. There was no evidence of physical imperfection, no outward sign of terminal disease. Yet there was no cause to doubt the diagnosis. He had seen the results of the ultrasound and the CT scan. And the exploratory surgery had been conclusive. Within six to eight weeks, this body would die of carcinoma of the pancreas. First the jaundice would appear, then increasing pain and physical weakness. There were drugs to control the pain, but death was inevitable. And when the body was wasted and useless, the mind would continue to function, the fine analytical mind that was the source of his pride. Dr. Theodore Elias would be fully capable of monitoring and cataloging his own demise until the very end.

His steps did not falter as he crossed the tasteful gray carpet and took his customary place behind his large polished desk. He could not afford the luxury of self-pity, not when there were decisions to be made. He had to think of his profession, of his duties to his patients. Something would have to be done with his group immediately.

Dr. Elias's eyebrows met in an impatient frown. This cancer could not have come at a worse time. Progress in his only current group was exasperatingly slow and it was the holiday season, a time when depression deepened and suicidal tendencies became severe. It was a time ripe for crisis. His eight patients, the last of his toughest cases, brought together over the years, were presently under control, but they would need help to get through the holidays.

The files were right where he had placed them after yesterday's session. Dr. Elias lifted the bulky stack and weighed it in his hands. So much paperwork, so much effort, and his patients were still far from the cure he had promised to spend his remaining career trying to achieve. His colleagues called him a miracle worker. A cure rate of 83 percent was more than impressive. But it was no comfort when he knew he'd run out of time with his last eight dangerous patients.

It was possible these patients could maintain their equilibrium for a while, even in this perilous season. Dr. Elias forced himself to look on the bright side. His patients might take months to break down, even longer if he could refer them to the best therapists. But eventually they would crumple. It was only a matter of time. And without the proper help, each of them was capable of violence that could destroy innocent people.

Dr. Elias remembered the late-night discussions of his college days. They were held in cluttered, smoke-filled student apartments, fueled with jugs of cheap red

A LETTER FROM JOANNE FLUKE

When I graduated from college with a degree in psychology, I toyed with the idea of going on for an advanced degree and becoming a therapist. Then I considered the enormous responsibility I would be shouldering for my patients' mental health, and I reconsidered. What if I turned out to be a bad psychologist and I hurt my patients instead of helping them? What if I let my patients become dependent on me and suddenly, I was not there to help them?

This line of questioning led me to make an abrupt turnabout in my career path. I decided that since I now had a plot for a new suspense novel, I would remain a writer for at least as long as it took me to complete the manuscript for *Cold Judgment.*

Cold Judgment is a suspense novel featuring a clinical psychiatrist who is diagnosed with a terminal disease. Every one of his patients has a severe and dangerous affliction, but they are living borderline normal lives thanks to his treatment. How will they fare when their therapist is gone? Will they self-destruct, hurting themselves and others in the process?

I never did go on for that advanced degree in psychology. Perhaps that's a good thing. I know that I wouldn't want to be faced with a decision like the one that Dr. Elias was forced to make in *Cold Judgment*!

Books by Joanne Fluke

Hannah Swensen Mysteries

CHOCOLATE CHIP COOKIE MURDER
STRAWBERRY SHORTCAKE MURDER
BLUEBERRY MUFFIN MURDER
LEMON MERINGUE PIE MURDER
FUDGE CUPCAKE MURDER
SUGAR COOKIE MURDER
PEACH COBBLER MURDER
CHERRY CHEESECAKE MURDER
KEY LIME PIE MURDER
CANDY CANE MURDER
CARROT CAKE MURDER
CREAM PUFF MURDER
PLUM PUDDING MURDER
APPLE TURNOVER MURDER
DEVIL'S FOOD CAKE MURDER
GINGERBREAD COOKIE MURDER
CINNAMON ROLL MURDER
RED VELVET CUPCAKE MURDER
BLACKBERRY PIE MURDER
JOANNE FLUKE'S LAKE EDEN COOKBOOK

Suspense Novels

VIDEO KILL
WINTER CHILL
DEAD GIVEAWAY
THE OTHER CHILD
COLD JUDGMENT

Published by Kensington Publishing Corporation

COLD JUDGMENT

JOANNE FLUKE

KENSINGTON BOOKS are published by

Kensington Publishing Corp.
119 West 40th Street
New York, NY 10018

Previously published by Dell Publishing

ISBN-13: 978-0-7582-8975-9
ISBN-10: 0-7582-8975-8
First Kensington Mass Market Edition: November 2014

eISBN-13: 978-0-7582-8976-6
eISBN-10: 0-7582-8976-6
First Kensington Electronic Edition: November 2014

10 9 8 7 6 5 4 3 2 1

Printed in the United States of America

wine and accompanied by loud, idealistic arguments. One in particular came back to him in vivid detail. An animal trainer had spent his whole life training a brilliant but vicious dog that only he could control. When the trainer was told he was dying, he was faced with a decision. He could destroy the animal and annihilate his life's work or he could let the beast live and hope that another trainer could carry on with his project. No profound resolution had been reached that night. Undoubtedly a new group of students was debating the same question with no better results. Theoretical discussions were diverting in college, but real-life decisions were painful to reach. The guidelines set down by his profession were clear. He was obligated to refer his patients to other therapists and hope for the best.

CHAPTER 1

Snow swirled past the office windows high above the city. The white, glittering particles seemed to have a life of their own, whirling gracefully above the city streets. The beauty of a snowflake was brief. Soon it would spiral inevitably downward to the street below, to turn to muddy slush under the wheels of traffic.

Dr. Elias opened his desk drawer and pulled out the list of alternate therapists he had prepared. These were the best psychiatrists in Minneapolis. He had to trust that they were competent to handle his patients. It would be inconceivable for one therapist to take over his entire group. That was a job only he could handle. His patients would be upset, but the group would have to be disbanded. He was forced to refer them individually to eight different therapists.

He would tell them tomorrow and give them the names of their new therapists. Out with the old and in with the new. It was appropriate for the season, but Dr. Elias doubted his patients would appreciate the irony. There would be tears and panic, but he would be firm.

Tomorrow would be their last group meeting, and the last time they would see him alive.

He opened the first folder and read the neatly typed synopsis he had stapled inside. *Kay Atchinson, age forty-two, wife of Charles Atchinson, mayor of Minneapolis. Diagnosis: paranoid schizophrenia.*

A photo was clipped to the sheet of medical background. Kay was a pretty black woman dressed in an expensive, well-cut suit, hair carefully styled. Everything about Kay was careful, from her fashionable but not pretentious home on Lake Harriet to her studious, well-mannered children. In the fall of 1980 Kay had been under a lot of pressure, caught between a conservative political party and the radical black caucus. Charles had made public his plans to run for the Senate, and both Kay and Charles had anticipated the governor's endorsement. It had been a shock when the governor had backed out at the last minute. The time wasn't right, he'd stated. It would split the party. The governor was sorry, but he felt obligated to endorse a white candidate.

The night of the announcement Kay had put a gun in her purse. She'd planned to assassinate the governor. He was a racist, just as the black caucus claimed. Luckily Kay had been intercepted by Charles, who'd managed to keep the news from the press. After his wife had had two months of unsuccessful therapy in another state, Charles had called in Dr. Elias. Now, after over four years of therapy, Kay was functioning well as the mayor's wife. Dr. Elias had successfully sublimated her hostility, but if the defense mechanism failed, Kay could be dangerous.

Dr. Elias selected a therapist for Kay and wrote a referral. The new psychiatrist might help Kay maintain a cloak of normalcy. Of course, no one but Dr. Elias could cure her.

The next folder was thicker. It contained years of notes. *Greg Davenport, age twenty-three. Single. Diagnosis: pyromania.*

Greg had not smiled for the camera. His elbow was propped on a table and his chin rested on his hand. A handsome young man with dark, intense eyes. Greg had the world by the tail, as far as anyone knew. His inheritance was considerable, and now Greg was making a name for himself as a songwriter. No one knew much about Greg's childhood, no one but Dr. Elias. And certainly no one but Dr. Elias knew that Greg had set the fire that had killed his father.

Dr. Elias remembered the day, eleven years ago, when the trustees of the Davenport estate had called him in to examine Greg. The boy had been twelve years old, his slight frame making a barely discernible bulge under the maroon hospital blankets. His face had been pale, eyes turned inward, seeming not to notice Dr. Elias at all as he'd conducted the examination. Greg had been catatonic, unable to move or speak. He'd been like that since the night his father had died.

After long months of treatment, Greg had finally broken his silence with a tortured confession. He had set the fire in a desperate bid for attention. He'd been lonely after his mother's death, and his father had been more interested in women and wild parties than he'd been in Greg. The boy hadn't realized the small fire would spread so quickly, and he'd been horrified at what he had done.

As Greg's therapy had progressed, Dr. Elias had discovered he was dealing with a classic pyromaniac.

Fire excited Greg. It made him feel powerful and compensated for his low self-esteem. Now, after eleven years of therapy, Greg's pyromania was under control. Dr. Elias had taught him socially acceptable ways to satisfy his need for power. But Greg was not cured. Under stress Greg could revert to setting fires that could kill anyone caught in their path.

Greg needed good maintenance therapy. Dr. Elias consulted his list and finally settled on a compassionate young doctor with the University Medical Facility. Now two of his patients were referred. Dr. Elias picked up the third folder and massaged the back of his neck as he read his notes.

Debra Fields, age thirty, widow of Steve Fields, newspaper correspondent. Diagnosis: postpartum depression, complicated by severe melancholia leading to a psychotic episode of kidnapping.

Debra faced the camera squarely, her classic features perfectly balanced. She was a beautiful woman who took pains to appear ordinary. Her short brown hair was cut in a no-nonsense style, large green eyes hidden behind tortoiseshell glasses. Her blouse was severely tailored, without lace or frills. Debra's femininity was masked by an aloof, professional exterior, but Dr. Elias knew it was fear that made her appear cold and unapproachable.

Four years ago, when he had first met her, Debra had been in restraints, screaming for her baby. She had totally lost contact with reality. The shock of her husband's death on assignment in El Salvador had sent Debra into premature labor. The baby had survived for a month, but then died suddenly in the night. Driven frantic by her grief, Debra had kidnapped another baby from the hospital nursery and fled in a cab to the airport. When the authorities had found her, she'd insisted she was taking her baby to her husband in El Salvador. The infant Debra had abducted was unharmed and the parents did not press charges. After Debra had received several weeks of unsuccessful therapy at the hospital, Dr. Elias had been called in by her employer, the *Minneapolis Tribune*. Since Debra's husband had been on assignment for the *Tribune* when he was killed, and because of her own employment by the *Tribune*, the newspaper had assumed the responsibility for her medical bills.

It had taken six months of intensive therapy to bring Debra back to her empty reality. After a year she'd been able to return to her work as a photojournalist. Dr. Elias used a process of substitution in Debra's therapy. A doll took the place of her baby; whenever Debra felt anxious, she rocked and cuddled her placebo. Even though Debra was performing well at work, her personal life was a void. She was afraid of social contact, afraid to get involved with anyone on a personal level. Unless she continued her therapy, Debra's depression could deepen and trigger another psychotic episode.

The list of therapists that had seemed so inexhaustible held only one option for Debra. The Psychiatric Institute had a pilot program for parents who had lost their children. Dr. Elias wrote the referral and moved to the next file.

The next case was critical. Dr. Elias read over his notes and frowned. *Doug Sandall, age thirty-six, wife and children deceased. Diagnosis: suicidal depression.*

Doug's sandy hair and clear blue eyes gave him a boyish appearance. To his coworkers at MilStar, he appeared to be a conscientious pilot, never complaining about long back-to-back flights. Only Dr. Elias knew the fear and the compulsion that rode with Doug, thousands of feet above the ground. Six years ago Doug had flown his wife and small daughter to Detroit, to visit relatives. The plane had crashed in a sudden storm, killing Doug's family. Doug's friends said it was a miracle he wasn't injured, but Doug thought it was a curse. He still relived the accident in his dreams, agonizing over whether there was some way he could have avoided the tragedy. He had killed his family and he should have died with them.

Flying was Doug's life, and after a month of intensive therapy, Dr. Elias decided it was safe to let him return to work. Now Doug had five years seniority at MilStar Corporation and a reputation as a dependable, dedicated pilot. Only Dr. Elias knew that Doug needed continual therapy to keep his suicidal tendencies under control.

The Swiss clock on the bookshelf chimed the hour softly as Dr. Elias completed Doug's file. He pushed back his leather chair and got stiffly to his feet. There was a dull pain in his abdomen, which he decided to ignore. If he took the powerful analgesic now, he would not be alert enough to finish his referrals.

With slow, careful steps, Dr. Elias crossed to the window. The pain diminished a bit as he stood looking out at the city. From his penthouse apartment, he had a view of the entire downtown area. Lights gleamed from the offices in the Foshay Tower and the surrounding buildings. The copper dome of the Basilica of St. Mary stood stark and solid against the darkening sky. A plane flew high above the skyline in the wide flight pattern that would take it to Wold-Chamberlain

Airport, midway between Minneapolis and St. Paul. And far off in the distance he could see the strings of headlights on the freeways that encircled the Twin Cities. It was the Wednesday before Thanksgiving and traffic was heavy. People were leaving work early to avoid the rush. The grocery stores would be packed tonight. Turkeys and cranberries would be in short supply. Tomorrow was the traditional day of celebration and feasting, and on Friday the downtown area would be crowded with Christmas shoppers. The Friday after Thanksgiving was the heaviest shopping day of the year.

Softly falling snow covered the grimy streets with a frozen blanket of white, and the traffic slowed on Marquette Avenue below. The double glass window was cold to the touch as Dr. Elias watched in the gathering gloom. The temperature would be in the low twenties tonight. In a few weeks the mercury would drop to the below-zero figures hardy Minnesotans had learned to endure. This was the last winter he would see. Suddenly the icy streets with their early Christmas decorations seemed oddly dear to him.

This year Christmas fell on a Tuesday. A bitter smile crossed Dr. Elias's face. Celebrating a holiday on a weekday had always made him feel vaguely guilty. The week was for working, and Christmas was an excuse for a lot of commercial nonsense. This year he was spared his guilt. His work was nearly over. By Christmas his patients would be resigned to life without him.

Two men in parkas and moon boots were putting the finishing touches on the strings of lights that decorated the roof of the Northwestern National Bank Building. Cables of bulbs were anchored to a huge circle on the roof and met at the top of a pole, thirty feet high. Dr. Elias saw the workmen step back and signal to someone below. A moment later there was a blaze of multicolor brilliance as the switch was thrown and a mammoth Christmas tree appeared against the night sky.

This would be his last Christmas, if he lived long enough to see it. The holiday was less than five weeks away. Chef Leon Lossing of the Orion Room was preparing a special holiday dinner for him, and Dr. Elias had been looking forward to it. Wild rice soup, lobster and sweetbreads with raspberry sauce, and black velvet torte for dessert. Dr. Elias smiled in anticipation.

It was convenient to have a fine restaurant in the same building. Every evening, at precisely five thirty, Jacques delivered and served his meal. Wednesday's menu was rack of lamb boulangère. Dr. Elias reminded himself to open a bottle of Château Margaux 1974 to complement the lamb.

Jacques had the perfect blend of deference and efficiency that Dr. Elias expected in a waiter. He would prepare Jacques's envelope with his yearly gratuity in advance this year, just in case.

On his way back to the desk, Dr. Elias turned on his favorite music. Gustav Mahler's Ninth Symphony would help him to concentrate. Mahler understood his anguish. He was a kindred soul. Mahler, too, knew torture and disappointment in his search for excellence.

There were four folders left. Dr. Elias flipped open the top file and stared at the photograph. The man's face was tanned and healthy—brown eyes, hair thinning slightly on top. His most striking characteristic was a wide smile that displayed a full set of perfect white teeth.

Jerry Feldman, age forty-four, married, no children. Diagnosis: sexual aberration—child molester.

Jerry was a successful dentist specializing in cosmetic reconstruction. He claimed that he had worked on every one of the city's leading newscasters. It was an in-joke. All the dentists in town knew they could switch to any channel to see Jerry's handiwork.

His wife, Dotty, was a typical midwestern woman, warm-hearted and eager for a house full of children. Jerry hadn't told her about his vasectomy. And Dotty knew nothing about Jerry's darker secret.

Jerry's trouble had started early in his marriage. In 1979, he'd come to Dr. Elias after he'd nearly raped a ten-year-old girl. After six years of therapy, Jerry still was not cured, but he had learned to avoid situations that put him into contact with young girls.

In two weeks, Jerry would face a crisis. His ten-year-old niece, Betsy, was coming to stay with him over the Christmas holidays. Dr. Elias knew he had to find a good therapist to help Jerry deal with his niece. Without help, Betsy could be in real danger from her uncle.

The light in the room was fading rapidly. Dr. Elias switched on the Tiffany desk lamp and wrote a short letter of referral for Jerry. The golden circle of light illuminated the next file as he opened it, hitting the photograph like a spotlight. It was appropriate. Nora Stanford was an actress.

Nora Stanford, age thirty-six (actually forty-six), single. Diagnosis: thanatophobia leading to episodes of psychotic aggression.

Nora was a classic beauty with high cheekbones and a mass of shining blond hair swept back from her marvelously mobile face. She had refused to pose for a snapshot and had insisted that Dr. Elias use one of her publicity pictures, heavily retouched to make her appear younger.

Ten years ago Nora had viciously attacked the young ingenue who'd replaced her in *The Debutante*. The young actress had been hospitalized and Nora had been referred to Dr. Elias by the court. She was a brilliant actress driven by her talent, desperately afraid of growing old and not being able to perform. Dr. Elias had discovered that Nora had other problems in addition to her fear of dying. She was terrified of her attraction to other women. Once Nora had accepted her lesbian tendencies, her therapy had progressed. She'd found a compassionate lover and opened a theater workshop within walking distance of the Guthrie. There were no more aggressive incidents, but Dr. Elias knew that Nora's jealous rages were barely under control. She needed constant therapy to keep from becoming violent again.

After he had chosen a therapist for Nora, Dr. Elias reached for his eel-skin tobacco pouch. He selected his favorite pipe from the rack, a handmade natural briar crafted by Ed Kolpin, founder of the Tinder Box. Every month he received a package of his personal blend of tobacco from the original store in Santa Monica. Several years ago Dr. Elias had voluntarily cut down on his smoking. Now that precaution seemed ridiculous. His smile was bitter as he lit the pipe and tamped it with the gold tool a former patient had given him. There was no reason to deny himself any of life's pleasures now. There was little enough time to enjoy them.

There were only two more patients to refer and he would be finished. Dr. Elias opened the next file. *Father*

Vincent Marx, age fifty-one, single. Diagnosis: violent schizophrenia.

Father Marx prided himself on being a modern priest. In the photo he was dressed in a blue-striped polo shirt and chinos. Only the small gold cross that he wore around his neck was an indication of his profession. Father Marx was streetwise. He knew all the current street slang and used it in everyday conversation. That made him especially effective in his church on lower Hennepin, relating to broken families and rebellious teenagers.

There was only one area in which Father Marx was not a regular guy. He hated prostitution and everything it represented. When he was forced to confront blatant sex, he turned into a religious zealot.

Father Marx had found Dr. Elias on his own, five years ago. No one, including the church, knew about his problem. A prostitute had propositioned him on the street, and Father Marx had assaulted and nearly killed her because she'd reminded him of his mother.

Father Vincent Marx was the illegitimate son of a prostitute. When he'd been barely old enough to walk, he'd been punished for trying to climb into his mother's bed. After that incident he'd been locked in a closet every night so he could not interfere with his mother's business. As soon as he'd been old enough to rebel, Vincent had run away. A kindly priest had found him and persuaded his mother to sign relinquishment papers. Vincent had grown up in a Catholic orphanage and had entered the priesthood out of gratitude.

The hatred was still there, but with Dr. Elias's help, the violent emotion was kept under control. Father Marx was now able to counsel his parishioners regarding sexual matters even though, in his heart, he still felt sex was dirty and wrong. If he suffered a setback, his hatred could erupt into violence again. Under the right circumstances, Father Marx was perfectly capable of cold-blooded murder.

Dr. Elias wrote a referral for Father Marx and turned to the file of his remaining patient. *Richard "Mac" Macklin, age thirty-four, divorced. Diagnosis: severe guilt complex resulting in impotence.*

Kind blue eyes looked out from the photograph. Mac had an engaging face, one that inspired immediate trust. Laugh lines crinkled the corners of his mouth, and his curly red hair was charmingly unruly. The only evidence of the deep problems that plagued him was the permanent dark circles under his eyes.

Mac had been a detective on the Minneapolis police force when the incident had occurred, five years ago. Several attacks had been made on police officers in the preceding week, and Mac had been wary when he'd answered the call to a tenement on Lake Street. Two armed suspects had been spotted there. Mac's partner had gone up the fire escape. Mac had taken the door. The apartment had been dark and the hall light out. Mac had overreacted when he'd seen the shadow of the gun. He'd fired, killing a twelve-year-old boy. The gun had been a toy. The boy had been playing a very real game of cops and robbers.

Naturally the press had had a field day, even though Mac was cleared by the department. There had been hate letters and anonymous phone calls in the middle of the night. Somehow Mac had managed to ignore the people who'd called him a kid killer, but the pressure had taken its toll. After the shooting, Mac had found he was impotent. At first Mac's wife had been understanding, but as time passed she'd become dissatisfied with the marriage. Six months later she'd filed for divorce. Mac had suffered a breakdown and been hospitalized.

The police department carried excellent insurance, and Dr. Elias had been called in. After a year's leave of absence, Mac had returned to the force. His crisis was over, but even with Dr. Elias's encouragement, Mac refused to put his potency to the test. He was terribly lonely, but he felt it was better to avoid women than to risk failure.

After several months at work Mac's impotence had taken on a new complication, one that affected his career. His service revolver, an obvious phallic symbol, became the source of his anxiety. Dr. Elias knew the risks involved with a cop who could not use his gun. At any time a situation could occur where Mac would have to shoot to save a fellow officer's life. It would be a murder by omission if he could not fire.

There was only one practical way to deal with the problem. Mac had studied nights and received his promotion to detective. Now the probability of his having to use his gun was greatly diminished. Both Mac and Dr. Elias were relieved.

Dr. Elias finished Mac's referral and stretched wearily. Technically, these eight patients were no longer his responsibility, but he was unable to relinquish the final thread that bound him to his group. He would ask for progress reports from the new therapists. It was only right that he follow his patients as long as he could.

Fifteen minutes remained before his dinner arrived. Dr. Elias uncorked the wine and poured a glass to let it breathe. Then he unlocked the door that led to his art gallery.

The long, narrow hallway was filled with portraits he had painted, one for every patient he had cured. Dr. Elias walked slowly to the very end, glorying in his successes. The portraits were the work of a talented amateur. Once he had wanted to be an artist, but he'd felt compelled to continue his father's work in medicine. His therapy work was his art. He took disorganized psychic material and transformed it into human masterpieces. These portraits were glorious testimonies to his talent as a psychiatrist.

His studio was at the end of the corridor. The outside walls were of glass, to let in the strong northern light. An easel was placed in the center of the large room. Resting on it was his only unfinished canvas.

It was a portrait of his group: Kay, Greg, Debra, Doug, Jerry, Nora, Father Marx, and Mac. They were seated in a half circle around the conference table in his office. The portrait was precise, correct to the smallest detail. Only the faces were unfinished, startling white ovals of blank canvas.

His fingers itched to take up the brush and finish the painting, but it was impossible. He could complete a canvas only when the case was resolved. Dr. Elias felt a stab of remorse as he gazed at his painting. It violated his sense of order to leave a project unfinished. If only he could find a way to close these cases.

CHAPTER 2

"Aw, Mom! I hate to go with Grandma!" Trish stood at the back door, hands on her hips. "I don't see why I have to get out of the house, just because you're having a meeting. I could stay in the den and watch a movie."

"It's not going to kill you to spend the afternoon with Grandma." Kay gave her daughter a stern glance. "She adores you."

"I know." Trish sighed extravagantly. "It's just so boring! I'm dying to hit the Walker to see DeBiaso's new film, but Grandma wants to go to the MIA for the Early American furniture show."

Poor Trish looked so perturbed. Kay couldn't help it. She started to laugh. The last DeBiaso film had been a documentary about a homosexual poet. It contained a nude shot of the man's buttocks. The furniture exhibition was a much safer choice. Charles's mother was easily shocked.

"I'll take you to the Walker tomorrow," Kay promised. "And I'll let you drive. Will that make you feel better?"

"Great, Mom!" Trish grinned, her good humor restored. "Can we go early? I want to see Aiken's installation, too."

Kay nodded. A car horn sounded in the driveway and she gave Trish a quick kiss. "Hurry up now. If Grandma comes in and starts talking, I'll never get ready in time."

In just a few minutes the living room was ready. Kay arranged eight comfortable chairs in a circle and set a carafe of coffee on a nearby table. She wondered about pulling the drapes on the picture window. The view of Lake Harriet was lovely today, but it did make the room seem cold. Kay lit a fire in the fireplace and nodded. The room seemed much cozier now.

"You'd better pull those drapes." Charles came into the room frowning. "If the press finds out you're holding a therapy group here, I might as well quit."

"Of course, dear." Kay bit her lips as she closed the curtains. Their house was built on a half acre of land and set well back from the street. No one passing by could see in, but Charles was paranoid about the meeting this afternoon. She guessed she couldn't blame him. The mayor's wife in therapy would be a headline story.

"I'll pick up James after his karate class." Charles buttoned his coat and clamped his fur hat on his head. "Make sure to have them out of here by five, Kay. You told the kids it was a political meeting, didn't you?"

"Yes, Charles." Kay sighed wearily. Even though Charles had been understanding about this emergency meeting, she felt like a criminal. Five years of sneaking around to go to therapy and hiding her problems from the press had been a real strain.

Tears began to form in her eyes and Kay blinked them back. She had been crying a lot lately, since Dr. Elias was gone, and the new psychiatrist didn't seem to be helping.

It was almost a relief to find that she wasn't the only one who was upset. Doug had called two days ago. He didn't like his new therapist and he missed the group. It had been his idea to get together once more to talk about it.

Ralph, the children's Scottish terrier, whimpered at her feet. Kay reached down to pet him. James had named him when they'd brought him home from the pet store, six years ago. He'd said he wanted a dog who could bark his own name. Ralph licked Kay's hand and she tossed him a cookie from the plate on the table. Ralph was a great comfort, and he always seemed to sense when she was upset. He sat and listened when she talked to him and he loved her even if she was a little batty. Sometimes she felt closer to Ralph than she did to the rest of her family.

The front door slammed and Kay was alone. She set out the ashtrays and coffee cups. They should start to arrive any minute now. Everyone had promised to come.

The doorbell rang and Kay rushed to answer it. "Nora! I'm so glad to see you!" She hugged the actress tightly. "Come in and sit down. Help yourself to coffee."

As she helped Nora with her floor-length fur cape, Greg's Jaguar roared up the driveway. Father Marx was next, in a Yellow Cab, and then Debra, followed by Jerry. Doug and Mac came in together, and Kay blinked back happy tears as they all sat in a circle once more. She had missed them. It was so good to have the group together again!

"I asked Kay to have this meeting." Doug set down his coffee cup and clasped his hands together nervously. "I don't know how the rest of you feel, but I don't like my new doctor. It's not right without Dr. Elias."

"Adjustments take time." Greg lit a cigarette and watched the match burn down in the ashtray. "My doctor says it takes months to get used to someone new."

"I feel like I'm wasting my time." Debra stared down at the rug, her voice barely a whisper. She held her arms tightly against her chest and rocked slightly. "They put me in a group and all we do is act out roles. I don't think it's doing me any good."

Kay sat up straighter. She had doubts about her new therapist, too. "I'm getting along fine with my new doctor, but he's got a different approach. He spent the last three sessions trying to hypnotize me. Last Tuesday I got so relaxed I fell asleep."

Nora tossed her hair back and laughed. "My doctor's crazier than I am! He's trying to switch me back to men. I'm going along with it. It's so amusing!"

"My new therapist's Catholic!" Father Marx fingered his cross nervously. "I just don't trust him. He's one of those young converts who goes to Mass twice a week and confession every time he farts. You know the type. The man's so unbelievably devout, he might write a letter to the archdiocese telling them all about me."

"Jesus!" Mac whirled around as a log in the fireplace crackled. Then he grinned sheepishly. "It looks like we all have the same problem. We don't like our new therapists. What do you think we should do?"

"You should quit!"

Jerry laughed at the sudden silence. They were shocked and that made him laugh even louder. They were acting like a bunch of sheep, following their doctor's advice without question. At least he had the guts to take charge of his own life. He supposed he should explain things to them. They were his friends. Maybe he could help them be independent, too.

"Dr. Elias was the best shrink in town." Jerry smiled as the group nodded in agreement. "And if I can't have the best, I don't want any at all. I quit therapy because I refuse to go to a second-rate shrink. I never showed up for my first appointment."

"You didn't go at all?" Doug sounded shocked. "Isn't that dangerous?"

"I don't think so. I feel just fine. Never better."

Doug shook his head. "I don't have the nerve to do that. My therapist says I'm in crisis right now. He told me I should quit flying."

"That's crap, Doug!" Jerry's voice grew louder. "Don't let some idiot doctor bully you that way. Dr. Elias never told you to stop flying, did he? Tell your therapist where to stick it and do what you want."

"But what if he's right?" Doug's hand trembled and coffee sloshed over the rim of the cup.

"Christ!" Jerry made a disgusted face. "Five years at MilStar, Doug, and you've got a perfect safety record. If you were going to crash, you would have done it a long time ago!"

"Maybe you're right." Doug began to smile. "Thanks, Jerry."

"I don't know, Doug." Mac frowned. "Maybe you ought to lay off flying for a week or so. Just to be on the safe side."

"You've got some vacation time coming, don't you, Doug?" Greg looked thoughtful. "It wouldn't hurt to take it now, just in case."

"Bullshit!" Jerry jumped to his feet. "I can't believe you guys! You're supposed to stick up for Doug!"

"We're not taking sides, Jerry." Kay tried to make peace. "We love Doug and we want him to be safe. If he has any doubts about his flying at all . . ."

"He doesn't!" Jerry's face turned red. "His doctor's

just wrong, that's all. Doug should keep right on flying and prove his doctor's an asshole!"

"Don't fight!" Tears began to course down Debra's cheeks. "I can't stand it when people fight! I just can't stand it!"

She gripped her hands tightly together and dug her nails into her palms. Mac looked over and his eyes widened. Debra's hands were bleeding.

"Hey, it's all right, Debra." Mac got out his handkerchief and wrapped it around her hands. "Just calm down. Everything's fine. We're not really fighting."

There was a sudden silence in the room. Debra's outburst had rattled them all. Even Jerry looked ashamed.

Mac looked up to find everyone watching him. He shook his head and sighed. "We've got to keep this orderly if we're going to do any good at all. We're all having problems, now that Dr. Elias is gone. We have to pull together here to try to make some sense of it all. No one is happy with their new therapist. Is that right?"

There were murmurs of assent and nods. Mac went on.

"I have a suggestion that might work. We'll keep on with our new doctors unless we feel they're doing us more harm than good. You have to make your own decision on that. And we'll meet together once a week, just for moral support. How does that sound?"

"It's a good idea." Father Marx nodded. "I was lonely without the group. Actually it'll probably do more good than going to that psychiatric mackerel-snapper that Dr. Elias recommended."

"We can meet here next week." Kay spoke up quickly. She had the largest house and it was located conveniently. Charles would just have to swallow his objections and realize how important these group meetings were.

* * *

Doug was going to do it. He threw his flight bag on the passenger seat and started the car. Jerry was right. He was practically cured. Nothing bad would happen if he took the flight to Dallas tonight.

The local news was on the car radio. Fifty families in White Bear Lake were without power, and a wrong-way driver on the ring road at the airport had managed to exit before any accidents occurred. Doug only half listened until the third story started.

"A local man died of self-inflicted gunshot wounds after his wife and two children were killed in an auto accident last Tuesday. Franklin Waters, thirty-six, left a note saying he didn't want to live without his family."

Doug pulled off the freeway at the nearest exit. His hands were shaking so hard, it was impossible to drive. He had felt that very same way after Barbara and Janie had died. Life hadn't seemed worth living without them. He had tried to kill himself twice, but each time he had failed. At least poor Franklin Waters was at peace now.

Not a day went by that he didn't wish for death. Doug shuddered as the realization hit him. Perhaps his doctor was right, after all. He'd better cancel his flight tonight.

Determined to do the right thing, Doug placed the call. What he learned wasn't good. The relief pilot was out with a winter cold. He had to take the flight tonight.

Twenty minutes later, Doug drove up in front of the MilStar terminal. Employees called out greetings, but his smile was forced. Only one question ran through his mind as he checked the passenger list and filed his flight plans. Was his doctor right?

The fear left him as he strapped himself into the cockpit. He smiled. It was going to be all right. He was confident again. Everything would be just fine. Doug didn't understand it, but it seemed the simple ritual of buckling himself in had put everything in perspective.

The roar of the engines made him laugh out loud as he taxied down the runway. There was no danger of crashing tonight. He felt calm, in perfect control, happier than he had ever been before. Jerry was right. Just as soon as Doug landed in Dallas, he'd call Jerry and tell him. Doug knew he was cured! And his new doctor had almost cheated him of this moment, the exhilaration of liftoff, the freedom of flight.

CHAPTER 3

Only three more to go. Dr. Elias resisted the urge to give up on his morning exercises. Surely he could do three more push-ups. He had followed a rigid program of exercise every morning for the past forty years. As a young man he had done sixty push-ups without strain. Now the twenty he had assigned himself were taxing his strength to the limit.

Slowly, painfully, he forced his body to obey. There was comfort in his daily regimen. He had to stay in shape. Dr. Elias was not ready to give up the fight yet. He would follow his normal routine until the very end.

Eighteen! He raised his body up from the mat with arms that trembled. In the walls of the mirrored exercise room his face looked haggard. The kindly, distinguished father figure was gone, replaced by the reflection of a tortured man. The disease was taking its toll. Now furrows of pain were permanently etched in his broad forehead beneath his styled silver hair. His eyes were deep wells of anguish. Two more. He could do it.

Nineteen! Where was the sense of inner peace that most victims of terminal illness claimed to experience?

He had drawn up his will and put his affairs in order, but still there was no sense of calm acceptance. Instead, Dr. Elias's lips twisted in a grimace of frustration. How could he be at peace? He had not finished his work.

Twenty! He let his tired body fall against the mat to rest for a moment. His group was at fault. Officially they were no longer his patients. He had assigned them elsewhere, washed his hands of their problems and their fears. But Dr. Elias knew he could never let go. They were his. And he would not rest easy until he had provided for each one of them.

The pain made him gasp as he pulled himself to his feet. The ancient Greeks were right in their naming of *Karkinos*.The Crab. Cancer. There was a crab in his belly, gnawing at his vital organs. He could feel its sharp pincers ripping at his tender flesh. It was impossible to ignore the pain of being eaten alive. It could only be dulled by ever-increasing doses of powerful analgesics that clouded the mind and gave a false sense of euphoria.

A hot shower did not help to ease the pain. Dr. Elias bent nearly double as he made his way to the room he used as an office. He had prepared a syringe and it lay ready in the center desk drawer. He ached to plunge the needle into his vein, but there was work to do and his mind had to be clear. His hand was shaking as he closed the drawer firmly, the contents untouched.

His coffee was waiting for him, hot and strong, the espresso beans ground fresh in his expensive coffeemaker. One perfect croissant waited also, on the corner of his desk, delivered earlier by the French bakery in the IDS Center. He took a sip of pungent coffee and sighed deeply. Then a bite of the pastry, the thin layers flaking and dissolving in his mouth.

It was better. The pain had dulled of its own accord. Dr. Elias picked up the stack of reports that had come by messenger and began to read. A bitter smile appeared on his face as he paged through them. He was right about the new psychiatrists. They were unable to deal with his patients.

The reports were meticulous, as he had known they would be. The new therapists were adequate but uninspired. The spark of creativity that made great healers was not present.

Dr. Elias tried to be fair. He had not expected miracles. The new therapists did not have his advantage. He had been working with his patients for years and he knew them intimately. It was an easy matter for Dr. Elias to read between the lines. Every one of his patients was regressing, just as he had feared.

Greg was chain-smoking again. That observation was made in passing, but Dr. Elias alone realized its significance. The action of lighting cigarette after cigarette would soon give way to lighting other objects not socially acceptable.

Father Marx's therapist was hopeful. The priest seemed a little nervous, but that was to be expected in any new patient-doctor relationship. They had not discussed sex or prostitution. The new doctor intended to build up mutual trust before tackling the root of Father Marx's illness. That was a mistake. Father Marx needed to confront his problem constantly to defuse his violence.

Kay had wept under hypnosis. Her new therapist had noted that Kay's tears were cathartic. It was far from the truth. Kay's angry tears were fuel for her delusions. The cycle of hatred was starting again.

Nora's report was lengthy and detailed. She had spent

most of the session discussing a young student and her handsome boyfriend. She confessed she was jealous of their relationship. Assuming that she was taking an interest in men, her doctor decided to foster Nora's heterosexual involvement. Even though the new therapist was wrong, Dr. Elias could not fault his conclusions. Nora had been devious. She'd been playing a part for her new therapist. And Nora was a consummate actress.

Dr. Elias poured himself another cup of espresso and frowned. His group was not responding to the new therapists. How could they be helped if they refused to cooperate? He had referred them to the best psychiatrists in the city.

Mac's report was next. The new therapist stated that Mac was jumpy and ill at ease. That could be significant. Although Mac did not seem to be regressing as rapidly as the rest, Dr. Elias held little hope for his recovery. Mac would break down, too. It was only a matter of time.

Debra's therapist believed she was making progress. She had entered willingly into role-playing therapy. The report was brief, only a quarter of a page. There were no alarming observations. Dr. Elias shook his head wearily. He knew Debra didn't have the strength to carry on without him. Surely she was crumbling. The new therapist had been unobservant, but it was not his fault. Debra was an expert at hiding her true feelings.

Jerry's report consisted of a single line. He had not kept his initial appointment. Efforts to reach him by telephone had been fruitless. His therapist was still waiting for Jerry to return his call.

Dr. Elias glanced at his calendar and frowned. Jerry's niece was due to arrive on Sunday, the sixteenth. If

Jerry had not gone in for therapy by Saturday at the latest, he would have to take action.

Doug's therapist seemed to have things well in hand. Dr. Elias nodded as he read the report. Doug's depression was deepening, but young Dr. Wilkenson had recommended that he stop flying for the duration. Doug's therapy schedule was increased to three sessions a week. If Doug took his doctor's advice, he would be safe for a while longer.

There was a sound in the hallway, the clanging of pails and a cheerful exchange in Spanish. Dr. Elias stacked the reports neatly and put them into a file folder. The cleaning crew was leaving.

"*Hasta luego, Doctor.* Have a nice day!"

Dr. Elias smiled in spite of himself. The new cleaning crew was Chicano. They knew little English, but somehow they had picked up the most banal of clichés.

By the time he'd made his way to the living room, it was deserted. His cleaning crew had left. Wooden surfaces gleamed. Windows sparkled. His newspaper was neatly folded on the arm of his leather chair.

Dr. Elias frowned as he straightened a picture and repositioned his marble ashtray in the exact center of the end table. It was unreasonable to expect complete perfection. Actually the new cleaning crew was very competent.

The temperature was in the low teens today. Dr. Elias stood at the huge window overlooking the bank building and watched the bank sign with its time and temperature flash on and off. The temperature was of no interest to him. His environment was thermostatically controlled at a constant seventy-six degrees, and he seldom left it. There was no reason to leave. It was a simple matter to pick up the telephone and order whatever he needed. There were six excellent restaurants within a four-block area. Dayton's department store delivered his espresso coffee beans and the cases of fine wine he ordered. His work was here, with his office and conference room directly across the hall. And if he occasionally felt like walking, the seventeen miles of climate-controlled connecting bridges between the buildings in the downtown area made winter clothing unnecessary.

The sun was bright today, glancing off the mirrored walls of the City Center building. Dr. Elias pulled the heavy drapes to block out the view. The patterns of traffic on the street below did not interest him. Women in fur coats, carrying parcels of Christmas presents, could not possibly identify with his agony.

It was nearly noon and time to choose his pipe for the day. In the early morning, with his espresso and croissant, he smoked imported Balkan Sobranie cigarettes. Choosing a pipe for the afternoon was habit, pleasure, and ritual. His glass-enclosed pipe rack was filled with over three hundred briars.

When things were going badly, he needed a pipe that would not disappoint him. Dr. Elias reached unhesitantly for his Peterson's bent. It was a big, solid, homely clunker of a pipe, but of all his briars it had never turned sour on him.

Dr. Elias sat down in his leather chair. He filled the Peterson's carefully and lit and tamped it. Then he opened his newspaper. There might be an article by Debra today.

The Social Security controversy was raging again. Dr. Elias read the lead story with some amusement. A couple in their seventies had refused to legalize their relationship, claiming they would lose a large share of their benefits. The grandchildren of both families were staging a demonstration against the ruling that forced their grandparents to "live in sin."

There was trouble in Lebanon again and another Mother's March for complete nuclear disarmament. And down at the bottom of the first page, tucked in a corner, was the account of a plane crash.

Dr. Elias read the article with a sense of dread. Doug's plane had gone down. There were no survivors. The Federal Aeronautics Board placed the blame on unusual weather conditions, but Dr. Elias knew the truth. Doug had taken the flight, despite Dr. Wilkenson's warning. And he had indulged his death wish, at last.

It was his fault! The paper slipped from Dr. Elias's hands. Doug would have listened to him. He would have refused to fly if Dr. Elias had warned him. Now Doug was dead and he had taken four innocent passengers with him.

Doug's crash was proof that the group could not function without Dr. Elias. They would break down, one by one, killing other innocent people in the process. Somehow he had to ensure that the rest of his group did not run amuck. He had a responsibility to protect society from his patients.

Dr. Elias felt his anger grow. Damn this disease that kept him from continuing his group's therapy! He was weak when he should be strong. Inwardly he raged at his own mortality. He could have cured them all, but there was no time.

His pipe was cold. The pleasure Dr. Elias took in the first pipe of the day was gone. He knocked it into the marble ashtray, not caring about the consequences. The dottle, the plug of wet and partially burned tobacco, should have been smoked completely to keep his good briar from souring, but Dr. Elias's mind was no longer on his smoking. The pain was back, sharper than before, and he clutched at it as he got to his feet and made his way to his studio.

Sunlight streamed in through the glass walls and highlighted his group portrait. The unpainted canvas ovals were naked and white. Dr. Elias stood in the center of the sunlight, feet planted slightly apart as he stared with unseeing eyes at his painting. His gaze was turned inward, remembering the beginnings, the first hesitant steps his group had taken toward recovery.

The room was warm. Beads of perspiration formed on his forehead and rolled down his face. He did not notice. Even the pain had ceased to exist. He was remembering, lost in the time when he had been omnipotent, omniscient, a god to his patients. He had controlled their destinies. He had given them life!

The room was so silent that the sound of muted conversation from the floor below was clearly audible. Dr. Elias was not listening. Other voices were echoing in his mind, the voices of the past, with Doug's among them. They filled his head with their pleading. He had to help them. He was the only one who knew how.

His mind shouted out for silence. They had no right to plague him with their piteous cries. He had tried to help them, but they'd refused to listen. They should have responded to their new therapists!

His hands began to tremble and he tightened them into fists. His anger was back in full force, and it spread to include his group. They were breaking down, one by one, and there was only one solution. He had nurtured and counseled them to the best of his ability. But now they were doomed.

Dr. Elias moved at last. He had come to a decision. His eyes were bright as he squeezed paint on the palette and took up his brush. Doug's case was closed. And when he finished Doug's portrait, he would deal with the others.

CHAPTER 4

"It was an accident!" Jerry set down his cup so hard the coffee sloshed out on Kay's rosewood table. "I know what you're thinking, but just forget it. Accidents happen all the time in those small planes. The paper said there were unusual weather conditions."

They faced him like a panel of accusers. Jerry had known this was coming when Mac had called the emergency meeting. He'd spent the whole night agonizing over Doug's accident, trying to convince himself that he was not to blame. And now he had to convince them.

"Stifle it, Jerry!" Nora's eyes were blazing. "We all know Doug crashed deliberately. And you're the one who told him to fly."

"You *did* talk him into flying, Jerry." Greg patted Nora's shoulder as she burst into tears. "We all thought he should cancel the flight the way his therapist suggested."

Jerry's face turned red and his hands shook. His eyes searched each face in the group for an ally. Surely they didn't all blame him. There had to be someone who was sympathetic.

Father Marx fingered his cross. His expression was kind, but that didn't count. Priests were supposed to be forgiving. It was their profession. Kay looked nervous as she mopped up the spilled coffee, and she made no move to come to his defense. Debra's eyes slid away as he tried to make contact with her. His friends and confidants were turning on him. They all blamed him for Doug's death, with one possible exception. Mac looked carefully neutral.

He met Mac's level gaze. The big Irishman was thinking. Jerry had always liked Mac. He was usually impartial and he never spoke unless he had considered his words carefully. Surely Mac would not condemn him!

"I can see you feel bad, Jerry." Mac spoke up at last. "We all do. And I know you didn't deliberately try to hurt Doug. Do you want to talk about it?"

Mac had turned on him, too! His statements were carefully couched in the proper psychoanalytic terms, but Mac blamed him as much as the rest. There was no use staying there. They all condemned him!

"There's nothing to talk about!" Jerry stood up and glared at them. "I've got a root canal scheduled for this afternoon, so you can have your stupid therapy without me. Trying to meet without Dr. Elias is crazy! You're all *meshuggenas*!"

He knew they were watching as he slammed out the door. The sidewalk was slippery and he had forgotten his boots in Kay's closet, but he wasn't about to go back. He'd never see any of them again. They were all sick, and he was the only one who had guts enough to get along without Dr. Elias.

Jerry didn't know why he was crying as he got on the freeway and drove toward downtown. They weren't worth it. Maybe the tears were for Doug. He had been a good buddy and the accident was a tragedy, but it *was* an accident. He had to keep on remembering that.

He got off at the Lyndale exit and turned onto Hennepin. He had to pick up a Christmas tree on the way back to the office. As he drove past the basilica, he had a crazy urge to turn in and confess his fears to a priest. He had seen *Going My Way* on television last night. Barry Fitzgerald was perfect as the Father-confessor, but real priests were probably more like Father Marx.

Jerry began to chuckle as the copper dome receded in his rearview mirror. His grandparents would spin in their graves if they knew he had been tempted to set foot in a Catholic church. They had been Orthodox Jews. Jerry had lived with them until he went away to school, and then he had shed his restrictive life gratefully. All those dietary laws and traditions were a bother. Now he was a confirmed atheist. Religion meant nothing to him.

The Christmas decorations were up along Hennepin. Giant six-pointed stars flanked by evergreen boughs hung from every light post. Jerry couldn't help it. He started to laugh again. Leave it to the goyim to use a Star of David for a Christmas decoration!

The Dayton building loomed on his right as he stopped for the light on Seventh Street. Each year Jerry and Dotty walked around the Dayton's block to see the animated displays. Last year the huge department store had done the Twelve Days of Christmas, one window for each scene. They would have to take Betsy with them this year.

Just the thought of his niece made Jerry's hands sweat inside his gloves. She had arrived last night, ten years old, with a sweet young body and a golden California tan. He kept Dotty by his side as a shield. Things would work out just fine as long as he was never alone with Betsy.

Cars were honking behind him. Jerry put his foot on the gas and his car jumped through the intersection. He could think about it later. Right now he had to pick up the Christmas tree and get back to the office.

"Dr. Feldman! You remembered!"

His receptionist smiled as he came through the door carrying the tree. Jerry supposed the girls would spend all afternoon decorating the damn thing. He still felt a twinge of guilt each time he passed the tree in his waiting room, but he had learned to live with it. Dotty even put up a tree at home.

"Mr. Jackson called, Dr. Feldman. He'll be a little late."

Jerry nodded and went to wash up. He hadn't done a root canal in years, but Herb Jackson was an old college friend. Cosmetic reconstruction was his specialty now.

When Herb arrived, red-faced from the cold, Jerry suffered through the hail-fellow-well-met routine. He put Herb on nitrous oxide as fast as he could and shot him up with plenty of Novocain. With Herb set up with two suction tubes and a tiny rubber dam in his mouth Jerry was safe from his corny jokes.

The root canal went off without a hitch. Herb got a huge kick out of the card Jerry gave him: *I'm not on drugs. I've just come from my dentist's office.* The cards were Dotty's invention, her Christmas gift to him last year. It was past four when Herb left, his face still stiff with Novocain.

At four-thirty the girls locked up and Jerry was

alone. He went to his office and reheated the last of the coffee. There was no work left to do, but he didn't want to go home yet. He was still too upset. Dotty would notice and he'd be tempted to break down and tell her about the group. Dotty had no idea he was in therapy. She had never guessed his carefully guarded secret.

There was a message on his desk. Dr. Pearson had called again. Jerry crumpled the pink sheet of paper into a ball and tossed it into his wastebasket. He refused to start up with a new shrink. His therapy had begun and ended with Dr. Elias. He was cured. Nothing bad would happen if he kept himself under tight control.

Even though he tried not to think about it, Jerry's mind slipped back to the girl and the awful secret that had sent him to Dr. Elias. Years later, he could still feel the sticky heat of that August night. Dotty had gone to visit her mother for a week. The apartment was lonely and stifling. The air-conditioning was broken. And Jerry was restless without his wife.

He needed some air. Jerry took the car out of the underground garage and zipped onto the freeway. He was wearing his oldest shorts and a thin shirt. The night air felt good on his body and he rolled down the windows all the way. He took an exit at random, Bass Lake Road. He'd never been out in that part of the suburbs before.

The streets were wide and lined with trees. In some places the branches almost met overhead. Old-fashioned lampposts stood on every corner. Their bulbs glowed softly. It was a stage setting of a small town, only fifteen minutes from the heart of the city.

There was a church, the old-fashioned kind with a bell tower and steeple, painted white. And a small corner drugstore, the kind he had only seen in movies.

As he turned the corner he could hear children laughing and splashing in the community swimming pool.

He pulled up and parked across the street. There was a breeze and the leaves rustled overhead. A rustic wooden sign told him this was Lawrence Park. Jerry got out to sit on a green slatted bench beneath a huge oak tree.

The lights at the pool across the street blinked three times. It was too dark to see his watch, but Jerry thought it must be about ten in the evening, obviously closing time. In a few minutes a group of boys passed him, carrying towels and wet bathing suits. They were laughing and friendly. One or two smiled at him as if they knew him.

Five minutes later, the lights went off at the pool. Now Jerry was alone again and he leaned back against the bench. The stars were bright and he heard the rustle of small animals in the park. A dog ran down the path, stopping to sniff at several bushes. It was so quiet and peaceful there that Jerry began to long for a house in the suburbs. Then he saw her.

She was lovely. A small blond girl, budding breasts hugged tightly by last year's swimsuit. She smiled at him, a complete stranger, in a very adult way. Jerry felt his heartbeat quicken. She took the path through the park, towel swinging lightly over her shoulder and just touching the rounded curve of her buttocks. She turned to look back at him once or twice. It was dark, but he was sure she was smiling.

Before he could think, he was following her into the heart of the park. It covered an extended city block, paths winding among huge trees and bushes. He could hear her footsteps on the path ahead, and the white towel she carried gleamed in the moonlight.

The lamppost in the center of the park was burned

out. Jerry watched as she stopped and trailed one slim hand in the fountain. Then she turned and looked in his direction. He was sure he saw her hand rise and beckon to him in the shadows. Could she be older than she looked?

Something seemed to snap inside him. All the dark urges surfaced and he was running. She was running, too, but that was only a game. She wanted him. Hadn't she deliberately beckoned to him in the darkness?

He caught her at the darkest spot in the park and wrestled her to the ground. Yes, she was playing at resisting. He could tell. His hand covered her mouth and she whipped her head from side to side, wet blond hair stinging against his fingers. Her skin was blazing with soft heat as he pulled down the top of her bathing suit and grasped her young breasts. As she squirmed and fought, he laughed, playing the game, taming her token resistance. She wanted him. It was her dream, her fantasy, and he would give it to her.

Hot and tight. He could not believe the power of her young muscles as he spread her legs. He was a match for her, his body hard and well-muscled from hours of tennis and racquetball. His fingers found her, explored her roughly, the way she wanted. She was so small and fierce beneath him. He threw himself on her, covering her completely.

As he lunged forward, his hand slipped from her mouth and she screamed. His mind cleared with the sudden shock. He looked down at her closely, without the cloud of his fantasy, and he knew the truth.

He ran and took the nightmare with him. How close he'd come! How terribly close to losing his wife, his career, his sanity.

Jerry had started with Dr. Elias the next day. He'd

paid the high therapy costs and never told anyone he was in the group. And everything had been fine until Betsy had arrived. Betsy, the same face, the same age as the girl in the park. What if he lost control and raped his own niece!

His coffee was cold. It was after five and Dotty didn't expect him home until nine-thirty or so. She approved of his rigid physical fitness program and she always had a light dinner waiting when he came in from the spa.

Jerry took out his running outfit and sighed. He didn't feel like jogging his usual six miles. He was still upset about the way the group had turned on him and he wanted to see Dotty. She had a knack for jollying him out of his bad moods. He put his Adidas back in the closet and locked up the office. Then he drove to his Lake Minnetonka home. He hadn't told Dotty he loved her in an awfully long time.

"Hi, Uncle Jerry!" Betsy was just coming down the stairs from her bath, wrapped in a fluffy towel. She ran to him and hugged him tightly.

"Hi, honey." Jerry kissed the top of her blond head and managed to disengage himself. "Where's Aunt Dotty?"

"Oh, she went out to get a pizza." Betsy watched as he sat down in his recliner chair and then hopped up in his lap. She reached over to get the remote control and turned on the console television. "What do you want to watch, Uncle Jerry?"

"The news, I guess." Jerry cleared his throat uncomfortably. He really wanted to tell Betsy to sit in another chair, but she was probably missing her parents and he didn't want to be abrupt with her.

"You smell like my daddy." Betsy giggled and squirmed on his lap. "That's Pierre Cardin aftershave, isn't it, Uncle Jerry? All the girls in my class think it's sexy."

Betsy moved to nuzzle his neck and Jerry noticed that one bare leg was completely exposed. He couldn't help but stare at it. Light blond hair glistened on her thigh. Jerry tried not to notice, but the towel was just tucked in on top and it was starting to come loose. He could see the budding swell of her small breasts. Even though he knew that his niece was not being deliberately provocative, it was all Jerry could do to hang on to his control as he put her down firmly and made a show of glancing at his watch.

"I'm going jogging, honey. Tell your Aunt Dotty to save a piece of pizza for me and I'll heat it in the microwave later. I'll be back as soon as I can."

He saw Betsy's face fall as he rushed out the door, but that couldn't be helped. He had to get away from her! His hands were shaking so hard he had trouble fitting the key in the ignition.

Jerry didn't relax until he was back on the freeway, heading toward downtown. He had thought that part of his life was over, but now it was happening again. All those years in therapy hadn't helped. For a moment he actually considered calling the new therapist, but that was ridiculous. If Dr. Elias hadn't cured him, no one could. He was better off with his own method of coping. He'd jog the full circuit and exercise until he was exhausted. And he wouldn't go home until Betsy was safely in bed for the night.

CHAPTER 5

"It looks like a church in here, Greggie!"

The girl giggled and Greg smiled back. She'd be all right if she stopped giggling like a teenager. She was at least twenty. He'd known right off that she had a great body under her punk clothes and she was more than willing to go home with him after the concert. Most girls played up to songwriters. And they all wanted a special song dedicated to them.

Greg lit another candle and placed it in the ring around the bed. It did look rather like the inside of a church, with all the votive candles in a circle. The girl thought it was kinky, and that was fine with him. She had been very eager to shed her clothes and play in the firelight.

"Do you want another glass of bubbly, Greggie?"

She ran one gold-tipped nail down the inside of his leg, and Greg nodded. It was easier than trying to remember her name. Sherry, Shelly, something like that. Her little-girl act was annoying, but he hadn't brought her up here for conversation. To be entirely honest, he hadn't been after sex, either. He'd just needed companionship tonight. Greg desperately feared being alone. And she certainly kept him from moping about Doug.

"I never had anyone write a song for me before!" She kissed him lightly as she filled his glass. "Will you sing it for me again, Greggie?"

Her face was very pretty in the firelight and Greg felt himself getting hard again. He went quickly to the piano and played the tune with a flourish. It was the standard little ditty he used for all girls. When he came to the part where the name belonged, he used *baby*.

The expression on her face was rapturous, and for a moment Greg felt guilty. She had moved to the bed and her skin was golden in the glow of the candles. Points of fire were reflected in her eyes, and he forgot all about his little deceit.

"Come over and play with me, Greggie."

Her voice was low and teasing. She gasped when he rose from the piano and then she held out her arms. She thought his excitement was for her, not the fire. It was best she think that.

Greg stepped over the flames. As he felt the heat on his legs, his passion grew. It was all he could do to contain himself as he joined her on the bed in the glowing, flickering light. The circle of light. The circle of flame. The circle of power—and he was at the center.

It was late and she was sleeping, curled up like a kitten in the center of the bed. Greg finished the rest of the champagne. He had been drinking for hours, wide awake and listening. The flames were calling him, singing to him to build them higher. Very slowly, so as not to wake her, he moved from the bed.

There was a gold box of Dunhills on the table. Greg took one and knelt down before the tallest candle. He held his breath as he pushed the end of the cigarette into the fire. His heartbeat slowed and a trancelike expression came over his features as he watched intently.

The flame licked around the edges of the cylinder, daintily tasting his offering. It split in two at the point of intrusion and then rejoined at the tip, stronger and higher than before. The Dunhill blackened and scorched. A pencil-thin column of black smoke rose toward the high ceiling.

There was a light curtain of smoke in the room when the Dunhill was finally gone. Greg could feel the flame's disappointment as it resumed its former shape. Fires were hungry things. They needed fuel to survive. Now the candle was burning low with only a thin wafer of wax to feed on.

The girl's scarf was draped over the end of the bed, brightly printed silk in a checkerboard design. He reached for it, feeling the thick, smooth material slide over his fingers.

At first he only held it close, so the flame could admire it. He saw the flicker of greedy anticipation. Closer. Closer. The tongue fluttered out to caress and scorch. Silken fibers resisted the fiery kiss, smoldering defiantly. The flame licked higher, spreading and heating the woven threads to the combustion point. The dyes turned translucent as the scarf burst into light, holding the pattern for an instant past consumption.

Greg fed the flame slowly. The scarf was long and they had plenty of time. Blackened threads dropped to the rug and turned to ash. The flame danced joyously, romping nearly to his fingers as it begged for more. The pile of ash grew at the base of the candle.

Only one hungry mouth of flame was left and Greg could not bear to kill it.

He laid it down carefully in the pile of clothing by the bed and watched as it gathered new strength. It was growing, changing before his eyes, turning into a bright, powerfully beautiful blaze.

As the smoke in the room grew thick, the girl coughed and began to wake. It was her scream that finally roused him.

She grabbed a heavy wool blanket from the bed and threw it over the flames. "Help me, Greg! Get some water! And then call the fire department!"

As he rushed to the kitchen, Greg realized she had dropped her little-girl act. They doused the blanket thoroughly and beat at it with their hands. By the time the fire department arrived, the blaze was wet and dead.

After the firemen left, the girl said she had to go home. She had an early class in the morning. She was a sophomore at the university, majoring in mathematics.

Greg gave her some money for a new outfit and called her a cab.

While they were waiting, she went to the piano and picked out her song with one finger. When she came to the spot for her name, she stopped.

"Just fill in the name of your current companion. You wrote this same song for half the girls in my dorm."

She laughed and gave him her telephone number. Then she kissed him. There was no giggle in her voice when she said good-bye.

The apartment seemed empty without her. Greg almost wished she had stayed. They could have started over, with no pretense. He put the candles in a garbage bag and carried them out to the trash.

It was only an hour until dawn. Greg spent the time in the kitchen, drinking coffee to stay awake. He didn't smoke a single cigarette. There were no excuses for the fire. He had set it deliberately. He shuddered to think what would have happened if the girl had not been there.

CHAPTER 6

Jerry pulled out to pass a laboring snowplow and the car fishtailed slightly as he guided it back into the slow lane. Traffic was heavy tonight. Wayzata Boulevard was jammed with cars going into the downtown area. The stores in the Nicollet Mall were open late tonight for the convenience of Christmas shoppers.

A left-hand turn seemed impossible, but finally there was a break in the traffic. Jerry pulled into the parking structure and used his card to open the gate. The half-hour drive had calmed him and now he felt a little silly for bolting from the house. Betsy certainly hadn't been in any danger from him. He had panicked. It was that simple.

He changed into his jogging outfit and stuffed his office key into the Velcro pocket of his right shoe. The exercise would be good for him. It would erase all the frustrations of the day and leave him drained of all emotion. Jogging was every bit as good as psychotherapy and it was a hell of a lot cheaper.

Jerry jogged effortlessly, blue Adidas pounding

against the carpeted floor of the connecting second-story bridges of the Skyway System. He had been jogging for a full twenty minutes and he felt almost restored. His body responded eagerly to the pace he set, every muscle synchronized to maintain his perfect form.

He stopped for a moment at one of the huge plate-glass windows, jogging in place, to peer out at the weather ball on the Northwestern building. It was red. That meant a sudden winter storm warning. The night had been clear when he'd driven in from Minnetonka. Now gusts of snow rattled against the window and he could barely make out the time and temperature. Six forty-five. Twelve degrees Fahrenheit.

Last winter a man in Mankato had been badly frost-bitten while jogging. He had gone out in shorts and long athletic socks. When he came back in, his thighs were frozen.

Jerry grinned as he looked down at his jogging outfit, old University of Minnesota gym shorts and a T-shirt. The connecting bridges were a boon to joggers. He was perfectly comfortable in the constant sixty-eight-degree temperature while the people outside the windows were bundled up in their coats with their car heaters going full blast.

Three miles to go. Jerry turned from the window and started to jog again. If he stuck to his schedule, he'd be at the spa by seven-fifteen. He'd play a quick game of racquetball, relax in the Jacuzzi, and shower and change before he headed for home. By the time he got there, Betsy would be sleeping.

Dr. Elias put down the phone and sighed. It had taken an hour of his time, switching from one airline official to another, spending long minutes on hold listening to insipid recorded music, but he had finally gotten the confirmation he needed. Betsy had come in on the eight o'clock flight last night from California.

The pain was worse tonight, but he could not afford an injection. He had to be alert. Jerry had not called his new therapist. Time was running out. Betsy's presence would surely precipitate a crisis, and the situation was volatile.

Dr. Elias picked up his prized possession, the meerschaum that had belonged to his father, and held it carefully in his hand. He remembered when it was new and white. Now the intricately carved bowl, a likeness of Hippocrates, was a rich, deep mahogany. It was his legacy, his only link with his father.

"What would you do, sir?" Dr. Elias said aloud as he looked down intently at the meerschaum. A casual observer might think he was waiting for the pipe to speak in the words of his brilliant father, but Dr. Elias would have chuckled at such a preposterous idea. His father had been dead for years. The dead could not give advice to the living. Only in memory could Dr. Elias revive the words of experience and wisdom his father had spoken. And only in imagination could he postulate what his father would tell him today.

"My oath, sir. Is it necessary to break it?"

Long moments passed, moments of doubt and dread. Pain twisted the corners of Dr. Elias's mouth as he nodded at last, a short decisive dip of his silver-haired head. He opened the leather case and put the pipe inside, closing it reverently. He would smoke it later, as he did every night, when his duty was done.

The clock on the mantel chimed half past six as Dr. Elias rose from his desk. Jerry was a compulsive jogger, never varying his pattern. At precisely seven he would jog through the bridge connecting Dayton's department store with Dr. Elias's building.

It took only a moment to load the gun, a small twenty-five-caliber automatic. It fit neatly in his topcoat pocket. He had purchased it when the security staff had cut their hours, and it had been stored in the drawer of his desk for three years. It had never been needed before.

Dr. Elias locked the door to his suite and took the elevator down to the connecting bridge on the second floor. The building was deserted. Office personnel had gone home for the night and the cleaning crews had not yet arrived. The switch was just inside the entrance to the bridge, and he reached up to turn off the bright fluorescent lights. Then he walked slowly to the center of the corridor to wait.

The bridge spanned Nicollet Avenue. Since the mall had been opened, the street was closed to all traffic except buses and taxis. Dr. Elias leaned up against the cold windowpane and watched the street below. Snow pelted against the glass as the wind picked up outside. Most people had heeded the storm warnings and gone straight home. An occasional pedestrian hurried by, bundled up warmly against the cold, but it was impossible for anyone at street level to see inside.

All was quiet and dark inside the glass-enclosed skyway. Dr. Elias stood motionless. It was almost time. His fingers tightened around the gun in his pocket as he heard footsteps approach. Jerry was coming, right on schedule.

* * *

The lights were out. Jerry stopped suddenly at the entrance to the Nicollet bridge. He reached up to feel for the switch, but nothing marred the surface of the bare wall. It was on the other side.

His heart was racing and it was not from the exercise. Jerry shivered as he faced the dark mouth of the tunnel. It seemed filled with menacing shadows. Headlights flashed briefly as a taxi turned into the mall and sped under the bridge. The interior flickered for an instant and then plunged into darkness again.

He wanted to turn around and find an alternate route, but that would put him off schedule. Jerry chided himself for being silly. He would stiffen up if he hesitated here much longer. He had to maintain his pace.

Jerry's breathing quickened as he stepped into the darkness. He would hurry on through and catch the lights on the other end. Some janitor had probably forgotten to turn on the lights. It was certainly nothing to get spooked about.

The tunnel was very dark now. The snow had turned to sleet and it blew against the windows in staccato blasts. Traffic was stopped for a light at the corner of Sixth Street and not even the strobe of a headlight pierced the darkness.

Jerry concentrated on his form, unwilling to admit that he was scared. The snow flurries driving against the glass sounded like muted snare drums, ominous and building to some terrible rhythm.

Instinct told him to turn around and run, but Jerry fought his fear. Dotty would laugh when he told her about this. Only kids were afraid of the dark.

Left. Right. Left. Right. Jerry quickened his pace in

spite of himself. He was almost halfway through. Only a few hundred feet and he would be in the light.

Traffic was moving again now. Headlights from a passing bus illuminated the shape that stepped out into his path. Jerry's mouth opened in startled recognition, but before he could blurt out a question, it was too late.

CHAPTER 7

"Damn machine's broken again!" Curtis Holt turned to Mac in disgust. "Every time I want a cup of coffee, the damn machine breaks down."

Mac grinned and unfolded his big frame from the city-issue steel chair. Curt was one of the finest detectives on the force, but he had a real problem with mechanical things. The coffee machine hummed defiantly in the corner of the squad room while Curt stared at it balefully.

"Watch me, Curt." Mac approached the machine straight on, swaggering a little. The fingers of his right hand brushed lightly against his service holster.

"This is the police," he announced in a steely voice. "Hand over that coffee you owe the sergeant or you're under arrest."

Curt laughed as Mac rapped the machine with a nightstick. Then his eyes widened in awe as the paper cup dropped into the tray and coffee poured out. "Son of a bitch!" he breathed. "How did you do that, Mac?"

"You got to show it who's boss," Mac explained sagely. He slid open the little plastic door and handed the cup to Curt. "It'd help if you watched a few more John Wayne movies."

"There's a homicide on the Nicollet Avenue bridge." Desk Sergeant Reinert stuck his head in the door. "It's yours, Curt. You wanna drop him off on your way home, Mac?"

"Sure." Mac picked up his file folders and grabbed his coat. "Come on, Curt. I'll keep you company for a couple of minutes."

Both men were tense as Mac turned on Seventh and parked behind the black and whites lined up at the curb. The connecting bridges were the chief's idea, his pet project to cut down on street crime. Now the expanded Skyway System was the scene of a homicide. Murder in the heart of the downtown shopping area would be bad for business. There would be plenty of pressure from the City Fathers to clean up this case in a hurry.

Mac and Curt flashed their badges and pushed their way past the officers at the entrance. They took the stairs to the second floor and stopped at the landing to make way for the police photographer on his way back to the station.

The bridge was a sea of blue uniforms, metal gleaming under the bright fluorescent lights. An area in the middle had been cordoned off and the victim's body lay in the center of the area, covered with a sheet.

Mac stood to the side as Curt introduced himself to the officer in charge. He reached for the sheet and flipped it down. It was the body of a man in his early forties, dressed in jogging shorts. Mac gasped when he saw the man's face.

"Gunshot wound to the head." Curt nodded and the assistant coroner moved to cover the body again.

"Looks like a small caliber from the entrance wound. No ID on the body. They're working on it now."

Mac swallowed hard. His voice sounded flat when he finally spoke. "The victim's name is Jerry Feldman. He's a dentist. I knew him."

Curt glanced at him sharply and then turned to the officer in charge. "Notify the relatives and then let the press in. We'll write it up as a routine mugging for now."

Mac nodded. Curt hadn't missed the fact that Jerry's expensive jogger's watch was still on his wrist. An accomplished thief would have taken it. Both Mac and Curt knew this was no ordinary mugging, but there was no sense in speculating at the scene. The real investigation would come later, after the press had left.

The reporters were arriving now and Mac knew he should leave. He had known the victim. The department had strict rules about emotional involvement in cases like this. He was just heading for the doorway when he saw Debra.

She was impeccably dressed in gray slacks with a dark blue blazer, camera bag slung smartly over her shoulder. She pulled out her camera and took several shots. Even though she looked every inch a professional, Mac had the feeling she had to force herself to focus on the white-sheeted body. By now Debra knew who was under the sheet. Her hands trembled as she interviewed the officer in charge.

Mac made his way to her after she had finished. "Debra? Are you all right?"

He took her arm and she flinched. Then she looked up at him and swayed slightly.

"Oh, Mac!"

Her voice was shaking and grateful. Mac patted her

arm and she did not pull away this time. She no longer looked cold and unapproachable. She looked scared, and he stayed by her side like a shadow as she took the rest of her pictures and called the story in.

"Do you need a ride to the paper?" Mac opened the door for her and they stepped out into the storm.

"Yes, please!" Debra pulled her collar up and slipped on her gloves. "I was going to call a cab, but I'd rather ride with you. I just have to drop off this film."

It took only a moment to drop the film at the lab. Debra seemed to be just fine as she gave instructions to the technician. Several people called out greetings to her as they walked down the corridor and left the building. Mac began to think he was wrong. Perhaps Debra didn't need him after all.

They stood in the parking lot outside the *Tribune* building. Blowing snow whipped at her hair and ice crystals stuck and glistened on her long, dark eyelashes. Her car keys were in her hand, but she was shaking too hard to unlock the door.

"I . . . I don't want to go home alone, Mac. Could we have a cup of coffee?"

"Sure." Mac felt a surge of compassion as he led her to his car. She was in no condition to drive. Debra had used the last of her courage to finish her story and now she was exhausted and frightened.

She started to cry the moment he drove from the lot, huge wracking sobs that she tried to hide by turning her face to the passenger window. It hurt him to see her so vulnerable, but he didn't know how to help her.

"I'm taking you to my house, Debra." The moment the words were spoken, he knew it was the right thing to do. In a brightly lit coffee shop, the waitress and customers would stare at them curiously.

Debra made no protest. She just nodded shakily. She was still crying, twenty minutes later, when he pulled into his garage, helped her from the car, and led her into the house. He got her settled on the couch in the living room and went to make coffee.

Debra heard the water run in the kitchen. A cupboard door opened and closed again. She sat there for several moments, her mind blank with shock, and then she began to smell the coffee. Mac was making real coffee. She used instant at home and it never smelled this good. It would be nice to have a cup of real coffee.

A part of her mind was separate, recognizing the small homey sounds he made in the kitchen and cataloging them. A floorboard squeaked. There was a clatter as he got out the coffee mugs. She had to stop crying before he came back.

Debra wiped her eyes with the small lace handkerchief she kept in her purse. The tears would not stop. The harder she struggled for control, the faster the tears fell. She had cried like this only once before, the night her baby had died. And the tears had stopped only when she'd done that awful thing, when she'd kidnapped another woman's baby to take the place of her own.

"It's all right, Debra. Cry it all out."

She had not heard him come back from the kitchen and she trembled in the hot, heavy circle of his arms. This was not right. He shouldn't be holding her this way. But she needed someone so badly, someone to hold her and brush back her hair and take the tears she had shed and turn them into the comfort she craved.

Debra crept, defeated, farther into his arms. The top

of her head fit precisely under his chin. She was like a small, hurt sparrow. Too tight an embrace would crush her. All her defenses had crumbled and she was naked in her need.

The tears stopped falling at last. Debra shivered as she left his arms. She dabbed at her eyes with her useless handkerchief and pretended great interest in the snow falling outside the window. He had been so kind, holding her while she cried like a baby. He probably thought she was a basket case. She was too humiliated to even look at him now.

"Debbie?"

She turned in surprise. No one had called her that for so long. She was Debra, the professional woman. The nickname made her feel like a child again, eyes red from tears, handkerchief wadded in a soggy ball in her hand.

He was holding out a giant box of Kleenex. Debra stared at it uncertainly.

"I've got two more boxes in the closet. If you go through them, there's a Seven-Eleven on the next block."

A laugh bubbled up through her deep embarrassment. She pulled out a Kleenex and wiped her face. "I'm sorry, Mac. I . . . I guess tonight was just too much for me."

Mac handed her a cup of steaming coffee. "Drink this and you'll feel better. I'll make a fire. That'll cheer you up."

For the first time since she'd entered the house, Debra looked around her. She was in a comfortable room, heavily masculine, with walls of books and softball trophies. A Remington print hung over the fireplace, and a television and stereo were built into a cabinet facing the couch. The room was cluttered, but it was a pleasing clutter that added to the room's character. It was a place to hide in, a retreat from a threatening world.

Mac turned from the fireplace to look at her. There was color in her cheeks now, and she had taken the time to straighten her hair. She smiled at him tentatively as he joined her on the couch.

"I'm sorry, Mac." She seemed to think she owed him an apology. "Everyone's dying and I guess I was scared. First Dr. Elias left and then Doug was killed. And now Jerry! Our whole group's dying, one by one!"

"Everyone's not dying." Mac took her hands and pressed them tightly. "It just seems that way. Sometimes horrible coincidences happen in real life."

His words of reassurance sounded hollow to him, but she didn't seem to notice. Unwittingly, Debra had put her finger on the pulse of his own doubt. He was a cop, trained to be suspicious of coincidence. Two deaths out of a group of eight was statistically unusual. Mac's instincts warned him of danger. Jerry's murder could be a vengeance killing. Everyone in the group had blamed him for Doug's death.

An uneasy silence fell between them. Mac realized he was still holding her hands and he wasn't sure what to do next. Debra made no move, either. They sat there barely breathing, pretending to be comfortable, as the tension grew.

It was a precarious situation, on the brink of something fearful and new. It reminded Mac of an awkward first date. They were both locked into motionless silence, not willing to risk anything that would endanger their tentative intimacy.

At last Mac moved. "Debbie? This is crazy."

"'Insanity runs in my family. It practically gallops.'"

The quote came out before she had time to think. Debra's face flamed with heat. Now she'd have to tell him how she and her college roommate used to trade movie dialogue back and forth to try to stump each other. It was a childish game.

She had just opened her mouth to explain when Mac threw back his head and laughed. "Cary Grant. *Arsenic and Old Lace*. Nineteen forty-four."

Debra laughed with him. He knew! Suddenly everything was ordinary and familiar again. He still held her hands, but now it felt right. It was such a relief to laugh!

"I didn't know you were an old-movie buff!" Debra smiled. Perhaps it wasn't such a silly game, after all. "I watch the late show on Channel Eleven almost every night. I'll bet I've seen the beginning of *Arsenic and Old Lace* twenty times, but I always fall asleep before the end."

Mac began to grin. "We'll have to do something about that, right now. I just happen to have it that movie. How about watching it with me, all the way through?"

"Yes." She jumped at the idea. Watching a movie would be the perfect way to escape the reality of this awful night.

"Come and help me make popcorn." Mac pulled her to her feet. "Could you be persuaded to have a drink, dear? Maybe just a tiny triple?"

Debra thought for a minute. Then she laughed and followed him into the kitchen. "Bea Arthur. *Mame*. Nineteen seventy-four."

It was long past midnight when Debra opened her eyes. There was an afghan tucked snugly around her and her head was pillowed in Mac's lap. John Wayne's voice growled from the television. It was the second reel of *True Grit*.

"You missed the end again."

Debra turned her head to look at him. He was smiling and there was something new in his eyes. Love. The thought flowed like warm honey through her sleepy body and lay half formed at the edge of her consciousness. She felt safe and cherished.

"Come on, Debbie. Let's go to bed."

His words jarred her and she sat up, alarmed. The illusion of intimacy was shattered.

"I . . . I have to go home, Mac."

He heard the panic in her voice and he drew her close as she struggled to rise.

"Debbie. Don't think. You're here, safe with me. Just relax and let me carry you to bed. I'll sleep out here on the couch."

It was better then. She remembered that he was Mac, her friend. Mac would never hurt her. He wasn't like the others, the men who'd tried to lure her into their beds for sex. She lifted her arms and locked them around his neck, trusting him to carry her down the hall to his bed. She was safe with Mac.

He tucked her in like a precious child, stroking her hair until she was nearly asleep again. But when he attempted to leave her there in the big, lonely bed, she clung to him.

"Please, Mac. Don't leave me alone."

He reached out to fold down the covers and slid in beside her. Then her arms were around his neck again as if they'd never left.

"Hold me, Mac. Hold me tight."

There was no awkward fumbling as she snuggled tightly against him, feeling the heat of his body through their clothes beneath the blankets. Was this what Dr. Elias had meant when he'd said it was time to trust someone? The question stayed in her sleepy mind for only an instant. Then his arms moved around her and she was at peace.

Sleep did not come to Mac quickly. He held her warm body and stared down at her face—the heavy, dark eyelashes that brushed her cheeks, the almost luminous quality of her skin in the moonlight. And the pallor that only exhaustion could bring. The small, even sounds of her breathing seduced him, made his body threaten to come alive again and change everything. Last year, last month even, he would have rejoiced in such a change, but not now. Now things were different.

She sighed once, a small childlike sound of contentment. Her body moved against his, pressing positive to negative, molding to fill the spaces between them. He ached to turn loose his fingers to roam over the sweet, soft skin of her body, to spread her warm, sleepy thighs, to hear her cry out as he drove forward, his betraying hardness sheathed in her trusting warmth.

He was grateful she did not know. It would only frighten her, drive her out of his bed and back to her lonely, terrified life.

Mac stared up at the ceiling. The irony of his struggle did not escape him. His lips twisted in a bitter grin as he battled the very thing he had sought, forcing it back until his aching desire was only a temporary aberration, until he was himself once more, the Mac she trusted. Friendly, comforting, sexless Mac. At last he slept in the darkness beside her.

* * *

Mac awoke in the cold, gray hour just before dawn. Debra was gone. Only a small indentation on the pillow next to his confirmed her reality.

He found her on the couch in the living room. Her eyes were wide and unfocused. She held her arms cradled against her chest, rocking, humming a lullaby. Her cheeks were wet with tears.

"Debbie. Honey. It's all right." Mac spoke gently. She was still asleep, locked tight in a dream, even though her eyes were wide open. "Come on, Debbie. Wake up. Everything's just fine."

He knelt down and warmed her cold hands with his. Still speaking softly, he folded his arms folded around her. It seemed to take forever for her to recognize him.

"Oh, Mac! I dreamed . . . I dreamed my baby was alive!" She shuddered deeply and clung to him. "I used to dream it all the time, but then it went away. Ever since Dr. Elias left, it's back. I . . . I think I'm going crazy again, Mac!"

"No. You can't." Mac's voice was hard as he gripped her shoulders. "That's the easy way out, Debbie. You can try to sink back down, but I won't let you go. I need you."

The words filtered down through the fog of her depression, clear and unemotional. A statement of fact. She couldn't go crazy. Mac needed her. She needed desperately to be needed.

"We'll form a club, just the two of us. A survival team. We can get through it, Debbie. I'll help you and you can help me. We'll be there for each other."

Before she thought, her head had dipped in a slight

nod. Hope grew in the coldness of her heart. He needed her.

"How about some breakfast, partner? There's a little café just around the corner."

"I'm a mess." Debra tried to smooth the wrinkles from her blouse, but sleeping in her clothes had taken its toll. "I really should go home and change."

"No problem." Mac grinned at her. "I'm sure I've got something around here that will fit you."

Debra waited as Mac searched through the closet and pulled out a faded police academy sweatshirt that was obviously much too large for her. Usually she took great pains with her appearance, but everything was different this morning. Mac had seen her at her worst and he still liked her. Debra slipped the sweatshirt on and grinned at her reflection in the mirror. She looked like a waif, but Mac didn't seem to mind at all.

"Now I'd better find you something nice and warm." Mac rummaged in the back of the closet and pulled out a fur-lined parka and a pair of yellow hand-knit mittens with purple thumbs. "It's really cold out there this time of morning."

Dawn was breaking as they left the house. A dazzling blanket of white covered the city, hiding the winter ugliness. The sun peeked over the tall buildings and made the powdery snow sparkle as they kicked it up with their boots.

As they turned the corner, her boot slipped on a patch of ice. He caught her, laughing. She leaned forward very slowly and looked up into his face. They were so close she could see the dark shadows of whiskers the razor had missed, the flecks of gold in his blue eyes, the way his lashes lightened to blond at the tips. His frosty breath mingled with hers and then caught and held. She tilted her head to the side and brushed his cold nose with hers. And then she kissed him quite naturally, a kiss to seal the pact, a kiss of hope and wonder and longing and promise.

CHAPTER 8

It was a terrible dream. Kay was late to class and she ran through a corridor in agonizingly slow motion. Her feet stuck in invisible pools of thick molasses. Books dropped in an avalanche from her arms. And through it all the tardy bell was ringing, once, twice, over and over.

Kay opened her eyes to see the winter sun stream weakly though the window. It was morning and she was alone in the house. Charles was attending a two-day political meeting in Duluth, and the kids had gone with him to take in some cross-country skiing. Even Ralph was gone. The vet was keeping him overnight for worming.

She was awake now, but the tardy bell was still ringing. It was the phone. Kay sat up in the bed and reached out to answer it. Her eyes felt scratchy and the dull pounding of a hangover nagged at the back of her mind. She had started drinking right after they'd left for Duluth last night. The house was too lonely without them and the snow rattling against the window had made her nervous and jumpy. Now it was morning already and she couldn't even remember going up to bed.

"Hello?"

The word was muffled and thick with sleep.

"I'm sorry if I woke you, Kay." It was Mac's voice. "I think we'd better call a meeting today to talk about Jerry."

"Jerry?"

"Jesus. I'm sorry, Kay! I thought you'd have heard by now. Jerry's dead. Somebody shot him last night."

For a moment she couldn't say anything. Her mind was still foggy. Mac said Jerry was dead. That was terrible!

She must have said something because Mac went on talking. Kay tried hard to concentrate as he mapped out the plans for the meeting.

"I'll notify everyone. You just make a big pot of coffee. Debbie and I'll be there a little early. Is that okay?"

"Yes. Fine."

Kay replaced the phone very gently in the cradle. Jerry was dead. Tears began to form in her eyes and she blinked them away. She didn't have time to cry now. It was ten o'clock already and they were coming at one.

It was noon by the time she'd finished vacuuming. Perhaps Charles was right, after all. They really needed a maid. Kay had balked at the idea, but the house was too large for her to deal with herself. She spent far too much time cleaning and dusting. But what kind of maid? Kay didn't want to hire a black. Blacks had been stereotyped as domestics. But if she hired another minority, she would be discriminating against her own people. A white maid was totally out of the question. Then she'd be accused of reverse snobbery. The whole situation was simply too complicated to sort out right now. She'd do the cleaning herself until she could make up her mind.

Her purse was lying on the table, the car keys beside it. Kay frowned. She didn't remember going out last night. The entire evening was a blank. She picked it up and started to close it when she noticed the gun.

Her .25 automatic was inside. What was it doing in her purse? The last time she'd had a gun in her purse was when she'd tried to kill the governor!

Kay couldn't bear to touch it. She closed the purse tightly and shuddered. She had been very angry with Jerry when he'd stormed out of the group meeting. She'd still been angry when she'd started drinking last night. What if she'd flipped out like she had six years ago? What if she had killed Jerry!

"No!" Her voice was a hoarse whisper of denial. Of course she hadn't killed Jerry. She was being ridiculous. She had to calm down before the group came and caught her behaving like this.

A drink would calm her nerves. Kay took out the gin bottle and started to make a martini. Then she stopped and frowned. She was simply too upset to go through the whole process. She couldn't cope with the shaker and the careful drop of vermouth, the properly chilled glass and the perfect olive. She needed a shot of gin, not an afternoon cocktail.

"The hell with it!"

Kay tipped the bottle to her lips and swallowed.

Mac and Debra were startled when Kay opened the door. She looked nothing like the fashionable mayor's wife today. Her hair was pulled back in an untidy knot and she'd obviously been drinking. Without her customary immaculate makeup, she looked old and tired.

"I'll bet I look like hell!" Kay managed a weak smile. "Hearing about Jerry was an awful shock."

"Is there anything we can do to help?" Debra hung her coat in the closet and followed Kay to the living room.

"You can start the coffee while I freshen up. Just carry the pot in from the kitchen and plug it in right here. I'm sorry I'm so rattled. I just can't seem to get it together today."

"We'll take care of everything." Mac gave her a quick hug. "You go and make yourself beautiful."

Debra plugged in the coffee and helped Mac push six chairs in a circle. Two extra chairs stood against the wall.

"Should we move those chairs to another room?" Debra's voice shook a little.

"Let's leave them right there." Mac patted her shoulder. "We have to deal with it, Debbie. Two members of our group are gone. Hiding their chairs won't change that."

Twenty minutes later, everyone but Father Marx had arrived. Kay seemed back to normal as she filled coffee cups and passed the tin of imported cookies. They were just starting to worry when the doorbell rang and Father Marx rushed in, red faced and breathless.

"Please forgive me!" He hurried to his place. "I'm afraid I lost track of time. I was praying. This business about Jerry. Terrible! Do they know who did it?"

"Not yet."

"Poor Jerry!" Nora blinked back tears. "Why didn't he just hand over his money and cooperate?"

"It wasn't a mugging." Mac watched them carefully

as his words sank in. "Jerry's wallet was in his office and nothing was taken from his body. Somebody wanted Jerry dead."

"But who?" Kay's voice was sharp.

"We might be able to figure that out." Mac leaned forward. "We knew Jerry better than anyone. He told us all his secrets. Can you think of anyone who had a grudge against him? Someone who hated him enough to kill him?"

There was a long silence. One by one they shook their heads.

"The father of that little girl?" Greg frowned thoughtfully. "No, that was too long ago. Besides, Jerry was sure he didn't really hurt her."

"Maybe it was just coincidence." Debra spoke up. "Remember that guy in the Texas bell tower? Maybe it's another case like that. Some nut who hated joggers could have hidden on the bridge and shot the first jogger to run through."

"That's possible." Mac sounded doubtful. "If you're right, Debbie, we're wasting our time. Random murders are almost impossible to solve. Let's put your theory aside for the moment and assume someone set out to murder Jerry. The killer knew precisely where Jerry would be last night. That means he knew Jerry's habits. He waited on the bridge and when Jerry jogged through, he shot him in the head with a twenty-five automatic. Why? And who?"

"Divine retribution?" Father Marx shrugged. "I really hate to lay a heavy on you, but the Old Testament tells us 'an eye for an eye.' Jerry killed Doug by driving him to suicide. A lot of guys in my business would say God evened the score."

"Cut the religious crap, Vinnie." Nora laughed. "God

didn't hide on the bridge with a gun. Let's get back to the facts. If the police find out about our meeting yesterday, we'll all be suspects! We knew Jerry's jogging schedule. He talked about it all the time. And everyone in this room had a motive. We all blamed Jerry for Doug's accident."

Greg shook his head. "That doesn't mean one of us killed him. You're getting carried away with this Sherlock Holmes stuff, Nora. We were plenty mad at Jerry yesterday, but none of us wanted him dead."

"But will the police believe that?" Nora shrugged elaborately. "Remember, Greg. Every one of us is a certified loony!"

There was a tense silence as they looked at one another. Debra shivered even though the room was warm. Had someone in the room killed Jerry?

Kay set down her coffee cup with shaking hands. She looked ready to faint. "Kay!" Mac caught her as she slumped forward.

Nora rummaged in her purse and handed Mac a small bottle of smelling salts. "For stage fright," she explained, "Some of my students drop like flies before a performance. Just take the cap off and hold it under her nose. She'll come around."

A moment later Kay coughed and tried to sit up. "I . . . I'm sorry!" she stammered. "I just couldn't face it! I . . . I think I might have killed Jerry!"

"Why, Kay?" Mac's voice was very gentle.

"You said he was killed with a twenty-five automatic and I . . . I found a gun in my purse this morning!"

"I'm sure you didn't kill Jerry." Mac put his arm around her shoulder. His tone was quiet and soothing. "Where's the gun you found? I want to look at it."

"It's in my purse in the hall closet. I couldn't bear to

touch it. I must have done it, Mac! I can't remember anything I did last night! I killed Jerry!"

Debra rushed to the closet and brought back Kay's purse. They all watched as Mac took out the gun and sniffed the barrel.

"You didn't kill anybody." Mac grinned at her. "There's no way this gun was fired last night."

"Are you sure?"

"The barrel's plugged up with Cosmoline." Mac pulled back the slide and released it. Grease splattered out on the table. "It'd probably blow up if you tried to use it."

"Thank God!" Kay took a deep breath and gave them all a radiant smile. "You don't know how scared I've been! I thought I was a murderer!"

Nora leaned over and kissed Kay on both cheeks. "We all knew you didn't do it, darling. You might be a little cuckoo, but you're not frigging crazy!"

The tension in the room evaporated as they started to laugh.

Eventually even Kay joined in. "Well!" She settled back in her chair and smiled. "Now that I've got that off my chest, what shall we talk about next?"

Everyone turned to look at Mac. They were silent and expectant, waiting for him to speak. The group had made a decision. It was unspoken, but they all understood. Mac was their new leader. They had chosen him to take Dr. Elias's place.

Mac gave a sigh as the heavy cloak of responsibility settled around his shoulders. Then he smiled wryly. They depended on him. It was an honor. Mac just hoped he was ready to handle it.

CHAPTER 9

Father Marx sighed wearily as he collapsed the folding chairs that lined the church basement and stacked them against the wall. The parish basketball games were great fun for the boys, but they left him exhausted. Actually, he wasn't even sure which side had won. He had been too busy thinking about Doug. And Jerry.

Even though he kidded around about religion with his friends, Father Marx truly believed in the wisdom of the church. He played the role of the modern and enlightened man of God because his superiors expected it of him. The church was losing its grip, so a parish priest was expected to be a good PR man. *Relate to everybody* was his credo. Be what they want. Promise them anything, but give them Catholicism. He was the wise father confessor to the old guard, a buddy to the kids, and a good-natured cynic with his friends and fellow priests. Father Marx played so many roles that sometimes he wondered who he really was.

Father Marx hadn't thought deeply about religious

issues for years. He was too busy recruiting new parishioners, raising money for building additions, and organizing youth groups. People didn't like to see their priests somber or thoughtful. They liked a joke, an easy answer, or a friendly pat on the back. The old religion was gone. No modern priests burned the midnight oil, reading heavy books on doctrine or anguishing over a tricky question of morality. Father Marx hadn't experienced a sleepless night since he'd left the rigors of the seminary.

Now all that had changed. In his despair over Doug and Jerry, Father Marx fell back on his deepest beliefs. He had spent long hours on his knees beseeching God in Doug's behalf, even though he suspected his prayers were futile. The church was very clear on the subject of suicide. A human life was sacred and to destroy it was a mortal sin. But was Doug's death a suicide? That was a moral question of another magnitude. One could argue that Doug had been an unwilling victim of circumstance, a true innocent who had not been in control of his own mind when he'd crashed the plane. If so, there was hope that God would take mercy on his soul.

Jerry's eternal fate was another concern. If Jerry had deliberately driven Doug to suicide, he would be a murderer in the eyes of God. But if Jerry had harbored no ill intent, God would absolve him. Jerry had tried to live a decent life. Father Marx knew how valiantly he had fought against his perversion. Would God take his struggle into account and balance it against the evil of Jerry's unholy lust?

The sound of sweeping had been going on for some time. Father Marx roused himself and turned to see Paul Littletree pushing the heavy broom across the floor. The boy was small for his eleven years and there was a perpetual frightened look in his eyes. Paul lived in the borderline area surrounding Loring Park. Rent was cheap and the once-stately apartments were filled with drunks and addicts. It was a terrible place to raise a child, but Paul's mother could barely afford the rent on her third-floor efficiency apartment. Moving to a more desirable neighborhood was out of the question.

Paul's mother had left the Red Lake Reservation when he was a baby. She was a fiercely proud woman who refused to accept charity. A recent state program had trained her to operate a power sewing machine. Now she worked the night shift at Munsingwear. Since there was no one to see that Paul got home safely, Father Marx always made some excuse to walk him home on basketball nights.

"Would you like some company on your way home?" Father Marx smiled at the boy. "It's about time for my evening walk."

"Oh, that'd be swell, Father!" Paul carried the broom to the closet and put it away carefully. He picked up his threadbare coat and slipped into it. Father Marx noticed that the sleeves were too short.

"No mittens, Paul?"

Paul jammed his hands into his pockets and shook his head. "Naw. I let my mom wear 'em. These pockets are nice and warm."

Father Marx pulled out the pair of gloves he had bought and handed them to Paul. "Try these on for size. They were a present from Sister Theresa and they're much too small for me."

Paul slipped on the fur-lined gloves and grinned. The frightened expression almost disappeared from his face.

"Geez, Father! They're great! Are you sure you don't want 'em?"

"No sense in keeping a pair of gloves that don't fit. You'll be doing me a favor if you wear them, Paul. I wouldn't want Sister Theresa to think her gift went to waste."

The boy turned up his collar as they left the church. Father Marx saw him shiver. The wind hit them with an icy blast and they hugged the buildings as they walked west on Hennepin. A snowplow rumbled past them in the opposite direction, blue lights flashing. It was a miserable night for a walk.

They turned on the corner of Thirteenth and headed toward Harmon. Father Marx leaned into the wind and pulled his fur hat down over his ears. The blowing snow drove needles of cold against his cheeks. He walked on the outside of the sidewalk, trying to shield Paul with his body. The boy needed a warm parka with a hood. That would be his next big project.

Paul shivered again as they neared Loring Park. Father Marx wasn't sure if it was from the cold or from fear. The boy was wary, and he had good reason to be. This was a dangerous part of town.

Tonight the park was deserted and peaceful. Snow covered the frozen lake and the swans had been moved for the winter. No one was out in the vast unprotected area, but danger still lurked in the bordering apartment buildings. The freezing cold drove the crime inside. The drunks and addicts had moved to a warmer arena. Some were lucky enough to afford apartments, and the rest made do with hallways and stairwells. Father Marx was alert as he followed Paul into his apartment building.

The small lobby was dark. The bulb had burned out.

Father Marx doubted that anyone would replace it. Metal mailboxes lined one wall, their hinges sprung and rusting. Paul pushed open the door to the stairwell and stepped over a man who was sleeping in the corner. There was an empty wine bottle in his hand.

The stairs creaked as they climbed. Someone had dropped a garbage bag, and beer cans and coffee grounds littered the steps. There was the odor of decay and old cooking smells. In the summer the stench would be unbearable. Father Marx was grateful when they reached the third floor.

"Thanks for walking me home, Father." Paul took out his key and unlocked the door. He switched on the light and Father Marx glanced inside. There was only one room. A kitchen table with two chairs sat at one end of the space and a cot at the other. The couch in the middle pulled out to make a second bed. Paul's mother kept the apartment immaculate. It was in sharp contrast to the filth of the hallway. "I'll wait until I hear you lock the door." Father Marx reached out and made the sign of the cross over Paul's head. "Bless you, my son."

He stood in the dark hallway and waited until he heard the lock snap into place. When Paul threw the dead bolt, Father Marx sighed with relief. Mrs. Littletree had scraped together the money for a good lock. It was the best investment she could have made in her son's future.

There was a loud party in one of the apartments at the end of the hall. Father Marx heard shrill laughter and the tinny blast of a cheap stereo. As he walked down the faded, filthy carpeting, he heard a door fly open. The music was suddenly louder. He turned and saw a woman step out. She was dressed in bright red satin.

"Lemme alone!" She pushed her companion back inside. "I gotta get some air."

The door closed behind her with a slam, muffling the music. The woman leaned against the wall and reached down inside her low-cut dress to pull out a crumpled pack of cigarettes.

"Hey, sweetie! Gotta match?"

It took Father Marx a moment to realize she was talking to him. He shook his head and turned to leave, but she weaved down the hall toward him. She was obviously drunk.

"Watsa matter? Did the party bore ya?"

Father Marx knew he should leave, but he stood there impassively, watching her approach. Her dress slipped down lower with every step until one huge breast slipped free.

"Oops!" She gave a raucous laugh and grabbed at it. "It's a free show tonight."

She grinned at him, adjusted her dress, and stuffed it back in again. "Where ya been, sweetie? We coulda had some fun."

Father Marx turned to leave, but she grabbed at his arm. Her soft body ground against him.

"Come back inside with me. We'll have a real good time."

"I'm a priest." Father Marx's voice was hard. "Go back to your friends now. I have to leave."

"Ah, come on!" She licked her lipstick-smeared lips and fluttered long fake eyelashes. "You got desires, ain't ya? I never did a priest before. It'd be a real kick!"

He wanted to push her away roughly. Turn and run down the stairs. Flee to the sanctuary of the church. But he couldn't seem to move as she reached for him. Her fingers slid under his coat, searching. Then she gave a triumphant laugh.

"Ya don't even have to pay me, sweetie. I ain't felt nothin' this big all night."

He saw her face through a red haze of rage. The mouth slack, lips parted in a grotesque parody of delight. Her fingers groped and clutched, pinching at the heat of him, sharp knowing claws that repulsed even as they drew him down to his lust-filled nightmare.

"GET AWAY FROM ME!"

His voice was a bellow of denial, and he pushed her back with all his might.

Her painted face was a mask of injured reproach as she staggered against the opposite wall and crumpled to the dingy carpet. Then she laughed and pulled up her dress.

"Ya like it rough, sweetie? I'll letcha hit me a couple of times."

The voice of the Lord was loud in his ears. "Punish this harlot for her sinful ways." The voice commanded obedience, but Father Marx resisted.

He turned and ran, pursued by her laughter. Down the stairs, out the door, into the freezing night.

Bile rose in his throat, bitter and scalding. He retched in the street. Dark spots of gall spattered against the pure white snow. The voice of the Lord was a delusion. A false prophet. A product of his sickness, as Dr. Elias had told him.

At last he straightened and walked back the way he had come. His head was bowed and he did not feel the cold. There were no answers in the silent streets, no divine voices to guide him in the blowing wind. Dr. Elias was right. He had almost given way to temptation. He knew he was weak. Not worthy of the office he held.

It was past eleven when he unlocked the door to the church. His body was stiff from the cold. He longed to crawl into his narrow bed and ease his pain, but his soul was too troubled for sleep.

Father Marx genuflected before the altar. He raised his eyes to the statue of the Blessed Virgin and knelt at the prayer rail. Her plaster face was impassive. Did she approve of his action tonight? Would the Holy Mother bless him for his restraint?

The sacristy was so silent he imagined he could hear the Sacred Heart beating. Votive candles flickered dimly at the Blessed Virgin's feet. The dark shadows they cast were moving, reaching out to him with blind, searching fingers.

"Holy Mary, Mother of God. Pray for us sinners now and in the hour of our death."

The statue was changing. Father Marx shuddered as the face of the prostitute appeared, layered over the divine features like a demonic projection. He saw the red-smeared lips, the long false eyelashes that veiled knowing eyes. Her painted body was shifting. Robes parted to reveal rosy, voluptuous flesh. Then she was moving, leaning toward him in obscene delight.

He reached back and grasped the heavy silver cross. Raised it high above his head. His arms were strong now, trembling with his holy duty. The wrath with which a vengeful God had smote the Philistines was strong in him, His servant.

"Vade retro, satanas!"

It was a battle cry, hoarse and powerful. He smashed the cross, like a sword, against her sinful flesh.

He struck again. And again. Righteous blows against evil. The statue toppled, then crumpled, until it lay in silent ruin at his feet.

Father Marx sobbed with exertion. Great gulps of air filled his lungs and he dropped to his knees in the rubble, hiding his face in his hands.

He knelt there for hours, lips moving in silent supplication. He prayed until the Blessed Virgin released him and lifted him up from his madness.

CHAPTER 10

"Hi! This is Greg Davenport. I'm sorry I'm not home right now but . . . oh, no!"

Greg made a face and started at the beginning again. The user guide said never to say you weren't home. It was an open invitation to burglars. He flicked the switch to record and started again.

"Greg Davenport is unable to come to the phone at this moment, but he'd appreciate it if you'd leave your name and number at the sound of the tone."

Why on earth had he done that whole spiel in the third person? It made him sound like a stuffy English butler. Perhaps he should try to be funny.

"Oh, boy, did you call at the wrong time! Whatever made you think I'd be home at this hour? Well, don't feel bad . . . you're the seventh person who's made the same mistake tonight. Just leave your—"

BEEP!

The tone cut him off and Greg swore. He had already wasted fifteen minutes with this stupid machine and he had to get to the studio. He'd just leave that number and the hell with it.

"This is Greg. I'm at the studio. Call me at 555-6347."

Ten seconds of silence passed before the beep. Greg didn't care. He switched the machine to the answer mode and slammed the door behind him. He was late and there was a lot of work to do tonight.

It was snowing again and the streets were icy. The Jag skidded as Greg swung out of the driveway. Towering snowbanks flanked Eighth Street. They had just finished plowing. At least the streets were clear.

Greg turned right on Hiawatha and put some Scott Joplin music on the car stereo. The "Maple Leaf Rag" was playing as he cut over to take West River Parkway. Huge old homes lined the wide street that ran parallel to the Mississippi River. The people who lived in this area had money.

A green sign for Minnehaha Park came up on his right. Greg slowed the car and turned in at the second set of gates. He took his remote sensor from the glove box and pressed it. The metal gates slid open. He drove through and entered his father's estate.

For years Greg could not bear to drive past the place. The burned-out shell of the old mansion haunted his dreams. With Dr. Elias's help he had conquered his guilt, and last year he had converted the old carriage house into a modern sound studio. It was the sole building on two acres of prime riverfront land.

Greg used his key to disarm the security system. He unlocked the door and stepped inside, smiling as he switched on the lights. His new studio had state-of-the-art technology. It was the envy of everyone in the field.

A beautiful Steinway grand commanded a place of honor in the main room. Greg sometimes preferred to work in the old-fashioned way, plunking out melodies and transcribing them by hand in musical notation. This made him an oddity among his peers. With the recent advances in microchip design, most modern songwriters worked on synthesizers.

Greg turned on the lights in the soundproof control booth and sat down in the swivel chair behind the computer console. He accessed a file and checked the score on Kid Xeno's new number. There was a problem with the intro.

Sound filled the room and Greg listened intently. A few minor changes in instrumentation would help. He punched out the codes and listened again. Yes, that was better. Then he stopped and laughed aloud. What would poor Beethoven say if he could see this setup?

Dr. Elias drew on his pipe and shivered. He could feel the chill of the grave in his bones. The thermostat was set at a constant seventy-six degrees, but tonight Dr. Elias had pushed it up higher. He needed the comfort of a warm room.

The disease was progressing normally, although *normal* was a poor choice of words. There was nothing normal about what was happening to his body.

He had logged the symptoms as they'd appeared: shortness of breath, tremors in the extremities. The pain had grown from an occasional sharp stab to a slow, steady twisting. His appetite had decreased and his weight loss totaled eleven and a quarter pounds. His cheekbones protruded sharply from the thin, jaundiced flesh of his face. He barely recognized himself in the mirror.

There were psychological symptoms as well, the same alienation that accompanied psychosis. He felt separated from the people out there beyond his windows. They lived their complacent lives, thinking seldom, if ever, about their own mortality. They were spared the knowledge of when death would happen, where, and precisely how. They could pretend it would never happen to them. It was easy to avoid the subject. It wasn't the sort of thing one brought up at the corner bar or in polite conversation at the dinner table. Death was a great, terrible secret that only happened to other people.

He smoked his father's meerschaum carefully, holding it by the amber stem. The smoke wreathed his head and floated up toward the ceiling. Death had come suddenly for his father, at the hands of the Fascists. It would come slowly for him.

The topic of death was popular with speculative minds. No theory could be proven erroneous. Dr. Elias leaned back in his chair and tried to remember what was written on the subject.

Freud believed that it was impossible to imagine one's own death. Karl Menninger agreed. But neither of them went as far as Goethe, who proposed that this very inability was proof of immortality.

Dr. Elias smiled. Immortality appealed to him lately. Jung raised the subject when he proposed archetypes, the unconscious inheritance from ancestors. Loosely interpreted, it was a form of reincarnation.

Reincarnation had always amused Dr. Elias. A person's soul, or psychic energy, was thought to recycle at death to live again in a new body. Supposedly this had been happening since the beginning of time. No one seemed capable of explaining the population increases. How could there be enough souls to go around? Were they divided, perhaps? Or were some people simply born without souls?

His pipe was finished. Dr. Elias tapped it out and replaced it in its cushioned leather case. He was weary of thinking about death. It did not matter which theory was correct. Death would come, and recognizing its nature would not change its effect.

The evening paper thumped against his door. Dr. Elias went to retrieve it. He had paid his subscription a year in advance. The irony made him smile. Would the paper still be delivered, even after his obituary was published in it? Or would a refund check be issued, one that would never be cashed?

Dr. Elias poured himself a small snifter of Courvoisier and settled down in his favorite chair to read. The item was so small, he almost missed it. Firemen had been called to Greg's apartment last night. It had been a small fire, easily contained. The item was of little interest to the average reader, but to Dr. Elias it was crucial. Greg was breaking down. His duty was clear.

There was no one home at Greg's apartment. Dr. Elias listened to the recording and hung up without leaving his name. There was no reason to leave a message. Greg would never hear it.

Greg was working on a new song when he heard the noise. It was a small sound, no more than a slight scratching. It came from his music library, where he housed his collection of old published sheet music. It was the largest of its kind in the Midwest, over eighty thousand titles, indexed and numbered. Occasionally music historians from the university asked to use his library for reference work.

He hated to stop in the middle of his work, but Greg

knew he had to investigate. If there were rodents in the walls, a few weeks of chewing could ruin his entire inventory.

Greg walked down the hall and listened at the doorway. The library was quiet. It must have been an animal outside, a rabbit or a dog scratching against the exterior wall. He'd order some traps tomorrow and set them behind the stacks, just to be on the safe side.

He went back to the piano and tried to pick up the flow again, but it was no use. After ten minutes of frustration he closed the piano. His concentration was broken. It was impossible to compose with one ear while he listened for every little sound with the other.

The wind had picked up and the old carriage house creaked and groaned. Windows rattled and snow pelted against the roof. Another winter storm was due to hit the Midwest before morning.

Greg picked up his jacket and slipped it on. There was a draft in the studio. It was even colder in the narrow hallway, and he swore impatiently when he found the door ajar. The wind must have pushed it open.

The lights dimmed briefly as he slammed it shut. Greg's heart pounded in fear and then he recovered and laughed at himself. The howling wind outside would make anyone jumpy. Perhaps he should call that college girl and give her a tour of the studio. At least he'd have company if the power lines were down.

Her card was in his wallet. Shelly Graham. He'd make a point of remembering her name this time.

Greg dialed the number and waited five rings. She picked it up on the sixth. She was just going out the door, a family party for her mother's birthday. It wouldn't last long. She could meet him at his studio by eleven.

It was amazing how much better he felt. Greg glanced at his watch. She would be here in less than two hours. That gave him time to write a little song for her, the real thing this time. He'd use her full name at least twice in the chorus. And he'd never play it for anyone else.

He had just finished the first verse when he heard it again, the stealthy scratching in the library. Greg ignored the sound, working instead on completing Shelly's song. He was in a generous mood. The mice could feast until tomorrow.

The last note faded away and Greg grinned. It was perfect. Shelly Graham would like her song. He added a title and centered the sheets on the music rack.

"Shelly?" Greg turned on the bench as he heard the outside door open and close. She was very early.

"In here, Shelly!" he called out. There was no answer.

Greg frowned and got to his feet. Had he imagined the sound of the door? Now the studio was perfectly quiet.

He checked the control booth. No one was there. The hallway was deserted and the tiny bathroom, empty. Then he smelled the smoke. Greg raced to the library and pulled open the door.

The room was in flames. Loose sheet music burned brightly, fanned by gusts of wind from the open window. Thick black smoke rolled up from the cataloged bundles, and one by one the smoldering piles burst into flaming torches. Bound stacks broke open and scattered in the wind, fluttering and rising like bright, searing bats.

Greg coughed as the smoke filled his lungs. "Don't

Sit Under the Apple Tree" whipped past his face. The picture of the Andrews Sisters on the cover was blackened and charred. Lifetimes of words and music were annihilated as they fueled the insatiable flames.

His shocked mind shouted out commands. *Shut the door to the library! Run outside! Call the fire department!* But his paralyzed body would not obey him. The fire held him captive, hypnotizing him with its destructive beauty.

Now the flames reached out for him, demanding their sacrifice. The room was an inferno, a furnace of blazing orange and yellow. A mighty blast of heat seared his face and Greg crumpled to the floor. The very element he had loved and courted had betrayed him. His last thought was of the girl and how she would never hear her song.

The fireplace was blazing cheerily in his living room when Dr. Elias came home. He rubbed his hands together to warm them and stood with his back to the flames. Gradually the heat took the stiffness from his body and he could move despite the pain. Fire was a comforting thing, a necessary element in the survival of the race. It was unfortunate that Greg had been forced to experience directly the destruction it could cause.

After the task was done, he had lingered in the freezing storm until sirens wailed in the distance. It was his duty to stand guard until it was finished. When the first flashing red lights had appeared at the crest of the hill, he left. He did not remember the details of the ride home. His mind was fogged with cold and pain.

Dr. Elias picked up the syringe he had prepared. The fact that he had proceeded without it was a testament to his courage. It would be so easy to increase the dosage, to ignore his final responsibilities and sink into the false security of a drug-induced euphoria. But he had resisted the easy way out. He had tested the strength of his convictions and he had triumphed. Dr. Elias smiled as he plunged the needle into his vein. His father would be proud of him.

Now it was late and there was one more task to complete. Dr. Elias walked down the hallway, flexing his fingers until they were limber enough to hold the brush. He unlocked the door to his studio and faced the group portrait, smiling a little as he saw how well it was taking shape. Doug was finished. He had captured the radiant innocence in his eyes. And Jerry. There was a serenity about him now that he had not had in life.

Dr. Elias picked up his brush. Greg had been haunted by the guilt he'd carried. He would not paint him that way. Now Greg was at peace and his face would reflect the calm acceptance of his fate.

His brushstrokes were the only sounds in the room as he applied paint to the canvas. Greg's lips seemed to whisper words of thanks as he painted them. His eyes were clear and unafraid. Dr. Elias smiled as he put down the brush.

It was finished. Dr. Elias stood back and nodded. Three were terminated now, and the world was safe from them. Five more patients to cure and his work would be completed.

CHAPTER 11

"Move in with you?" Debra turned to look at him in amazement. "Mac! Is this a proposition?"

Mac laughed. "In a way, I suppose it is. I just thought you might feel nervous staying all alone. My house is big and it'd be nice to share it with you. As far as the proposition goes, I solemnly promise not to attack you in the middle of the night."

Debra swallowed nervously. If Mac had been any other man, she would have refused immediately, but somehow Mac was different. It wasn't just the sex thing, either. She felt safe with Mac and she hadn't felt that way with any man since her husband.

"I . . . well . . . yes!" Debra blushed to the roots of her hair. "I'd like to move in with you, just temporarily, of course, until things settle down. It's really nice of you to ask me, Mac."

It took only fifteen minutes to drive to Debra's apartment. Mac was grinning as he followed her up the stairs. The apartment building was old, but it was in good repair. Mac wandered through the apartment while she packed a couple of suitcases. Debra's living room was tidy and bare of more than minimal decoration. There were no family photos, no pieces of memorabilia to clutter her bookshelves. Mac looked in vain for some evidence of her personality, but even the magazines on the end table were standard and unexciting.

He poked his head in the small kitchen. There were no grocery bags or coupons lying about, no hastily written notes tacked to the refrigerator. The sink was clear of dishes and the porcelain was scrubbed to a dazzling white. All the pots and pans were highly polished, lined up on their shelves in precise geometric order. Even her Tupperware fit. Every lid sat on its matching container.

The bathroom was perfectly nondescript. Matching towels hung on the rack. A bottle of shampoo and one of conditioner sat on the shelf over the sink. The level of liquid in both was the same. Mac shook his head. Such precision was almost frightening. Debra's whole apartment looked like the models that builders showed to their clients. There was nothing personal anywhere.

Suddenly Mac understood. Debra was hiding. If there was nothing of Debra on display, that meant there was nothing to criticize. She was too frightened to put the stamp of her personality on these rooms. Somehow he would have to change that.

"Mac?" He heard her call out to him. He found her in the bedroom, trying to close the lid of the suitcase. "I can't get it shut!"

She looked endearingly untidy. Her hair was mussed and there was a smudge of dirt on her cheek.

"Sit on it." Mac grinned and lifted her up. "Just wiggle a little and I'll do the rest."

Debra laughed as Mac snapped the suitcase shut. "Gary Cooper and Audrey Hepburn. Nineteen fifty-seven. *Love in the Afternoon!*"

Mac loaded her suitcases in the trunk and dropped her at the paper. He had to spend a couple of hours at the station. They'd meet later for dinner and then go home. He found himself looking forward to the end of the day.

Now it was evening and they were sitting in his living room watching television. Mac smiled. It was surprising how much more he enjoyed his movies when he shared them with Debbie. Just having her next to him on the couch was a pleasure. He had never realized how lonely he had been.

"'I suppose I was in your way going down the rapids. Then what you said to me back there on the river was a lie about how you never could have done it alone and how you lost your heart and everything. You liar! Oh, Charlie, we're having our first quarrel!'"

Mac grinned as Debra mouthed the words along with Katharine Hepburn. She was staring at the screen intently, her crocheting forgotten on her lap. They were watching *The African Queen,* but Mac found himself watching Debra instead of the movie. She was so beautiful sitting there with the brightly colored skeins of yarn stacked at her side.

It was almost like being married. There had been only one awkward moment when they'd first gotten home. Debra had been standing in the doorway of the spare room, staring at the single bed.

"It's way down here at the end of the hall." Her voice had quivered slightly.

"Why don't you sleep with me?" Mac had taken the

suitcases from her and carried them into his room. "I got used to you last night. It's nice to have someone to cuddle in the middle of the night."

She had blushed and nodded, not quite meeting his eyes. Her hands had trembled as she'd opened the suitcases and started to put away her things, but Mac had noticed her grateful smile.

Bogie and Hepburn were going through the marriage ceremony now. Mac watched for a moment. This movie was one of his favorites. He knew every scene. Debra was so absorbed she didn't even notice when her crochet hook slid off her lap and dropped to the rug.

It was good, having Debbie here. Her clothes hung in his closet on the side that was empty after Mary had left. Now there were bright, feminine colors to balance his browns and grays. The scent of her perfume made the whole house smell wonderful. Her makeup sat on a tray in the bathroom, precisely arranged to take up the least amount of room. The bottles of shampoo and conditioner were in the shower, and Mac grinned. He had used the shampoo when he'd gotten home from work. Now the levels were no longer even.

Mac hoped his untidy habits wouldn't drive Debra up the wall. He was a notorious slob. Even though he tried, his clothes never seemed to wind up in the laundry basket. On wash day he had to check every room for forgotten items. And he wasn't very good about doing the dishes. Mostly he made do with paper plates and TV dinners. He noticed that Debra had straightened up the refrigerator, and the bathroom sink was almost white again. Luckily Debra hadn't found his beer can collection. He had 114 different labels on the top shelf in the spare room. They hadn't been dusted in three years.

The house was beginning to benefit from a woman's

touch. Pretty soon he wouldn't be able to find anything without asking her. Mac was a little surprised to find it didn't bother him a bit. He even promised himself that he'd try to be neater. Having Debra stay here was the best thing that had happened to him in a long time.

Mac turned back to the movie in time to see the German gunboat blow up. Hepburn and Bogart were swimming to safety. There were tears in Debra's eyes.

"I just loved it!" She leaned back and sighed. "Our lives are so ordinary in comparison. There's no romance anymore."

"Maybe there could be if two people were willing to take a chance."

Debra turned to look at him. She saw the warmth in his eyes. Mac wanted to make love to her.

She knew she could put him off, misinterpret his meaning. It would be easy to pretend not to understand. But that would put a lie between them. She had to decide quickly before Mac noticed her fear.

She wanted to make love with Mac. She felt a warm shudder of anticipation when she thought of it. But what if he couldn't? What would happen then?

"Let's go to bed, Mac." Debra tried to hide her nervousness as she smiled. She got up and a skein of yarn rolled to the floor. She left it there. Being neat and tidy wasn't important right now.

Debra's hands were trembling as she went to the bathroom to put on her new nightgown. It was a thin silk negligee, totally unsuitable for winter. She had dashed into Dayton's this afternoon to buy it, while Mac was down at the station. She had picked it on a whim, without even trying it on. It was totally unlike her to be so expensively spontaneous.

Debra gasped as she faced her reflection in the

mirror. The peach color made her skin seem rosy and enticing. Her breasts were barely covered by the lace of the neckline. Every curve of her body was revealed. The thin, clinging material was shamelessly transparent, falling over her hips in a sleek, unbroken line. She looked voluptuous and ripe, like an accomplished paramour.

Suddenly Debra felt ridiculous. The negligee was so blatantly seductive that she was afraid to face Mac. How should she act? What would she say?

Debra shivered in the cold bathroom. Perhaps she should have worn her old flannel pajamas like Doris Day in *Pillow Talk*. She looked too much like Maggie the Cat in this ridiculous negligee.

That was it! Debra practiced a pose with her hand on her hip. She'd be Elizabeth Taylor tonight. She'd pretend to be wise and experienced, a professional courtesan. She would take the initiative and be sexy and enticing. Mac would be unable to resist her.

Mac tried to calm down as he waited for her. He was more than a little nervous. In a way, he almost wished that she hadn't caught his meaning out there in the living room. What if he failed?

He heard the bathroom door open. She was coming. Mac looked up as she walked to the bed and his heart pounded loudly in his chest. She was gorgeous! That negligee was the sexiest thing he'd ever seen.

Debra looked so different, he barely knew her. She moved like a practiced seductress as she snapped off the light and slid into bed. She reached out for him and folded her arms around his neck, kissing him deeply. She was ripe and beautifully wanton as she pressed her body against his. The heat of her came through the thin silk and he could feel her need surround him, demanding and urgent.

He wanted to, but nothing happened. Mac kissed her back, but something was wrong. Then she reached out to fondle him and he shuddered at her touch. Her motions were calculated and cold. It felt almost as if she had memorized a sex manual and was flipping through the sections, trying one technique after another.

"I need you, Mac." Her voice was low and sexy. Mac frowned in the darkness. Everything she was doing was right, but he couldn't respond. His frustration grew as she tried, again and again, rubbing against him, grasping with desperate fingers. There were long minutes of agony as she went through all the motions, trying to arouse something that was dead and useless.

"Debbie, stop!"

Finally he pushed her away. There was no life in him, nothing to satisfy her need. She was a woman and he was a eunuch. The farce was too painful to play out any further.

He knew they should talk. Mac tried to find the right words, but his disappointment was too great. He had failed. He turned away from her and hid the source of his agony. He wanted to be alone in his misery.

"Mac, please!" Debra tried to put her arms around him, but he pushed her back. Her pity was the last thing he wanted. Why couldn't she leave him alone? It was clear the whole thing was over between them.

He heard her start to cry, but he was powerless to comfort her. There were no magic words to bridge this gulf. He could not give her what she needed. It was as simple as that. Now she would leave him and he couldn't blame her.

It took a long time before he was able to speak again. His voice was flat and emotionless. "I'll help you move back home in the morning, Debbie. There's nothing for you here. I'm sorry it didn't work out."

There was a moment of silence. Then she started to sob again. "I don't want to go, Mac. I . . . I love you! I'll sleep in the other room. Or out on the couch. But please, Mac, let me stay!"

Mac rolled over to look at her. She was serious. She really wanted to stay. And she loved him!

"I love you, too, Debbie." He reached out to hold her. "I just thought you wouldn't want to stay after—"

"Oh, God, Mac. That was all my fault!" Debra's voice was shaking. "I made a terrible mistake. I was Maggie the Cat and I should have been Doris Day!"

Suddenly Mac laughed. Everything was clear now. Debra had been nervous and scared, too.

"You should have been Debbie," he corrected her gently. "I don't want Doris Day or Elizabeth Taylor. I just want you."

Mac held her tightly then. They rocked back and forth, laughing and crying.

What they had between them was stronger than this crushing disappointment. It was going to be all right.

"Mac?" Her voice was small and tentative. "This might sound unromantic, but I'm hungry."

"Me, too." Mac grinned and pulled her to her feet. "Let's go make triple-decker sandwiches. There's a robe in the bathroom you can wear. That nightgown's gorgeous, but it can't be very warm."

Debra grabbed Mac's terrycloth robe and slipped it on. She tied it tightly around the waist and turned up the collar. She felt better now, almost her old normal self. She was not cut out to be a seductress. There was no use in pretending. She'd throw the negligee in the garbage tomorrow and concentrate on being just herself.

Mac was working at the butcher block table when she got to the kitchen. Jars of mayonnaise, mustard, and plum jam stood open on the counter. There were three kinds of bread stacked on the table and Debra watched, wide eyed, as he opened a can of sardines.

"Ham? Peanut butter? And sardines?" She shook her head and shuddered.

"Hey! Don't knock it until you've tried it." Mac grinned and slapped a sandwich together. He put it on a paper plate and handed it to her with a flourish. "'Years from now, when they talk about this—and they will—remember to tell them it was my idea.' Faye Dunaway. *The Towering Inferno.* Nineteen seventy-four."

CHAPTER 12

Father Marx knew he should stay away from the meeting. Old habits were strong and he would be tempted to blurt out his problems. When he answered the phone he firmly intended to make some excuse, but Kay's voice was too familiar and comforting to resist.

"I'll be a little late," he heard himself say. "The statue of the Virgin Mary was smashed last night. I'll have to take care of it before I can leave."

"Oh, Father! What a shame! Was it vandalism?"

For a moment he hesitated, but Kay had provided the answer. "Yes. Vandalism."

Father Marx sighed as he hung up the phone. He didn't like to lie, but it was important that none of them guess the truth. They had enough on their minds right now. He couldn't add to their burden.

He found Thomas McCrea in the front of the church. The old man had swept the plaster into a neat pile.

"It's a sad day, Father." Thomas stepped back and crossed himself. "Did you call the police?"

"No, Thomas. The Lord will deal with it. Divine justice is surer than any law made by man."

They worked in silence, pushing the rubble into trash bags and carrying it out to the street. Finally it was done, and there was a large empty spot where the statue had been.

"Here's something for your trouble." Father Marx pressed money into the old man's hand. Thomas lived on a pitifully small pension and picked up odd jobs in the neighborhood. He was always on hand when there was work to be done.

"Will we be locking the doors now, Father, to protect our holy saints?"

It was an old argument and Father Marx was weary of it. Thomas had been trying to get him to lock the church doors for years.

"No, Thomas. We must put our trust in the Lord and not in locks and bolts."

There was disapproval in Thomas's eyes, but Father Marx refused to back down. It was true that other churches were locked at night. Most priests thought it was a necessary precaution. Locks kept the vagrants out and made the church less vulnerable to vandals and thieves. But Father Marx knew locks barred the parishioners as well as the criminals. They were denied a refuge in time of trouble. And trouble could come at any time, not just in the daylight hours. As long as he was the priest at St. Steven's, the doors would remain open.

"Whatever you say, Father." Thomas gave a curt nod. "I'll be leaving you then, until the evening Mass."

The old man grumbled to himself as he walked off. Thomas had been a member of the parish for so long that sometimes he felt he had the right to dictate church policy.

Father Marx rushed to his office to call a taxi. He

pulled off his work boots and replaced them with a dress pair. Then he took his heavy camel's-hair coat from the closet. It was cold today. The thermometer outside the window was stuck at five degrees below zero.

It took a long time for the cab to come. Father Marx watched the street so he would be ready. He could see the green plastic trash bags by the curb, waiting for the afternoon pickup. The Virgin Mary lay crumbled inside. Would Thomas change his mind about locking the church doors if he knew that vandals were not to blame?

The taxi driver pulled up and beeped his horn. Father Marx clamped his hat on his head and rushed out into the cold. Now he must think only of the group. His own guilty secret would remain in the hands of the Lord.

They sat in a tight circle around the coffee table. There were only five of them now. Mac noticed that they unconsciously drew together, as if for protection. They reminded him of frightened deer, forming a circle to fend off the wolves.

"What next?" Nora shook her head sadly. "Our group has been haunted by tragedy since Dr. Elias had to leave us."

Kay shivered. "It's frightening. Another one of us is dead. I know this is going to sound crazy, but it . . . it's almost like someone is killing us off."

"That's exactly how I feel!" Debra clasped her hands together nervously. "First Doug. Then Jerry. And now Greg. I keep wondering if I'm going to be next!"

Nora slipped a cigarette into her holder and laughed. "You two make it sound like a production of *Ten Little*

Indians. You're just letting your imaginations run away with you."

"That's probably true." Mac nodded. "But three fatalities out of a group of eight is really unusual. I think we should check in with each other every night. It'll make us feel more secure. You three call me at my house. If I'm not home, Debbie'll be there."

"Mac! You got it up!"

There was a shocked silence, and they all turned to stare at Nora. She had the grace to blush.

"I'm sorry. It just slipped out. Vinnie, darling? I need your help. My tongue is possessed by the Devil."

Debra couldn't help it. She started to laugh. Nora was so outrageous.

"An exorcism?" Father Marx chuckled. "Nora, my child, if I took away your devilment you'd have no personality left."

"Back to the telephone calls." Mac grinned sheepishly. "Call me any time. I mean that. Day or night, it doesn't matter."

"Like a paranoids' hotline?" Kay gave a nervous laugh. "You're right, Mac. That would help. I get awfully nervous when I'm here all alone."

"You're never alone, Kay." Father Marx reached out to pat her hand. "God is always with you. And He doesn't charge long-distance rates."

Kay gave him a tentative smile. Father Marx was doing his best to cheer her even though he had troubles of his own.

"Thank you, Father. I know you must be terribly upset about your church being vandalized, but still you haven't lost your sense of humor. I wish I could be like that."

"What happened to your church, Father Marx?" Debra leaned forward.

"The statue of the Virgin Mary was smashed last night." Father Marx looked down at the table so he wouldn't have to meet their eyes. He would have to be very careful not to slip up now.

"People don't have respect for anything anymore!" Nora frowned. "It takes a real sicko to vandalize a church!"

"Did you call the police, Father?" Mac was concerned. "If you request extra surveillance, they'll keep an eye on the church."

"I think I know who did it, Mac. Believe me, it's not a matter for the police. I'll have to handle this my own way."

Mac nodded, but he watched Father Marx closely. The priest was hiding something. His hands were folded together so tightly that his knuckles were white, and he stared down at the table, visibly upset. His jocularity had vanished the moment they'd started to talk about the statue, and he acted almost guilty. It wasn't like Father Marx to be secretive about anything.

"I wish I could help." Debra sighed deeply. "There must be something we can do."

Nora reached into her purse. "You know I'm not a religious person, Vinnie, but I'd like to start a fund for replacing your statue."

"Nora?" Father Marx looked up in surprise. "That's very kind."

"Just don't start trying to save my soul." Nora

laughed. "I want to help you, that's all. If we don't help each other, we'll all go down the tubes."

"Count me in." Kay nodded emphatically. "Our accountant said we needed a tax write-off. Charles doesn't know it yet, but he's just made a big healthy contribution."

Debra stopped at Byerly's when she got through at the paper. Mac was working until eight and she had plenty of time to get home and fix dinner. *Home? Fix dinner?* Debra laughed out loud as she pushed her cart to the meat case. She was thinking the thoughts of a suburban housewife and she didn't even know how to cook!

The cuts of meats in the case were a mystery. Debra had no idea what to do with a rolled rump or a boneless blade Boston. She'd probably be safer with hamburger or hot dogs, but she wanted to make a special dinner for Mac tonight. It was her way of saying thank you for being there when she needed him.

A Strauss waltz was playing on the store's music system and Debra danced down the aisle to the cookbook section. She picked out an illustrated Betty Crocker edition and put it in her basket. Several people stared at her as she went back to the meat case. For the first time in years, Debra didn't care what they thought. She was happy and that was what counted.

Debra stood at the meat case and paged through the cookbook. There was a complete menu for a family dinner that looked delicious in the illustration. She rang the bell and asked the butcher for the right cut of beef to make a Yankee pot roast. If it didn't turn out like the picture, she'd do an exposé on the General Mills test kitchens!

She found fresh carrots and russet potatoes in the produce section. The book said to arrange them around the meat. The celery was expensive, over a dollar a bunch. No wonder people bought canned vegetables in the winter.

Betty Crocker suggested apple pie for dessert, but Debra didn't feel confident enough to tackle a pie crust. She settled for a gallon of Lady Kemps French vanilla ice cream and a Swanson frozen pie. At least she could claim she baked it herself.

Byerly's bakery was crowded, but Debra took a number and stood in line. She wanted the very best rye bread for Mac. The cinnamon rolls were lying in state at the front of the glass display case. Éclairs dripping with rich glazed chocolate tried to seduce her. The aroma of warm doughnuts did foolish things to her head and suddenly Debra was starving. She'd never be able to hold out until Mac got home.

"A loaf of dark rye, one of those gorgeous éclairs, two great big cinnamon rolls, and . . . that's enough." Debra laughed along with the girls at the counter. "Put the éclair and the rolls in a separate bag, please. They're not going to make it home."

Debra checked out and took her plastic claim tag. She started her car and drove to the pickup area. There she had to wait again, in a long line of cars. The new Cadillac in front of her sent up towering plumes of white exhaust in the freezing air.

"I'd better put these in the backseat." The pickup boy grinned as he brought out her groceries. "Your milk'll freeze in the trunk. Cans even burst when it gets this cold. One of our new guys loaded up a trunk last week and the customer had two cases of popped Diet Pepsi by the time she got home."

Debra tipped the boy a dollar and smiled at his amazed reaction. She reached into the white bakery bag and took a huge bite of the éclair. She finished it before she got out of the parking lot.

It was rush hour, but Debra didn't mind. She was grinning as she got on the crowded freeway and headed toward Mac's house. It was wonderful to be alive.

It hit her with the force of a physical blow. Greg was dead. Debra's smile vanished and she was suddenly contrite. It wasn't right to feel joyous. She should be mourning for Greg.

Debra shivered. It was growing dark and she snapped on her headlights. The yellow beams picked up the high snowbanks on the side of the road and she felt very alone in the cocoon of her car. Where was Greg now? Did he know she cared? Was he glad she was denying her happiness in honor of his death?

She thought deeply through four miles of traffic. Greg had believed in happiness. He had actively pursued it in his own brief life. Debra reached out to turn on the radio. Then she started to sing at the top of her lungs. She didn't know the song, but that didn't matter. Greg would definitely approve.

CHAPTER 13

When Nora opened the door to the loft, the first thing she saw was the tree. It was a huge spruce, six feet tall, flocked in pastel pink. It had pink twinkling lights and pink satin balls. Little pink birds perched on the branches, and a huge rose-colored star glowed at the very top.

Nora clamped her hand over her mouth and shook with silent laughter. Elena had decorated while she'd been gone.

"Elena?" Nora called out, but there was no answer. The stereo played soft Christmas music and two wine-glasses sat on the ivory table in front of the couch. The ashtray was filled with cigarette butts, Eve 120's with little flowers on the filters. They were Hope's brand. Hope had been here, visiting Elena.

"Elena?" Nora called out again, a little louder this time. She walked over to the alcove that served as their bedroom, but it was deserted. Elena's tote bag lay in a heap on the floor. The toe of one dance shoe stuck out the top. Her black leotard was draped carelessly over the bathroom door and her scarf was tossed on the dresser.

Elena must have brought Hope home with her after dance class.

Nora tried to think positive thoughts. Elena loved her. She had decorated their loft for Christmas. Hope had merely come along to help her with the surprise. Nora knew she should be grateful, not jealous.

Even though she tried not to give in, Nora's eyes were drawn to the bed. It was unmussed. Of course they could have straightened it, after.

Nora went back to the living room. She did her best to ignore the pink atrocity as she picked up the ashtray and emptied it. Where was Elena? She was always home on Wednesday afternoons.

Elena's sheared beaver coat was on a chair in the living room. That meant she was probably downstairs in the workshop. Elena never went outside without her coat. She'd probably insist on wearing it in the middle of August.

Nora hung the coat on a padded hanger in the closet and sighed. Elena never picked up her clothes, and half the time Nora felt like a mother instead of a lover. In some ways Elena was still a child. She was half Nora's age, only twenty-three.

The coat had been a birthday present. Elena had squealed in rapture when she'd opened the box. Her first fur coat! Wasn't Nora a darling to buy it for her? She had worn it through the whole party and she'd kept it by the bed that night. Nora knew it was well worth the money she had spent.

Nora rinsed out the two wineglasses and made a cup of tea for herself. When it was ready, she carried it down the stairs to the workshop.

The stage lights were on and Nora tiptoed to a seat in the back row. They were near the apron, going over a scene. Elena's long black hair fell over her face in a shining wave as she leaned forward and laughed. Her arm was around Hope's shoulders as she led the girl back to center stage and gave her a cue.

Nora gasped with shock as she realized what they were rehearsing. It was her play, *The Heretic Mother*! She was opening in the lead role at the Guthrie on Friday. Elena must have given Hope the script.

There was no way she could control her jealousy as Nora heard Hope deliver the lines that she had rehearsed for so many months. Her hands started to shake and she clenched her fingers around the arms of the seat.

It took every ounce of self-control she had to sit quietly in the darkened theater. She wanted to jump up from her seat and kill that blond bitch on the stage. And Elena! Elena had betrayed her! Everything was perfectly clear now. Hope was trying to steal her role and Elena was helping her!

"You've got it all wrong, Hope. You owe me five bucks. I told you that scene was too difficult for you."

"How does she do it?" Hope shook her head. "I watched Nora in rehearsal and I thought I picked it up."

"Nora's a genius, it's that simple. If you ask her after the opening, she might coach you. Don't bother her now, though. Even great actresses like Nora get opening night jitters."

"Do you think she'd come to a party tonight?" There was an eager expression on Hope's face. "I told some of my friends that I was in her class and they're dying to meet her. They say she's a living legend."

A living legend? Nora had a mental picture of an ancient Chinese, glazing pots in some mountain cave. She wasn't sure she liked the image, but she wasn't about to quibble with terminology. Living legends certainly didn't sit in the back rows of theaters, spying on their lovers.

Nora didn't wait to hear any more. She got up quietly and went back up the stairs to the loft. She was still shaking, but it was from relief, not anger. She had almost made a dreadful mistake.

"Thank you for the gorgeous Christmas tree, darling." Nora hugged Elena as she came in the door. "Pink's my favorite color."

"I wasn't sure about that, but Hope convinced me." Elena hugged Nora back and kicked off her shoes. "She says they have one just like it in the lobby of her bank."

Nora grinned. She wanted to make a joke about First Flamingo Federal, but she bit her tongue. The tree would look better once they got some packages under it.

"I picked up something for you this morning." Nora pointed to the box on the table.

"It's not Christmas yet." Elena looked puzzled. "Why did you buy me a present?"

"Just because I love you so much."

Elena lifted the lid on the box and gasped. "An ounce of Pheromone? Oh, Nora! You shouldn't have!"

She opened the bottle and sniffed at the stopper. "It's heavenly! I'm going to wear it right now. We don't have to go out tonight, do we? I'd rather spend a nice evening here and go to bed early."

"That's fine with me."

Nora smiled as Elena dabbed the perfume behind her ears. She hadn't even mentioned Hope's party. It was good to know Elena preferred to spend the evening at home with the living legend.

* * *

Debbie was waiting for him when he came in the door. Mac grinned as she held out her arms.

"As chairwoman of the reception committee, I welcome you with open arms."

Mac stopped in the doorway and thought for a second. "'Is that so? How late do you stay open?'"

"Right on! Groucho Marx and Margaret Dumont. I just caught the last of *Duck Soup* on Channel Nine."

They laughed and hugged for a moment. Then Debra pulled Mac inside and shut the door.

"Something sure smells good!" Mac hung his coat on the hook by the door and kicked off his boots. "Don't tell me that besides being beautiful, you know how to cook."

"Well . . . I'm not sure. If it doesn't taste right we'll eat the picture. It's supposed to be Yankee pot roast. Do you want a beer while you're waiting? There's a six pack of Newcastle Brown Ale in the refrigerator."

"Newcastle Brown Ale? Where'd you get that? I've never heard of it before."

"It's imported from England. The man at the liquor store thought you'd like it. It's on the top shelf, right next to the milk."

Mac grinned as he sat down at the table and poured beer into the mug Debbie had chilled. It was almost frightening the way she was doing everything right. Dinner smelled fantastic. There was cold beer in the refrigerator. His sink was clean. He wasn't sure how he'd stumbled into this whole thing, but he wasn't going to give it up without a fight. If Debbie thought he was ever going to let her move back to her own apartment, she was crazy!

The phone rang as Debbie was dishing up his second

helping of pot roast. Mac picked it up on the kitchen extension. “Hi, Kay. Did the family get back yet?”

Debra listened to the one-sided conversation. Mac was really good on the phone.

“You tell Charles he’d better keep an eye on you. You’re too pretty to leave alone for two days. Is Ralph glad to be back from the vet’s?”

Debra grinned as Mac held the phone out to her. She could hear Kay’s little dog barking in the background. Mac always seemed to know what to say to people to make them feel good. Some people would call it Irish blarney, but Debra knew it was more than that. Mac cared. It came across in everything he said.

Nora called as they were finishing dessert. Everything was fine. She was just checking in. She and Elena were spending a quiet evening at home.

“Two down, one to go,” Debra said as Mac hung up the phone. “I wonder why Father Marx hasn’t called yet.”

“I think I’ll call him.” Mac frowned. “He seemed different today. Did you notice it, Debbie?”

“He was upset about his statue. Other than that, I thought he was all right.”

“Just a crazy hunch, I guess.” Mac shrugged. “I’ll call him anyway. Then we’re through for the night.”

Debra scraped the plates and put them in the dishwasher while Mac was on the phone. It was a short call.

“Father Marx says everything’s fine.” Mac came back to the kitchen and leaned up against the refrigerator. “He just forgot to call, that’s all. Get your coat, Debbie. We’re going for a little ride.”

The snow had stopped falling and the night was crystal clear as they drove down the silent streets.

“Oh, look!” Debra pointed as they passed houses that

were decorated for Christmas. "There's a sleigh with reindeer on that roof!"

"The people on the next corner always have a big Santa up by their chimney. There it is, Debbie. See?"

"We're getting a Christmas tree?" Debra laughed as they drove into the Golden Valley YMCA lot. "Oh, Mac! It's been years since I've had a Christmas tree!"

They stomped through the snow, trying to pick out the best tree. It was hard to tell. The trees were tied into tight little bundles to prevent the frozen branches from snapping off. Mac had a theory about the right tree. It had to be shaped like a carrot and it had to have an exact ratio of two to seven for its width and height.

"I certainly hope you brought your tape measure." Debra tried to keep a straight face.

"Right here." Mac pulled a Stanley collapsible steel tape out of his pocket. "You figure out the math and I'll measure 'em."

Mac measured trees for forty-five minutes before they found exactly the right one. It was twenty-seven inches wide and ninety-four and a half inches high.

"Oh, no!" Debra started to laugh as Mac picked up the tree. "That's almost eight feet tall, Mac. We'll never be able to get it in the house!"

"You just leave that to me, Debbie. We'll lop a little off the bottom and a little off the top and it'll fit just fine."

Debra was still laughing as they tied it on top of Mac's Toyota and drove toward home. She snapped on the radio and tried to find some Christmas carols, but all she could get was news. Finally she settled for *The Nutcracker Suite* on KSJR.

"We'll put the tree up tonight and trim it tomorrow after it thaws out a little," Mac promised. "Do you mind using my parents' old decorations? Mary took all the new ones with her when she left."

"I think that's even nicer." Debra smiled. She thought about the old decorations her father had given her. She'd run over and get them out of storage tomorrow. The Scandinavian straw angel would look perfect on the top of their first Christmas tree.

CHAPTER 14

It was going to be a good Christmas this year in spite of everything. Kay smiled as she wrapped a red and green tree skirt around the bottom of the lovely Scotch pine. It stood in front of the mirrored wall and the reflection of the lights would make it look like two trees. She'd have to watch the kids to make sure they did a good job trimming the back.

Kay glanced at the grandfather clock that had belonged to her parents. It was noon and she had been up since six this morning. She had mixed up two batches of rum balls and baked all the sugar cookies before breakfast. Trish and James could frost them later. Last year James had been into ethnic origins. He'd insisted that all the Santas be black. He had mixed all the food coloring together and added it to the frosting. The cookies had looked so awful that no one had eaten them. James hadn't mentioned the black movement for a while, but Kay had stocked up on chocolate frosting, just in case.

The holiday season was busy this year. Kay sighed as she thought of her schedule. Sometime this afternoon she had to go to the Children's Medical Center and the Sister Kenny Institute to deliver toys. It was one of her annual duties as the mayor's wife. The other hospitals got pots of poinsettias. There were fourteen hospitals in all. She'd have to recruit Trish to help with the carrying. Later tonight the whole family was attending a performance of the *Messiah* by the Minnesota Symphony Orchestra.

Tomorrow was just as busy. She had a League of Women Voters luncheon and a drop-in at the Swedish Institute's holiday tea. Her therapy appointment was at three. Then she had to rush home, pick up the kids, and make an appearance at the city employees' Christmas party. From there they'd go directly to the Guthrie for Nora's opening night.

She couldn't do it. Kay got out her calendar and checked Friday's appointments again. Something would have to be scratched. There weren't enough hours in the day. She stared down at the blocks of time and arranged her priorities. There were want-tos, should-dos, and must-dos. Everything for tomorrow was a must-do, except for her shrink's appointment. She'd have to call and cancel again.

When could she work in her hour with the new therapist? Kay turned the page. On Saturday she was modeling in a charity fashion show at Dayton's Sky Room and she had to save the morning for a hair appointment. That night was a duty appearance at the governor's mansion for his annual Christmas party. Saturday was out.

Sunday was relatively free, but that didn't help. Her psychiatrist's office was closed. Monday was Christmas Eve and Tuesday was Christmas. There was no way she could reschedule her appointment until next Wednesday, at the earliest, and even that was inconvenient. Actually, she'd be better off waiting until the first of the year. The week between Christmas and New Year's was heavily booked and she had entertaining of her own to do.

Kay closed the book with a snap. Her therapy could wait. She was sure she'd be just fine without a shrink to hold her hand. Mental health was all a matter of positive thinking. If she was determined to stay cheerful and stable, she would.

"Another live Christmas tree?" Charles came into the room, carrying a stack of boxes. He stopped in the doorway and made a face.

"Oh, Kay! That means I'll have to chop a hole in the backyard and plant the damn thing after the holidays are over. It's a waste! You know they always die by the middle of February. Why don't you get a dead one in the first place? Everybody else buys cut trees."

"But, Charles . . . that's not humane!" Kay took the boxes of ornaments from his arms and set them down on the table. "You know how I feel. I don't even like cut flowers."

"You're too tenderhearted for your own good." Charles laughed and ruffled her hair. "I wish I could stay home and help trim the tree, but I've got a council meeting this afternoon."

"The kids'll help." Kay rose up on her tiptoes and kissed him. "Don't forget to bring home a collar with bells for Ralph. He just loves Christmas."

"I'd better make a list." Charles took out his leather-covered Daily Reminder. "Collar for Ralph. String of outdoor lights for the patio."

He looked up and sighed. "I know you're busy, honey,

but could you pick up my gray suit at the cleaners? I need it for the symphony tonight."

"I'll stop in on the way to the florist's. Trish and I are doing the hospitals this afternoon."

"While you're there, pick up a poinsettia for Rob's secretary. You'd better get one for Shirley, too. And I wouldn't complain if you brought home some mistletoe for our bedroom."

"That sounds nice and festive!" Kay laughed and kissed him again. "Hurry up now, honey, or you'll be late."

Twenty minutes later the living room was in shambles. Boxes of decorations lay open on the rug, and tissue paper was everywhere. Kay replaced the last bulb that had burned out last year and stood back to look at the tree.

"See those two greens together up there at the top? Switch the colors around, Trish."

Kay turned around in time to see James with a fistful of tinsel. She knew exactly what he was going to do.

"Don't you dare throw it, James! Hang each strand separately and evenly from the branch."

Kay grinned as she remembered her own mother saying the very same thing. The urge to throw tinsel must be hereditary.

"When I was a girl we had to tear the tinsel apart. It was made of real metal then, not the plastic we have now. My mother used to tell us to—"

"Count ten icicles for each branch so they were even!" Trish and James finished the sentence for her.

"Sorry." Kay laughed. "I guess you've heard that one before. Did I ever tell you about the birds' Christmas tree?"

"I don't think so." Trish looked interested.

"We used to trim a special tree outside for the winter birds. We hung apples and pieces of suet from the branches. That way the birds had a holiday, too."

"That's sweet, Mom!" Trish grinned. "What's suet, anyway?"

"It's fat. Birds have a high metabolic rate and they need lots of fat in their diet to keep from freezing in the winter. Every time we fried meat, we poured off the grease in a jar by the stove. We saved it all year long for the birds' Christmas tree."

"Oh, gross!" James made a face.

"I don't think it's gross at all." Trish gave James a withering look. "Maybe we should make a birds' Christmas tree. We could trim the little spruce in front of the picture window. Can you buy suet in the store, Mom?"

"Probably not, but raw bacon would work just as well."

"Can we do it, Mom?" James wore a devilish grin and Kay noticed that he had thrown some tinsel at the back of the tree while she'd been talking to Trish. She'd have to straighten it out later. Ralph was also decorated. He was chasing his tail, trying to get rid of the tinsel.

"Ralph! Calm down!" Kay grabbed the little dog and took off the tinsel. She managed to put a smile on her face as she turned to James. Sometimes it took every ounce of patience she had to be a good mother.

"We can make a birds' tree if you want to, James. It's a good way to learn the names of the winter birds. You might want to do a paper on ornithology for science class."

"Well . . . maybe." James shrugged. "I just thought it would be fun, that's all. Ralph'll go bananas when he jumps up at the bacon."

* * *

It was four o'clock when the young couple left Father Marx's office. It would be a good marriage. Father Marx was convinced they took their responsibilities seriously. He glanced at his watch and saw he had two hours before confession started. It was just enough time to decorate the church for Christmas.

Father Marx smiled as he got out the boxes of artificial trees. He felt better today. He had read over the church's position on psychotherapy last night. For the first time, it made sense. He understood why it was impossible for a secular psychiatrist to counsel a priest. Father Marx realized he had erred when he'd gone to Dr. Elias. He wouldn't make that mistake again. He could get along just fine without therapy.

The boxes were very light. Father Marx picked up all four at once and carried them to the front of the church. He noticed that the trees were made in Taiwan, of non-allergenic manmade materials. Joyce Kilmer had been wrong. Someone besides only God could make a tree.

Buying the plastic trees was one of Father Marx's wisest investments. He had used them for the past three years and they would hold up for another six or seven. They had paid for themselves by the second year and now the Christmas tree fund could be used for other, more charitable purposes.

Father Marx chuckled as he opened the boxes. Not one of his parishioners had guessed that the trees were artificial. That was a secret between Father Marx and the Almighty.

It took a minimum of effort to assemble the trees. The branches fit into neat little holes on the plastic trunk. They were numbered. Branch eight fit precisely into hole eight. Of course it was possible to see where they joined, but Father Marx solved that by spraying a light coating of flocking over the joints.

The lights were still in their original packages, purchased at an after-Christmas sale. Father Marx started at the peak of the first tree, winding the lights around as he worked his way down to the base. There were three strings of bulbs for each tree and they connected to a large extension cord that ran behind the baptismal font to the wall socket.

The ornaments came next. There were eight boxes of shiny gold bells, molded in one piece of unbreakable plastic. Father Marx hung two bells on each branch, one at the tip and another near the trunk. A traditional flaxen-haired angel perched at the top of each tree, snowy-white wings spread gracefully, peering down on the pews with benevolent blue eyes.

Father Marx stepped back to look at his handiwork. The trees were perfect. Now St. Steven's was dressed in its Christmas finery. Only one final touch remained to complete his little deception. Father Marx put an aerosol can of pine-scented fragrance behind the altar rail. He would spray the church before every Mass and no one would suspect his trees were fake.

"Thank you, sir!" The young delivery boy grinned as he looked down at the size of the tip. "Make sure to ask for me when you order your tree next year."

Dr. Elias closed the door behind the boy and locked it. There would be no Christmas for him next year. His shoulders were stooped with pain as he walked back to the living room and sank down into his chair. The tree stood there in all its splendor, lights twinkling brightly, the symbol of a holiday he would never again see.

He had ordered the tree this morning, the first Christmas tree he'd put up since he was a boy. It was the foolish whim of a dying man. He had pictured himself sitting in front of a huge tree blazing with lights, sipping a hot toddy while snow fell silently outside the window. There would be Christmas carols playing softly in the background and a cheerful fire in the grate. Obviously he had read too much Dickens.

He supposed the tree looked festive enough. The branches were symmetrical and every ornament hung in perfect balance. The boy had done a fine job of trimming, but Dr. Elias experienced none of the nostalgia he'd expected. The tree was merely a decoration, a dead one at that. Soon the needles would begin to fall and it would be relegated to the trash bin.

Dr. Elias took a deep breath of the pine-scented air. It reminded him of the cleaning compound the crew used on the kitchen floor. The Christmas tree had been a mistake.

The delivery boy had rigged a switch by his chair and Dr. Elias turned off the colored lights. He had wasted the whole morning on foolishness. Now there were important things to do.

The moment he sat down behind his desk, Dr. Elias felt better. A stack of reports had come in the morning mail. He knew the material they contained would be distressing, but it was his duty to read them. His father had often said that duty was the basis of all morality. Dr. Elias prided himself on being a moral man.

The first report was as he'd expected. Nora was still playing games with her therapist. Dr. Elias nodded as he read through the closely typed pages. There was nothing he needed to do at this stage. Nora's problem had not yet become critical.

Mac's therapist reported he was adjusting quite nicely. At least there were no obvious problems. Mac's case could safely wait. He would maintain on his own for a while.

Debra appeared relaxed and happy. Her therapist was confident she was making progress. Dr. Elias shook his head sadly as he read the glowing report. Debra's therapist had a lot to learn. The report glossed over the fact that Debra's illness was cyclical. There was always a period of euphoria preceding the onset of depression. Debra might be on an upward swing, but she would spiral inevitably downward into melancholia. Her happiness was nothing but a warning signal of the depression to come.

Kay had canceled her Wednesday appointment, but she had booked another for Friday afternoon. Dr. Elias knew that, as the mayor's wife, Kay was very busy over the holiday season, but her therapy should take top priority. He circled the new date in red on his calendar. He would check to make sure Kay kept her appointment tomorrow.

There was no report for Father Marx. Dr. Elias paged through the sheets of paper again, but it was clear the priest had not kept his Wednesday appointment.

There was more than a warning here. Dr. Elias straightened in his chair and his hands shook slightly as he gripped the sheaf of papers. This was a crisis situation. Father Marx was much too conscientious to forget an appointment and he had failed to cancel or reschedule. Father Marx was in trouble and he was deliberately avoiding his new analyst. Dr. Elias knew he had to intervene before it was too late.

CHAPTER 15

Debra sat on the floor in Mac's living room with the big box of Christmas decorations in front of her. It felt odd to be there, instead of at the paper. Her boss said it was a Christmas present, two days off in a row. She didn't have an assignment until Saturday afternoon.

The box was dusty and she brushed it off. Her father's spidery handwriting was on the label: *Xmas Decos*. How long ago had he written it? Both her parents were gone now. Her mother had died eight years ago and her father had followed within a year. These decorations hadn't been used since they'd moved from the family house in Mankato. That meant it had been at least ten years since this box had been opened.

The masking tape was starting to peel and it came off easily when Debra pulled on it. The ornaments were packed in layers of excelsior, each one wrapped in its own square of soft cloth. Tears came to Debra's eyes as she recognized the white flannel patterned with tiny blue flowers. It had been one of her mother's favorite nightgowns. The worn yellow cotton with frolicking lambs had once been a sheet for her own crib.

Debra smiled as she unwrapped the delicate blown-glass baskets of strawberries. They had belonged to her grandmother. The porcelain elves were next, all eleven, including the one she had broken as a child. Her mother had mended it with Duco cement. Debra still remembered holding the little head with its peaked cap and asking her mother to make it all better. She had been very young then and she had still believed in the magic of grown-ups. Later that year she had encountered a dose of reality when her mother hadn't been able to fix a broken balloon.

There were the walnut shells they had glued together and painted gold. Colored pinecones were in another box, each wrapped individually in tissue paper. They had gone out in the fall to gather them, picking out the perfect ones from a bed of fragrant pine needles in the park. They'd had enough to fill five Red Owl grocery sacks, and when Christmas came, they'd dipped them in tempera paint and decorated the tree.

There were more treasures in the second layer of the box. Her parents had saved the star she'd made out of cellophane soda straws. And the red and green paper chain linked together in circles with untidy dabs of school paste. The paste still smelled faintly of peppermint. Debra knew from experience that it didn't taste that way.

She had been in the first grade that Christmas. She'd memorized all three verses of "Up on the Housetop" and gone caroling with the rest of her class. On Christmas Eve she'd played the Virgin Mary in the Lutheran Sunday school pageant. Her favorite doll had stood in for Baby Jesus. She had rehearsed for weeks, saying her line over and over, to anyone who would listen. *And she brought forth her firstborn son and wrapped him in swaddling clothes, and laid him in a manger, because there was no room for them in the inn.* Her parents had been so proud when she'd done it perfectly.

There was a package in the bottom of the box. The tag on the outside was in her mother's perfect Palmer penmanship: *For Debra's Little One at Christmas.*

Debra's hands shook as she tore off the faded Christmas wrapping. There was a baby doll inside. A card was pinned to the blanket. *This was your mother's first doll. We saved it for you.*

Her baby would never see this doll. Debra picked it up and cradled it in her arms. She didn't realize she was crying until she saw the wet splashes of her tears on the dusty lid of the box. Her mother and father had packed her childhood away for her, sealing and saving all the warm memories of her past for a grandchild they would never see. And now that grandchild was dead. Steve was dead. Her baby was dead. What had ever made her think she had the courage to start all over again?

Mac pulled the mail out of his box. It was late, as usual. The desk sergeant usually recruited a rookie to handle it. That meant it was always screwed up. It was after three in the afternoon and Reinert's rookie had just finished the distribution.

There was a flyer for a basketball game: The Cops vs. the Rubbers. Firestone was sponsoring a charity game for muscular dystrophy. Any officer who wanted to play was urged to sign up.

The Policemen's Relief Fund was asking for donations again. They did a good job. Mac slipped some bills in an envelope and sealed it. He'd drop it off at the desk later.

A special equipment catalog was stuffed in the box. Mac paged through it even though he'd never gone in for sap gloves and weighted batons. The department frowned on special equipment, but some officers claimed a cop needed every advantage he could get.

Feet hurt? Try our special arch support shoes. Made with the man on his feet in mind. Mac chuckled as he read the brochure. A hundred and fifty bucks for a pair of shoes. And they probably weren't any better than department regulation.

A pink notice was tucked in the back of his box. Mac wondered how long it had been there. It was his yearly notification. He had to qualify on the shooting range by the first of the year.

Mac sighed and glanced at his watch. Fritz Gunderson was on duty until five. If he went right down to the range, he could get by again this year.

The MPD range was one of the finest in the country. The winter months made it impossible to use a walk-through combat range, and the old swivel-target type was outdated. Now Minneapolis had an expensive video projector setup. Scores were recorded electronically from the grids in the screen. It even measured velocity. The whole thing reminded Mac of a sophisticated computer game.

The illusion of reality was frightening. It felt just like being out on the street, encountering targets at random. Old ladies with shopping bags got in the way when you tried to take out the man with the shotgun. There were dark shadows in a deserted alley, two dogs knocking trash cans over, and a killer with a gun pointed at your head. A man leaning out a window blocked your aim when a robber took a shot at your fellow officer. There was even one point where your own partner got in the way as a murderer faced you with a revolver. Your shots were counted and cataloged by computer and points were subtracted when you hit a civilian. Mac had shot on the range only once and logged a perfect score. For the past four years he hadn't been able to shoot at all.

Mac signed out for the range and got his coat out of his locker. He backed the car out of the lot and sighed impatiently as he waited at the light. The Christmas traffic was heavy. It would be worse when he came back. Then he'd hit the five o'clock exodus from the downtown offices.

He gripped the steering wheel tightly as he drove to the range. Perhaps it would be different this time. He wasn't as nervous as he'd been last year.

"Hey, Mac! It's good to see you!"

There was a big smile on Fritz's round face. He was putting on weight and his uniform stretched tightly over his stomach. He'd always been heavy, but now that he was off the street, his wife's cooking was catching up with him.

When Mac had first met Barbara Gunderson, she'd been working her way through the Time-Life *Foods of the World* series. She had just started *The Cooking of Germany*. Mac's mouth watered as he remembered the wooden table in Fritz's kitchen loaded with potato pancakes, sauerbraten, roast duck with stuffing, red cabbage with apples, Black Forest cake, and five different kinds of strudel. Fritz had brought Mac home for dinner at least twice a week when they were partners. Mac wondered which volume Barbara was working on now.

"Set it up for me, Fritz." Mac ejected his service rounds and loaded his revolver with wad cutters.

"You don't need to, Mac. There's nobody here. I can just sign you off again."

"I've got to try it, Fritz." Mac shook his head. "Maybe I can make it on my own this year."

Fritz patted his shoulder and went into the control booth. Mac took his place in front of the screen. He tried to breathe deeply and fight down his nervousness. It was only a target range. This wasn't real.

Mac's hands started to sweat as he waited for the targets. The scene was a city street at night. He could see a man lurking in a doorway as he approached. The man stepped out. There was something in his hands. An umbrella. Mac held his fire.

Another figure appeared on his left. It was a big man with a shotgun pointed directly at him. Mac tried to squeeze off a shot. It was no use. He couldn't do it.

A third target appeared, a woman with a revolver. She cocked it and aimed at Mac. She was so close, Mac could see down the barrel of her gun. He tried to shoot, but his finger was frozen on the trigger.

It was impossible. Mac let a teenager with a shotgun and a burglar with a handgun get away. It was no different from last year. He still couldn't pull the trigger.

"Damn! I can't do it, Fritz." Mac's voice was shaking.

The screen went blank and Fritz came out of the booth. "Hey, it's all right." He draped a friendly arm around Mac's shoulders. "You could do it if it was real. I'll bet on it."

"I hope you're right." Mac took the form that Fritz had signed and put it in his pocket. His hands were still shaking.

"Come on in the booth and have a cup of coffee with me. If I don't tell somebody about the captain, I'll bust."

"His gun was dirty again this year?" Mac managed a grin.

"Of course it was dirty. There's no reason why he should change the habits of a lifetime." Fritz laughed as he poured coffee for Mac. "And Schuman and Tomczik are just as bad. The only time their guns get cleaned is when I do it down here. Schuman's was green inside. I swear to God, Mac."

"What did the captain do?" Mac got ready for a good one. Captain Meyers was notoriously bad on the range.

"He took a stance like one of those western gunfighters. I should'a had the sound track from *The Good, the Bad and the Ugly*. And his score was even worse than last year. He missed every target but one and shot four civilians through the head. How's that for setting an example for the rest of the force?"

"Jesus! I'm glad he never has to use his weapon." Mac chuckled. "So what did you do, Fritz?"

"I told him he qualified. What else could I do? He's my boss!"

"You were wonderful, Nora!" Elena hugged her tightly as she came into the dressing room. "Tomorrow night's going to be fantastic!"

"Tomorrow night's going to be a disaster!" Nora slapped a glob of cold cream on her face and rubbed it in.

"Nora, be reasonable." Elena handed her a box of tissues. "Remember what you tell your students. If the dress rehearsal goes off without a hitch, you've got legitimate cause for worry."

"This one's the exception!" Nora snatched a tissue and wiped off her makeup with angry strokes. "I'll kill

Harry if he doesn't get the light cues right. That baby spot was all over the place!"

Elena moved to stand behind Nora's chair. She started to rub Nora's tense shoulders with strong, even strokes. "Just relax now. You're all upset over nothing. Would you like a little glass of sherry?"

"I'd like a gallon of vodka!"

Suddenly Nora started to grin. Elena was the soul of patience. And she was right. Everything always worked out perfectly on opening night.

"I'm fine now, darling." Nora reached back to squeeze Elena's hand. "It's just an attack of nerves, that's all. Why don't you run to the office and see if the playbills are ready? I promise to be in a better mood by the time you come back."

After Elena left, Nora stared at her reflection in the harsh lights of the dressing table. Without the makeup, she looked dreadful. Age lines crinkled the skin at the corners of her eyes and the creases were deep around her mouth. Age was supposed to give a face character, and Nora thought she'd like a little less. Laugh lines were not laughable when they happened to be hers.

She slipped out of her costume and tossed it over a chair. Then she faced the mirror again. Her upper arms were still firm and her legs were good. Her breasts didn't droop because they were small to begin with. The centerfold cuties in *Playboy* would look like cows when they were her age.

Her hair was nice, no gray at all. There had been a few gray strands, but she was ruthless about pulling them out. Nora Stanford, at her publicized age of thirty-six, could not be seen with gray in her hair.

"Not bad for an old broad." Nora stuck out her tongue at the mirror. It was a childish act of defiance.

Inwardly she was terrified. She was aging with every breath she took and there was nothing she could do to stop it. Someday she'd look in the mirror and face her nightmare. She would be old. What would Elena do then? Would she leave to find a younger lover?

"You're so beautiful, Nora!"

Nora jumped as Elena's image appeared in the mirror behind her. She hadn't heard her come in. She watched Elena's hands reach out to caress her gently.

"I locked the door, Nora." Elena's voice was soft in her ear.

Nora turned to kiss her gratefully. Elena was wonderful. Suddenly she felt young and sexy and not over the hill at all.

Confession was over for the night. Father Marx checked the poor box on his way to the altar. It held five dollars less than it had this morning. Another negative donation.

Father Marx did his best to be charitable. Someone must have needed the money very badly to steal from the church. Perhaps it had been a man with hungry children to feed, or a renter who needed five dollars to avoid eviction. Charitable thinking was so difficult to maintain at St. Steven's. More likely it was a teenager needing a fix.

His back hurt as he bent over to shut off the Christmas tree lights. It always hurt after a two-hour stint in the confessional. When he'd been young he'd believed that discomfort was good for the soul. He had disapproved of the old priests who'd had cushions installed on the hard wooden bench in the priest's cubicle. Now Father Marx's convictions had weakened along with his back. He would bring a pillow with him tomorrow night.

Father Marx frowned as an old man entered the church and walked toward the confessional. Technically confession was over. The man had not seen him. Father Marx knew he could escape to the parish house and the comfortable recliner that was waiting for him, but something in the old man's halting steps aroused his sympathy. He was here to serve his parishioners. Hearing the old man's confession wouldn't take that long and it would be a change of pace. Most of the evening's penitents had been teenagers with impure thoughts to confess. Father Marx was afraid he'd scream if he heard that phrase one more time tonight. Thank God this man was too old for that!

This was probably a Christmas nostalgia confession, an old man seeking penance for a long-forgotten venial sin. Father Marx hurried to the priest's cubicle and pushed back the curtain. He kissed his stole and took his place on the bench. It was still warm from the heat of his body. This couldn't be more than five Hail Marys and Our Fathers, and a good Act of Contrition. One more absolution and he could quit for the night.

Father Marx made the sign of the cross and opened the screen. There was no response. He leaned closer and nodded encouragement.

"Yes, my son?"

The knife entered his eye socket and penetrated his occipital lobe. Death was instantaneous. His rosary rattled as it struck the marble floor.

CHAPTER 16

It took long moments for the sound to sift down through the thick layers of her depression. Finally Debra recognized it. The phone had been ringing for some time. She had to answer it.

At first she didn't know where she was. She blinked as she looked around her. Everything was happening much too slowly. It seemed to take forever to recognize the softball trophies, the rack of vintage movies, the tree in the stand in front of the window. She was sitting on the floor in Mac's living room and she had to answer the phone.

At first she couldn't seem to move at all. She told herself to get up, walk across the floor, pick up the phone, but her body didn't seem to get the message. She concentrated hard on making her legs move and at last they obeyed her. She stood up painfully. Her legs were stiff and sore. She must have been sitting there for hours.

She reached the phone at last, wincing at the pain in her knees. "Hello?" It was Mac.

"Hi, Debbie. I'm on my way home. I just wanted to let you know."

"Oh. Thank you for calling." Debra frowned. Her voice had the quality of a recorded message.

"Debbie? Are you all right?"

"I'm just fine." Debra tried to sound bright and cheery. "Hurry home and I'll see you in about forty-five minutes."

Her hands were trembling as she hung up the phone. The depression was lurking in the back of her mind, threatening to come back with full force. She could feel it there, like some predatory beast, stalking its prey.

She couldn't give in this time. Debra shook her head hard. She had to fight it. Mac was coming home.

The best thing to do was to keep moving. Debra knew she had to keep busy. If she occupied her mind with ordinary tasks, she could keep the beast at bay. Fix dinner for Mac. That was good. She'd concentrate on cooking and she wouldn't have time to let the depression creep in.

She went into the kitchen and switched on the lights. Everything was a little out of perspective. The room looked like a Salvador Dalí. The colors were too vivid. The yellow paint on the kitchen wall was so bright it made her head hurt. And the refrigerator was no longer rectangular. Its harvest gold sides tilted crazily toward the stove.

Debra blinked hard. She remembered a friend offering her a tab of acid and describing the effects it would have. Now she was glad she had turned down the offer. No one in her right mind would want to experience this deliberately. The familiar kitchen was frightening. It reminded her of *The Cabinet of Dr. Caligari.*

The cookbook was leaning against the flour canister. Debra reached out for it gingerly. It looked puffy and soft like a pillow, but once she opened it, the pages were fine. She would ignore everything that was wrong, and things would straighten out by themselves. They had to.

Debra read the title out loud. "Quick Chili." The recipe was circled in red. Vaguely she remembered buying everything she needed to make it.

She walked to the refrigerator and pulled open the door. The shelves slanted steeply, but nothing had fallen over. That proved it was only an illusion. If the shelves were actually tilting at a thirty-degree angle, the pickle jar would tip over.

There was the hamburger, on the second to the bottom shelf. Debra swallowed hard as she looked at it. The ground beef was bleeding. A pool of blood had congealed at the bottom of the refrigerator. She squeezed her eyes shut and forced them open again. The blood was still there.

She told herself what to do. *Touch it, Debra. See if it's real.*

She reached out and touched the pool of blood. It was cold. Then she pulled back her finger and looked at it. The tip was red. It was real. Of course it was real. The hamburger was fresh and there was a cut in the bottom of the package.

Debra sighed gratefully as she got a sponge and cleaned the bottom of the refrigerator. Now she had to fry the meat and onions.

It seemed to take a long time to put the hamburger in a pan and cut up the onions. Debra deliberately avoided the clock on the kitchen wall. It might be running backward or something equally bizarre. She'd just do what she had to do and not worry about the time. Now she had to open the kidney beans.

The electric can opener seemed to be working just fine. It whirred when she pressed the lever, and the cans opened without incident. When the hamburger was brown she poured off the grease and dumped in the beans.

"Two cans of stewed tomatoes." It helped to read each step out loud. Debra opened the tomatoes and added them to the pan.

"Two teaspoons of chili powder." She took the measuring spoons from the nail by the sink and measured carefully. "Salt and pepper to taste."

Debra knew she'd better not think about this one or she'd never be able to do it. What constituted too much salt? In her confused state of mind, it was a mystery. She held the salt shaker over the pan and sprinkled automatically. It was done. Now all she had to do was let it simmer until Mac came home.

Before she thought, she turned to look at the clock. Mac would be here in twenty minutes. The clock was running just fine. It wasn't melting like Dalí's. It was a normal, perfectly round kitchen clock. The minute hand was sweeping in the proper direction and all the numbers were consecutive.

Everything was fine now! Debra sighed in relief as she glanced around the kitchen. The refrigerator had straightened, the walls were the same pale yellow they had been before, and things were familiar and safe. The cloud of depression had lifted and suddenly she felt happy again. She had worked her way out of it, all by herself!

The cookbook lay open on the counter. Debra smiled as she paged through to find a recipe for baking powder biscuits. She really ought to do a story on Betty Crocker therapy. You could beat depression along with your eggs.

"Kay's just leaving for Orchestra Hall to hear the *Messiah*." Mac smiled at Debbie as she took the biscuits from the oven.

"Nora called when you were in the shower. Elena's taking her to the Sofitel for dinner. She said it was a night-before-opening-night celebration."

"Nothing from Father Marx?" Mac glanced at the clock.

Debra shook her head. "Not a word."

"If he doesn't call by eight, I'll call him. I can't shake the feeling that something's wrong. He acted so distracted when I talked to him last night. It's not like him to forget to call."

"You're right, Mac." Debra set the bowls of chili on the table. "Father Marx is usually late, but he always calls or shows up. Maybe he's still upset about his statue."

A half hour later, the chili was completely gone. The recipe said it served six, but Mac was a big eater. And he obviously liked her cooking.

"No answer at the rectory." Mac came up behind her and kissed the back of her neck. "Throw me a sponge, Debbie. I'll wipe off the table and then I'll try again."

There was no answer at eight-thirty or at nine. Debra could tell Mac was getting nervous.

"Let's drive over to the church," she suggested. "We could drop in on Father Marx and then look at the Christmas decorations downtown. The stores are open until eleven tonight."

The minute they got on the freeway, Debra reached

for the radio. It wasn't Christmas without the music. She turned it on and the strains of "O Little Town of Bethlehem" filled the car. She hummed along with the Norman Luboff Choir until they reached the Highway 12 interchange. She hadn't realized that there were four verses to "I Saw Three Ships."

Mac parked in front of the church and shut off the ignition. "Let's try the parish house first. It doesn't look like there's anything going on at the church."

They rang the buzzer and stood on the steps in the cold. The wind whipped past Debra's face and she turned up her collar. Then she shoved her hands back into her pockets and shivered.

"I don't think he's here, Mac. The lights are all off inside."

"Let's try the church."

Debra took Mac's arm as they walked down the icy sidewalk to the church. "Do you think we should disturb him if he's praying?"

"We'll just take a quick peek inside." Mac opened the heavy church door. "If he's up at the altar, we'll know he's all right."

The church was dark inside. The flickering candles at the feet of the saints were the only illumination. Debra gripped Mac's arm tightly as they walked down the aisle. The empty pews and the huge plaster statues reminded her of the setting in *Murder in the Cathedral*.

"He's not here." Mac's voice was unnaturally loud in the stillness. "Could he be in there?" Debra pointed to the confessional.

"Not unless he fell asleep hearing confessions."

Debra saw it first—the crumpled figure on the floor by the side of the confessional. She gripped Mac's arm and pointed. She seemed to have lost the ability to speak.

"Sit right here, Debbie." Mac pushed her down in a pew. "I'll check it out and come right back."

Father Marx was dead. There was no need to feel for a pulse. Mac swallowed hard as he stared down at the priest's body. There was blood everywhere. On Father Marx's vestments. On the curtain of the confessional. On the marble floor. Even though he'd encountered violent death many times in his job, Mac shuddered and turned away. He felt sick. Father Marx wasn't just another murder victim. He was a friend. And he was the fourth member of the group to die.

Debra looked up as he came back to the pew. Her face was white and her eyes asked the question.

"Come on, Debbie." Mac pulled her to her feet. "I have to call the station."

Debra stood next to Mac as he made the call. She was cold and numb.

Mac's words seemed to take forever to register in her brain, but she heard snatches of the conversation. Mac said they'd wait for someone called Holt. Debra hoped Mac wouldn't expect her to go back inside the church. She knew she could never bear it. She just wanted to go home so she could cry.

It didn't take long for the police to come. Debra hung back as Mac took them inside. Her feet felt frozen as she paced back and forth on the sidewalk in front of the church.

The thought hit her suddenly, and she stopped in her tracks. Someone was killing the members of the group and she was standing here all alone in the dark. She should run back inside the church where it was safe.

The murderer could come along and kill her with Mac and the police only ten feet away.

She turned back toward the church and got as far as the door before she realized that she couldn't go in. She was terrified. There was no way she could face the sight of Father Marx's body again. She was caught up in the limbo between her two fears.

Debra huddled up against the door. Suddenly the irony of the situation struck her. Dr. Elias would call it an inappropriate emotional reaction, but Debra started to laugh anyway. She knew she was heading for hysteria, but she couldn't seem to stop the brittle laughter that bubbled up out of her throat.

Someone pushed against the inside of the door. Debra moved to the side, still shaking with laughter. It was Mac. She tried to stop laughing, but it was impossible.

"Debra?" Mac shook her shoulders gently.

"I . . . I was just thinking about how the murderer could kill me when you were in the church with the police. It's funny, Mac. Really it is. I'd be dead on the outside while you were trying to solve a murder inside."

"That's enough, Debbie." Mac put his arms around her. He could feel her body shaking as he held her. "Come on, honey. We can go home now."

"A smart killer could get us both right now. Two birds with one stone." Debra's words were muffled against the front of Mac's coat.

"We're going home now, Debbie." Mac turned her around and propelled her toward the car. "One foot in front of the other. That's right, honey. Don't think. Just get in the car."

It was better when they were inside the car, and better

yet when Mac started to drive. Debra reached out to lock her door. She had to pull herself together.

St. Steven's was four blocks behind them before Debra calmed down enough to speak. She drew a deep breath and swallowed hard.

"I'm all right now." She buckled her safety belt and sat up straighter. "What did you tell the police, Mac? Do they know about the group?"

"Not yet." The streetlights flashed across Mac's face as a car passed them. He looked tense and worried. "We'll call a meeting first thing in the morning. If we go to Captain Meyers as a group, he'll give us all police protection."

"But what about Kay? She can't admit she's in therapy. It'd be sure to leak out."

"Someone out there is trying to kill us! We can't ignore that, Debbie. Nora and Kay need protection. I'll ask for three men. One for each of you."

"But I've got you! I don't need any other protection."

Mac saw the expression on Debra's face as they turned onto the freeway. She had blind faith in him. She really believed he could protect her better than anyone else. He knew he should feel proud and honored. But Debra's life was in danger. The stakes were too high. All he felt now was scared.

CHAPTER 17

At last Debbie was asleep. Her arm was resting on his chest and Mac moved it very gently. He was surprised at how much it weighed. Debbie was small. The top of her head just fit beneath his chin and she couldn't tip the scales at much more than a hundred pounds, but when she was sleeping, her arm was dead weight.

Dead weight. That phrase brought up all sorts of gruesome images. Mac slid out of bed, slowly, so he wouldn't wake Debbie. There was no way he could go to sleep now. He had to decide what to do.

Mac froze with one foot on the floor as Debbie rolled over. She reached out toward his side of the bed. For a moment Mac thought she'd awaken, but she just sighed and wrapped her arms around his pillow. She was still sound asleep.

He inched his other leg out from under the covers, careful not to pull the blankets with him. He found his robe on the chair and slid his arms into the sleeves. His slippers were under the bed and he felt around in the dark until he located them. Then he tiptoed out of the room, holding them in his hand.

The kitchen floor was tiled. Mac knew how cold it could get in the winter.

He stopped in the hallway to pull on his slippers, first the left and then the right. He guessed that meant he was still left footed. When he'd been in third grade, Miss Wozniak had tested him. He'd held the pencil in his right hand, so he was right handed. He'd looked through the toy telescope with his right eye and that meant he was right eyed. He'd put on his jacket right sleeve first. That meant he was right armed. Then she had asked him to put on his gym shoes.

Mac had been tired of the tests by this time. He'd wanted to join the rest of the kids on the playground. He'd grabbed the sneaker that was nearest and put it on. It was the left.

"Richard Macklin? You're inconsistent!" She had frowned and written a note on his pink health record card. "It's a wonder you read as well as you do!"

Mac had decided to put on his left shoe first from then on. Miss Wozniak watched him for the whole year, especially when they got ready for recess or gym. Mac had been very careful always to put on the left first, in sneakers and boots and ice skates. Miss Wozniak had covered his little pink record card with her notes. Mac supposed it was still in his file, somewhere in the basement of Whitney Elementary School.

The thermostat was turned down for the night and Mac pushed it up a little. Reddy Kilowatt, the NSP cartoon character, advised homeowners to turn their heat down at least ten degrees at night. That worked just fine if you stayed in bed under the covers, but there was a cold draft out here in the hall.

The cold didn't usually bother Mac, but tonight he

was shivering. A bowl of Debbie's chili would warm him up.

The chili was gone. Mac sighed as he remembered polishing off the last at the table. He had eaten three enormous bowls. Debbie's cooking was great. If he wasn't careful, he'd have to buy bigger clothes.

He switched on the light over the kitchen table. Some hot soup would do the trick. There was a collection of Cup O'Noodles in the bottom cupboard and Mac picked out a chicken flavor. He'd practically lived on this freeze-dried stuff before Debbie had moved in. It was quick and easy, and it filled him up. That had been his criteria for eating at home. There were also no dirty dishes, a definite plus.

Mac boiled water in the tea kettle and poured it into the white Styrofoam cup. While he was waiting the three minutes for it to do what it was supposed to do, he went to the refrigerator for a beer.

The top shelf was filled with bottles and cans. Mac grinned. He had kidded Debbie about buying the Newcastle Ale. He'd said he felt guilty drinking imported beer when so many good brands were made right here in Minnesota. Debbie had obviously taken him seriously. Now he had a choice between Hamm's, Grain Belt, Cold Spring, Kato, North Star, Old Milwaukee, and New Ulm. The whole top shelf was stocked with local brands.

Mac pulled out a Cold Spring Export and opened it. His soup was ready and he peeled off the lid. He looked at the list of ingredients as he stirred it, but he stopped reading abruptly when he came to xanthan gum. It was probably something perfectly ordinary, but he didn't want to lose his appetite.

The soup didn't taste as good as he remembered.

Mac finished half of it and threw the rest in the garbage. Debbie's cooking had spoiled him for anything else.

He had delayed long enough. Mac pulled out the silverware drawer in his old-fashioned table and took out a notebook and pen. Before he could sleep tonight, he had to make a decision. He divided a blank page into four sections, one each for Doug, Jerry, Greg, and Father Marx. Under Doug's and Greg's he wrote *Accident/Suicide*. Jerry's and Father Marx's were labeled *Murder*.

Two out of four. Would Captain Meyers believe him if he voiced his suspicions? There was no evidence of foul play in Doug's death. And none in Greg's. The group knew that Greg was unlikely to burn his collection, but an investigation would reveal that Greg had a long-standing problem with fire. It was only natural to assume that Greg had set the fire himself, and there was no proof to the contrary.

That was the problem. No hard evidence. Jerry's death was obviously a murder, but nothing linked it to Father Marx's. Jerry was shot while jogging. A random killing. Father Marx was stabbed. The moment Captain Meyers heard about the smashed statue, he would suspect the murderer was some nut with a hard-on against the Catholic Church.

Mac knew the captain would at least listen to his theory of group murders. He might even believe that someone was killing the group off, one by one, for some crazy reason. But first he'd have to discount Mac's emotional involvement with the victims and his possible impaired judgment because of that involvement. He'd have to overlook the fact that there wasn't a shred of hard evidence, that all Mac had were hunches and suspicions.

Assuming the captain didn't conclude that Mac was having another mental breakdown, what would he do?

Captain Meyers would ask for the names of the remaining members of the group. It was only logical that he'd assign police protection to each member until the killer was caught.

Mac flipped over the paper and frowned as he drew a line down the middle.

He had two choices. He could give the captain the names. Or he could refuse. What would happen if he gave out the names?

Kay would certainly suffer. If the news leaked out that the mayor's wife was in therapy, Charles would be dead at the polls.

How would it affect Nora? Mac stared down at the paper and sighed. Nora's gay life would be exposed, but Mac doubted it would ruin her career. Actresses were allowed some leeway by virtue of their profession. They were expected to be exotic. Nora would cringe at the publicity, but that was about it.

And Debbie? Of course she'd be upset, but her career wouldn't suffer. The real problem lay in Debbie's reaction to him. If he went behind her back and gave her name to the captain, she'd never be able to trust him again. She'd leave him. Debbie wouldn't live with a man she couldn't trust.

Trust was the big problem. If he went to the captain without the group's permission, they'd all suffer, one way or the other. The group would have to disband. Mutual trust was what kept them together, and it would be sacrificed in the interest of safety.

Mac drew a heavy *X* through the left side of the

paper. He couldn't give the captain the names. What would happen when he refused?

The captain would be angry, of course. He'd probably accuse Mac of withholding evidence and he might even put him up on charges. That would be bad for him personally, but there was an even greater danger. The killer would be free to strike again. And again. How would he feel if Kay were killed because he'd refused to give her name to the captain? Or Nora? Or, God forbid, Debbie?

Mac shuddered. Suddenly he felt very exposed sitting in the circle of light at the table. Someone could be watching out there in the dark, planning a nice quiet way to kill him.

He reached up and found the light switch, plunging the kitchen into darkness. He listened alertly, cataloging every sound. The furnace kicked in. It was loud in the stillness. The roof creaked. Mac stood up cautiously and looked out the kitchen window. The snow was fresh and unbroken outside. No one was there. He was being paranoid.

Mac snapped on the light again. The killer always struck when the victim was alone. He would have to operate under that assumption or this constant vigilance would drive him up the wall.

Back to the paper. He couldn't give the captain the names of the surviving members. That much was clear. Would the captain assign him to the case anyway?

Not a chance. Mac sighed. He'd probably be on suspension pending investigation by the board. He could still work on the case on his own, but he'd have no direct access to police records or sources of information. His hands would be tied on the most critical case of his life.

He couldn't bring it up to the captain at all. Mac drew

another *X*, this time through the right side of the page. There had to be something else he could do.

What would happen if they went to the captain in a group? Then the captain would have to do something. At least Kay, Nora, and Debbie would have police protection.

It wasn't a perfect solution, but it was the best of the lot. Mac really doubted that he could talk them into it, but he'd bring it up in the morning. If they all agreed, there'd be no breach of trust.

He had the first option now, but Mac believed in being prepared. He still had to decide what to do if they refused to go to the captain.

Of course he'd try to protect them himself. That went without saying. And he would conduct a personal investigation on his own time. If he could discover the identity of the killer, there would be no need to bring the captain in until the very end.

It was three in the morning when he finally crawled into bed beside Debbie. He inched over and curled his body around her warm back. Debbie mumbled a word in her sleep. It sounded like *darling*. Mac smiled in the darkness and closed his eyes.

CHAPTER 18

Kay hung up the phone and went straight to the bottle of Baileys Irish Cream that was sitting out on the counter. Charles had suggested a nightcap when they'd gotten home from the concert last night. Even though it was barely nine in the morning, Kay poured a generous shot in her coffee. She needed something to steady her nerves.

Mac had called just after Charles had left for the office. The kids had gone with him to do some Christmas shopping downtown. In a way, Kay was glad she was alone. At least she didn't have to pretend that nothing was wrong.

She sat down at the kitchen table and gripped the mug with both hands. Trish had made it for her in ceramics class last year. It had a yellow smiling face on one side.

Ralph whined at her feet. He knew something was wrong. Kay tossed him the toast from her plate. The eggs had congealed and the sausage was cold and greasy. The thought of eating it made her gag.

"Here you go, boy." Kay set the whole plate down on

the floor. Ralph's tail thumped ecstatically against the table leg. At least someone was happy this morning.

Kay raised the mug to her lips and drank. Tears rolled down her cheeks and she didn't know how to stop them. The group would be here in thirty minutes, but for the first time, she didn't care about the mess. The breakfast dishes could stay piled in the sink. The unmade beds could wait. Poor Father Marx. What had he done to deserve such a violent death?

Ralph finished the last of the eggs and lay down at her feet, his head resting against her blue satin slipper. Kay picked him up and cuddled him. His little pink tongue came out to lick her cheek.

They could meet right here, in the kitchen. There was plenty of room at the table. There were only the four of them now. The thought made her start to cry again. Kay gave Ralph one more pat and got up resolutely. She'd try to stay busy until they came.

First she'd wipe off the table. There were crumbs from Trish's English muffin, and her jar of clover honey had left a sticky ring on the Formica. A capless bottle of Louisiana Hot Sauce sat by James's place. He refused to eat his eggs without it. A pile of fatty bacon pieces were rolled in his napkin. James had a disgusting habit of tearing the bacon apart and only eating the lean parts. Charles never left a mess when he ate, but his newspaper was in its usual untidy pile.

Kay tossed the whole napkin on the floor. It would keep Ralph busy for a while. She ran hot water in the sink and washed off the honey jar. Then she put the cap on the hot sauce and stuck it back in the cupboard. The newspaper went in the trash. She didn't feel like reading about world problems today.

Her eyes were puffy and it was hard to see as she

wiped off the table. If she thought about Father Marx anymore, she'd never be able to make the coffee. At least Nora couldn't make any cracks about overactive imaginations this morning. She'd have to admit they were right. Four of them were dead and even Mac was nervous now.

Kay ran water in the pot and ground the coffee beans. Two of the filters were stuck together and she used her fingernail to separate them. She moved the dial on the basket to Strong and flicked on the switch. It seemed she was acting in slow motion. Even routine tasks took twice as much time as they usually did. There was no way she could make her appointments this afternoon. She was barely functioning on a minimal level.

At last the coffee was ready. Kay set out cups and saucers. She didn't have anything to serve with the coffee, but no one would feel like eating, anyway. She grabbed the bottle of Baileys and set it in the middle of the table. That was more like it. Maybe she wasn't the only one who felt the need for a drink.

"I'll drive you over there, Nora." Elena took the car keys from Nora's shaking fingers. "It's no problem. Hope can take my dance class this morning."

All Elena had to do was look at Nora to tell she was in no condition to drive. She moved like a sleepwalker as she took her cape from the hanger and slipped it on. Her eyes were red from crying, and her voice quavered as she gave Elena directions. Maybe the group meeting would help, but Elena doubted it. As she wound her way through the morning traffic on Hennepin, Elena began to plan out what to say if Nora couldn't go on tonight.

"They were right, Elena." Nora turned toward her on

the seat. "Kay said someone was killing us off and I laughed at her!"

"You're forgetting about the vandalism, Nora." Elena deliberately kept her voice calm and emotionless. "Maybe the same person who smashed the statue came back to kill Father Marx. It could be some nut who hates the Catholic Church. He might not know anything about your group. The whole thing could be a total coincidence."

"Four dead out of eight?" Nora's voice had a hysterical edge. "Do you know what the odds are on something like that, Elena? They're astronomical!"

"Easy, Nora. It's all right." Elena pulled up behind the Toyota in the driveway and shut off the engine. "I'll wait for you right here."

"Oh, don't be an asshole, Elena! Come inside where it's warm."

Nora saw the hurt expression that crossed Elena's face and she reached out to hug her. "I'm sorry, darling. I didn't mean to snap at you. I'm just so damned upset! Come inside with me. I'll feel a lot better if I know you're not freezing out here."

"Well . . . if you're sure it's all right." Elena got out of the car. "I don't want to intrude, Nora. Really I don't. I know your group meetings are private."

Nora took Elena's arm and pulled her to the door. "No one'll mind, darling. Kay'll give you a cup of coffee and you can wait for me in the den. You might as well meet the group while there's still a couple of us left."

"Absolutely not!" Kay set her coffee mug down so hard it rattled. "You know my position, Mac. I can't admit I'm in therapy!"

"At least let me try to get you a security aide, then. We can make up some story about a threat on your life."

"I turned down a security aide when Charles took office three years ago. I told the press it was a waste of the taxpayers' money. There's no way I can accept one now."

"How about you, Nora? We could leave Kay out of it and you and Debbie could go to the captain with me."

"Count me out." Nora frowned. "Elena and I can't afford to have our private lives exposed. Minneapolis is still provincial in a lot of ways. Parents would pull their kids out of our workshop."

"But you'd be a lot safer with a security aide."

Nora stuck a cigarette in her holder. Her hand was shaking so hard she had trouble lighting it.

"I can't live my life with a cop following me around. I'd go batty, Mac! Look at me. I'm a wreck already. And I've got an opening tonight!"

There was a crash from the living room and Mac jumped up. A second later Ralph raced into the room. There was a plastic Santa Claus in his mouth.

Mac went to check the living room. When he came back he was grinning. "Ralph must think Christmas is over, Kay. He's taking down the tree for you. All the ornaments are gone from the bottom branches."

"Oh, Ralph! You scared me half to death!" Kay's laughter was very close to hysteria. She scooped up the little dog and held him tightly.

"We tried to train him, but it didn't work. Now we hang plastic ornaments on the bottom for him. Ralph takes them off and we put them back. It's turned into his favorite game."

Mac took Debbie's hand. She had turned white when

she'd heard the crash from the living room. Now the color was slowly returning to her face.

"You'll go to Captain Meyers with me, won't you, Debbie?"

"You know I'll do anything for you, but I don't see the point. I've already got my police protection."

Nora ground out her cigarette in the ashtray. "I know what's going through your head, Mac. If you go to the captain without our permission, I'll never speak to you again!"

"If I don't tell the captain, you might not speak to anyone again."

Nora shuddered. The coffee sloshed from her cup and her hands shook as she mopped it up with a napkin.

"There has to be another way, Mac." Debra swallowed hard. "Isn't there anything we can do that doesn't involve the police?"

"We can make sure we're never alone. So far the killer's struck only when the victim is alone. That's about it, Debbie. If someone really wants to kill you, they can think up a million ways to do it."

"You have to catch him, Mac!" Kay held Ralph so tightly, he whimpered in protest. "I . . . I can't stand it much longer. He's going to kill us all!"

"I'll stay on top of it, I promise." Mac reached over to rescue Ralph. "Let's all calm down and use our heads. Try to think of anyone you know who'd want to kill off our group."

Debra clasped her hands together to keep them from shaking. "Maybe it's like *The List of Adrian Messenger*. Without realizing it, we may know something about the killer that could hurt him if it got out. That could be the motive for . . . for getting rid of us."

"Oh, my God!" Kay looked ready to faint. "I know who it is!"

"Easy, Kay." Mac put his arm around her shoulders. "Just take it nice and slow. Deep breaths. Nice and easy, that's right."

It took a full minute before Kay could speak. Tears of fright rolled down her cheeks. "It's the governor! He knows the party will suffer if anyone finds out I'm in therapy. He's got to kill all of us so nobody can talk!"

"Oh, forget it, Kay! You're flipping out again." Nora slid her chair closer to Kay's and reached for her hand. "Be reasonable now. The governor's not a killer."

"Yes, he is!" Kay's voice shook with terror. "He knew you wouldn't believe me. He counted on that!"

"I believe you, Kay."

There was a long, tense moment as Kay stared into Mac's eyes. She swallowed hard.

"You do?"

"You bet I do! That's the first thing you learn when you're a cop. Everyone's a suspect—until you clear them. Let's see if we can find out where the governor was last night."

"I'll call the paper." Debra jumped up from her chair. "They'll know his schedule."

Nora slid another cigarette into her holder and lit it. She laughed and blew a cloud of smoke toward the ceiling. "A killer runs amok in high government circles, terrorizing a cop, a reporter, and an actress. Only the mayor's wife knows the truth."

She patted Kay's hand. "All right, Kay. It sounds like a bad soap opera, but I'll try to keep an open mind."

Debra came back to the kitchen, shaking her head. "The governor was in St. Cloud last night for a jazz festival at the college. He introduced Woody Herman and the New Thundering Herd. The car left the capitol at five and didn't get back until midnight."

"I . . . I guess I was wrong." Kay dropped her eyes and stared at the table. She was clearly embarrassed. "I'm sorry. In the back of my mind I knew it was crazy, but I just couldn't help it."

Mac refilled Kay's coffee mug and handed it to her. "That's all right, Kay. Tell me if you have any more suspicions. I don't care how crazy they sound. We'll check everything out. It's the only way to be sure."

Nora took a deep breath. "I think we should call Dr. Elias. I know it's wrong to bother him now, but he might be able to help."

"It's too late." Debra blinked back tears. "I tried to call him this morning, but the answering service said he was gone. He's paid up through December, but he told them to stop taking messages."

"He could be in a hospital somewhere." Kay's voice was a whisper. "Or maybe he's already dead. It's so awful!"

"That means we're really on our own." Mac cleared his throat. "There's nobody else to help us, unless you reconsider. I still think our best bet is to go to the captain and level with him. He'll do his best to keep it under wraps."

"But, Mac!" Kay looked up, suddenly alarmed. "Won't he suspect one of us?"

"I've got an airtight alibi, but it's slightly embarrassing." Nora began to smile. "Elena and I went out for an early dinner and then we stopped at a bar downtown. I got so smashed I danced on the table."

Even though she was still scared, Kay started to grin. She could guess what kind of bar it was and the type of dance that Nora had done.

"Trish and I made the rounds of the hospitals in the afternoon. Last night we all went to the *Messiah.* I didn't get home until after eleven."

Debra looked worried. "What time was Father Marx killed? I was at Mac's house all afternoon by myself."

"I checked on that this morning. The coroner says between six and seven."

"That means I don't have an alibi!"

"Yes, you do." Mac nodded. "Your car was parked on the street when the snowplow came through on the afternoon run. It was completely blocked in. I dug it out this morning."

"Well! We're all in the clear!" Nora sighed extravagantly. "You were at work, right, Mac?"

"Nope. I signed out at four to go to the range. I was there an hour. Then I drove around running address checks until seven. I had plenty of time to stop by the church and kill Father Marx."

"But you didn't!" Debra looked shocked. "We don't believe that for a second, Mac!"

"I didn't . . . but I could have." Mac sighed. "Looks like I'm the only one without an alibi."

"You're in the clear." Nora grinned triumphantly. "The killer shot Jerry with a gun! We all know you can't shoot your gun!"

Mac winced. "You know that, but the department doesn't. According to my records, I qualified on the range again this year. Fritz Gunderson signed me off."

"That means we're all in the same boat. You can't afford to go to the captain either!"

Mac nodded glumly. Nora was right. It was up to him to catch the killer. And he was completely on his own.

CHAPTER 19

Living with death was an intriguing experience. Dr. Elias found that the ordinary facets of his life had taken on an immense importance. The very act of taking a shower was revealing. The tingle of hot water against his skin was a confirmation of life. His nerve endings were still alive and functioning. The steam that rolled up to cloud the bathroom mirror was a kindness that hid his wasted body from view. The soft texture of a freshly washed towel seemed to absorb his pain as well as the moisture. Life was filled with small miracles if it was viewed from this perspective. He did not know which particular shower would be his last and he intended to enjoy each one to the fullest.

Dr. Elias stepped on the scale. Recording his weight was critical. He had dropped another three pounds last week. It was not surprising. Actually his weight was holding well. The body could function quite adequately at a fifteen percent reduction of normal weight. Laboratory rats were kept at that level as standard procedure in reinforcement studies. He had a comfortable cushion of eight pounds before he would experience any ill effects.

Shaving only took a moment with the electric razor. Dr. Elias remembered how fascinated he had been as a boy when his father had stropped his straightedge. He had watched as his father whipped up the lather in the shaving mug and brushed it on his face to soften the whiskers. And then came the part he had loved best, when the razor flashed expertly in his father's hand. It'd made a sound like crunching snow underfoot as it scraped off the stubble. Dr. Elias remembered how he had held his breath, afraid that his father would cut himself. But that had never happened. The hand that was so brilliant with the scalpel had never faltered.

Perhaps he should try it once before he died. Straightedge razors and leather strops must still be obtainable somewhere. He'd heard that barbers learned their craft by shaving lather off balloons. The technique would be difficult to master. He could cut himself quite badly if he slipped.

Dr. Elias chuckled as he recognized the irony. It was ridiculous to worry about injuring himself when he was dying anyway. In any event, the straight razor could wait. He had much higher priorities.

He had already selected his clothes for the day, and Dr. Elias dressed as quickly as he could. His right arm hurt, but the pain was a reminder that he had accomplished his duty last night. It had taken all his strength to wield the knife, but he had ensured that Father Marx would die instantaneously.

Dr. Elias sighed as he massaged the stiff muscles in his arm. It would have been much easier to use the gun, but the risk was too great. Then there would be an obvious connection between the murders. He had calculated that Mac would not tell the police about the group. After four years of therapy, he knew that Mac was unlikely to breach a confidence.

Father Marx's death would bring the group together again, but panic would cloud their thinking. Mac would urge them to ask for police protection, but they would refuse. Kay was too fearful of jeopardizing Charles's career, and the others had their own good reasons. They would decide to handle things on their own.

Dr. Elias knew that no one in the group would suspect him. It was psychologically impossible for them to doubt the psychiatrist they had trusted for years. They'd been too dependent on him, and they were too unsure of themselves to ask the right questions. They might try to contact him to ask for his help, but they would be told that he had left town. Naturally they'd conclude that he was dead or close to it.

It was all working out precisely as he had planned. His only uncertainty was Mac. It would be simpler to kill him now, but the police would go into high gear if one of their own was murdered. Another detective might recognize the ultimate link between the murders. Dr. Elias was counting on the trust that existed between patient and psychiatrist to blind Mac to the obvious conclusion. It was a calculated risk.

Dr. Elias smiled as he slipped into his jacket. He looked quite dashing for a dying man. Dressing in a suit every day was an important psychological ritual. If he stayed in his robe and slippers he would feel like an invalid. He had made only one concession to his illness. He no longer wore a tie.

His breakfast was waiting for him. Dr. Elias had increased his order in spite of his failing appetite. It was imperative to try something new every morning, in addition to his usual croissant. So little time remained, and there were many new things left to sample. He could not eat all that he ordered, but Dr. Elias found it gratifying to taste a bit of each.

A sticky bun was his treat for this morning. The top of the roll was covered with a brown gluelike substance and the waxed paper stuck to the bun as he lifted it from the box. Dr. Elias frowned. As a rule, he did not care for confections, but sticky buns were a Minnesota tradition and he felt he should try one before he died.

The bakery had included a little plastic fork. Dr. Elias pulled the paper away from the bun and cut off a small piece. The taste was pleasant enough, but it was much too sweet. The caramel stuck to his teeth and his fingers were tacky. He wrapped the roll back in its paper and went to wash his hands.

It was an experience he did not care to repeat. Dr. Elias dried his hands and went back to his chair. A real sugar addict might overlook the mess, but sticky buns were not to his liking. Perhaps it was too late in his life for innovations.

A sip of espresso helped to cut the sweetness. Dr. Elias settled down again and opened his morning paper. Father Marx had made the first page. VANDALS SUSPECTED IN PRIEST'S MURDER. Dr. Elias smiled as he bit into his plain croissant and began to read.

The window was fogged and Kay wiped a place clear with the kitchen towel. Mac and Debra were outside, talking to Charles in the driveway. Charles had a very serious expression on his face.

Even though she knew Mac was right, Kay still felt

guilty for calling Charles home from the office. He had canceled his speech. The League of Women Voters would be upset.

Mac was opening his car door now. He reached inside and pulled out a plastic scraper. He was still talking to Charles as he lifted the wipers and scraped the ice off the windshield.

Charles did not smile as he shook Mac's hand. Kay knew he was upset. Handshakes were always paired with smiles in politics.

They were leaving now. Debra gave a little wave toward the house and got into the passenger seat. Mac backed his Toyota out of the driveway and turned onto the street. Charles stood there watching until they were gone. Then he hurried toward the house. Kay drew a deep breath and got ready for the argument that would be sure to come when he got inside.

Charles didn't say a word as he came into the kitchen. He just hugged her hard. He held her so long that the snow from his boots began to melt and drip in a puddle on the spotless kitchen floor. Kay felt safe with Charles's arms around her. It was the first time she'd felt safe in days.

"You should have told me, honey." Charles brushed back her hair. "You must have been terrified."

Kay nodded. She didn't trust herself to speak. It was such a relief, she felt like crying. Now she wished she'd confided in Charles in the first place.

"We'll get some protection." Charles sat down at the table and slipped off his boots. "I'll call Captain Meyers and he'll assign the best men on the force to guard you."

Kay drew a deep breath. She had to be firm now. She knew she was right.

"It'll leak out, Charles." Kay faced him squarely.

"You know it will. I refuse to let you ruin your career for me!"

"My career doesn't mean a damn without you, Kay!" Charles reached out to take her hand. "Look, honey, Lieutenant Macklin seems to be a pretty levelheaded guy. If he says your life is in danger, I'm not taking any chances."

"No!" Kay stood firm. "There's got to be another way, Charles. Isn't there anything else we could do?"

Charles sighed deeply and rubbed his forehead. He looked tired and defeated. Kay knew what was running through his mind. They had talked about it before.

As the only son of a black judge, Charles had grown up with politics. There'd been no question about his major in college. He had a BA in political science from the University of Minnesota and a law degree from William Mitchell. His ultimate goal was Washington and a position of power in the federal government. What would Charles do if his political career collapsed?

Kay knew there would be plenty of job offers from industry, but Charles would be miserable in a corporate atmosphere. He could teach, but the academic life would be stifling for him. Charles was born to be a politician.

Charles sighed and squeezed Kay's hand. He still looked worried, but the defeat was gone from his eyes.

"Well . . . I suppose we could just leave town until they catch him. Everyone expects us to be here over the holidays, and we could sneak away before they got wise. It's only a ten-hour drive to your mother's. What do you think?"

"Perfect!" Kay smiled gratefully. They'd load up the kids and go to her mother's for Christmas.

There was a whimper from the corner of the kitchen. Ralph was trying to get her attention by pushing his food bowl across the floor. It was empty.

"I think he's trying to tell you something, Kay."

"All right, Ralph. I get the message." Kay took out a sack of kibble and gave him a generous scoop. His water bowl was empty, too. Ralph preferred spring water and Kay filled the bottle with Glenwood. Ralph went through one five-gallon bottle every two weeks. He really had a cushy life.

"Let's take Ralph along." Charles managed a smile. "He could chase your mother's cats."

Kay grinned. A cat would probably scare Ralph to death, but it might do him some good to see how the other half lived. There was no Glenwood dispenser or sack of kibble under the sink at the farm. Her mother's cats ran wild, existing on whatever they could catch.

The kids would grumble a bit about leaving the city. James had tickets for the big hockey game next week and Trish was looking forward to a New Year's Eve dance at the Capp Towers, but the prospect of doing some cross-country skiing would appease them. Going to her mother's was the perfect solution, and best of all, no one would think to look for them there.

"I love you, Charles." Kay kissed the top of his head where his hair was beginning to thin. She felt much better now and her energy had returned. She'd wrap the gifts tonight and pack them in the trunk of the car. And somehow she'd find the time to bake Charles's favorite pecan cookies to eat on the trip.

"I'm insensitive?" Nora picked up the cut-glass decanter and poured iced tea into a whiskey glass. She made sure the liquid spilled out in a visible splash. Then she crossed to the wing chair, stopped halfway, and took a drink before she sat down.

"Listen to me, Robert! I was sensitive long before . . ."

Nora stopped and blinked. She trembled in the glare from the baby spot.

What was the rest of the speech? Her mind was blank.

"Long before you could spell . . ." Elena's voice prompted gently.

"I was sensitive long before you could spell the damn word! Your father came to me one day in . . ."

Nora faltered again. The spot was so bright it blinded her. She couldn't see Elena in the middle of the house and the wings were filled with deep moving shadows. Someone could be hiding there, waiting for her exit.

The familiar theater seemed suddenly threatening. Nora was alone and vulnerable, caught in the spotlight. She felt like a deer, targeted in a hunter's scope. The killer could see her, but she couldn't see him. He could be watching her now and she'd never know it.

Elena was there to protect her, but she couldn't be everywhere at once. Elena wouldn't see the killer if he waited backstage. He could be crouching behind the piles of flats or lurking in back of the second-act scenery. There were too many shadows, too many places to hide, too many ways to kill her.

"I can't!" Nora's cry was panic-stricken.

"It's all right, Nora." Elena ran for the stage. "Hold on! I'm coming!"

There was no point in continuing. Elena could see that Nora was too frightened to rehearse. Nora clung to her like a frightened child as she led her from the theater. The only thing that seemed to ease her panic was the physical contact of her fingers on Elena's arm.

"Please tell me I'm paranoid, Elena!"

"No. I think you're right." Elena started the car and drove from the lot. "Just let me figure out what to do."

It was only a few blocks from the Guthrie to their loft apartment. They covered the distance in silence. Shivering, Nora stared out the window at the snowbanks that lined the street. The trees were stark and bare. The ground was covered with icy snow. How would they dig Father Marx's grave if the ground was frozen? She really didn't want to know.

"We've got to get you out of town." Elena pulled into the alley behind their studio and parked. "Forget the play, Nora. April can take your part. That's what understudies are for. Nothing's as important as your life."

Nora nodded. Elena was right. There was no way she could go on tonight. Even if she remembered her lines, her performance would be ruined by fear.

"It's been twenty-five years and I've never missed an opening before." Nora sighed deeply as she followed Elena up the stairs. She held her breath until they were inside the loft with the doors double locked behind them. Then she sank down on the couch and gave a pale imitation of her famous laugh.

"Maybe the killer'll get April instead of me. She always says she's dying to take my part."

Curtis Holt pulled out a crumpled handkerchief and blew his nose. He had a rotten winter cold. The bright fluorescent lights in the squad room hurt his eyes and his throat felt scratchy. He had taken a timed-release cold capsule before he'd left his apartment, but maybe it was time for more vitamin C. He'd wash it down with a cup of coffee. He could use the caffeine.

Curt felt around in his pocket for change. The Feldman murder case was getting him down and now he had the priest on top of it. Two murders at once were a pain. He needed some help, but today was Mac's day off and Curt didn't want to bother him at home. Mac would tell him to look for connections, but there didn't seem to be any. As far as Curt could tell, the murders were unrelated. Mac had known Feldman, so he couldn't be officially assigned to the case. And he had known the priest, too. Curt frowned. The only connection between the two murders was Mac!

For a moment Curt was alarmed. Then he grinned sheepishly. St. Steven's Church was on lower Hennepin. Mac had walked that beat when he was a rookie. And Feldman was a dentist. Mac was probably a former patient. Of course he'd run a routine check, but it probably wasn't important at all.

Curt sneezed and blew his nose again. His wife had filled a Baggie with high-potency vitamin C, and Curt chuckled as he took it out of his pocket. If the narc boys came in, he'd probably be busted for possession.

The coffee machine buzzed loudly. Curt knew it was daring him to put in his money. This time he had it licked. He knew exactly what to do.

Curt dropped his money in the slot. The machine accepted his coins with a series of clicks. Curt whacked the metal frame exactly as Mac had done and stood back, grinning. The coffee splashed out and ran down the drain. No cup.

"Aw, shit!" Curt groaned loudly. He was debating the

wisdom of investing another fifty cents when the new female rookie walked into the room. She was a gorgeous redhead in her twenties. The guys called her Bazookas.

"Hello, Sergeant Holt."

Curt smiled back and nodded. For the life of him he couldn't remember her real name. He opened his mouth to warn her about the coffee machine, but it was too late. She had already dropped in her money.

The machine whirred smoothly. The cup dropped into perfect position. Coffee filled it to within a half-inch of the rim and stopped.

"Uh . . . Carol?" Curt grinned as he remembered her name. "Would you get one of those for me, too? I'm up to my neck in this paperwork."

"Sure, Sergeant Holt." She took his coins and gave him the world's sweetest smile. "I had trouble with the coffee machine, too, at first. You just have to show it who's boss."

CHAPTER 20

"Believe me, Debbie, it's a lot safer if you stay with Elena. I'll put Nora on the train and meet you at the theater."

Debra gave in reluctantly. She was so scared, she hated to let Mac out of her sight, but he was right. She'd be perfectly safe if she stayed close to Elena.

All their plans were made. Nora was leaving tonight on the train to Chicago. She had phoned to reserve a compartment. Elena would fly to meet her tomorrow. As the show's choreographer, she was required to attend the opening night and make notes on any last-minute changes in the dance numbers. She would be free to leave in the morning once the show was set.

Mac glanced at his watch. "We'll leave in a minute, Nora. You'd better get ready. Put on Debbie's coat and scarf. If anyone's watching, they'll think Debbie and I are leaving and you're still inside."

"It's early, Mac!" Nora looked puzzled. "If we leave now, I'll get to the station an hour before I can board."

"I want to drive around for a while and make sure

we're not tailed. Let's see what you look like in Debbie's clothes."

Nora put on the cloth coat and frowned at her reflection in the mirror. With Debra's scarf wrapped around her head, she looked like a frump. She almost told Mac she wouldn't be caught dead wearing a scarf, but the time for joking was over. She'd wear galoshes and overalls if it meant she could get out of town safely.

"You can have my sealskin to wear while I'm gone." Nora took a coat from the hanger and tossed it to Debra. "I guarantee it'll change your life." Debra was stunned. Nora's coat was obviously expensive.

"Are you sure, Nora? I've got another coat at my apartment I can wear."

"Of course I'm sure. Live it up a little, darling. You'll look gorgeous in it."

Debra smiled as she stroked the soft fur. She had refused to wear animal skins of any kind for conservationist reasons. It was an easy commitment to make. Fur coats cost much more than she could afford.

"Thank you, Nora." Debra gave her a grateful kiss on the cheek. She hoped none of the Greenpeace people would be at the Guthrie tonight.

"Bring my full-length mink cape when you fly up tomorrow." Nora hugged Elena hard. "And tell April to break a leg. You don't have to mention that I mean it literally."

"I love you, Nora." Elena hugged her back. "I'll meet you at four tomorrow afternoon."

There were tears in Nora's eyes as she kissed Elena good-bye. Debra swallowed past the lump in her throat. They really loved each other. She thought about how she'd feel if she had to leave Mac and she almost burst into tears.

Mac cleared his throat. "Come on, Nora. You don't want to miss your train."

Elena handed Nora her tote bag. "Have the porter make up your berth right away and take two Valiums the minute the train pulls out of the station. You can sleep all the way to Chicago."

Elena's smile stayed in place until the door had closed behind them. Then her shoulders slumped and she brushed the tears from her cheek with the back of her hand. She turned back to Debra and tried to smile.

"I thought we'd open a bottle of Chardonnay to celebrate Nora's escape. We've got an hour before we have to leave. Then we'll splurge and take a taxi to the Guthrie."

"That sounds fine." Debra smiled back. She noticed that Elena's hands were shaking as she took out the wine. "Do you want me to open that, Elena?"

"I think you'd better." Elena sighed as she handed over the corkscrew. "I'll probably stab myself with the damn thing. That'd be poetic. Nora flees on the train in the midst of danger and I do myself in with a corkscrew at home."

Dr. Elias had just finished an excellent dinner. The coq au vin from the Orion Room had been perfect tonight. He poured himself a small glass of port and placed the leather case containing his father's meerschaum on the table next to his chair.

An evening of relaxation awaited him. Dr. Elias tuned the radio to KSJN. They were playing Mahler's

Symphony no. 2 in C Minor. It was one of his favorites. It addressed the *why* of human existence. Mahler told a German critic that it was a sequel to his First Symphony, written five years earlier. The first movement, "Celebration of the Dead," bore the hero from his First Symphony to the grave. Mahler said it asked the great questions: *Why have you lived? Why have you suffered?* And, *Has it all been only a huge, frightful joke?*

Dr. Elias particularly looked forward to the graceful Austrian folk dance in the second movement and the horns of the apocalypse in the fifth. The symphony climaxed with a burst of shattering power that he always found invigorating.

The theme from *All Things Considered* was just ending. Dr. Elias adjusted the volume. There would be a brief series of public announcements and then the symphony would start.

"The Guthrie Theater announces a change of cast in tonight's opening performance of The Heretic Mother. *April Forrester will replace Miss Nora Stanford in the leading role. Call 555-2224 for advance tickets."*

Dr. Elias hurried to the phone as the music critic began to give the program notes. Nora was missing her opening night. He had to find out what had happened.

It took twenty minutes to get through to someone who had the necessary information. The first movement was just ending as Dr. Elias was connected to the manager's office. Miss Stanford had been called out of town for a family emergency. Her mother was extremely ill. The theater manager didn't know when she would be back. He expected Miss Stanford to contact him tomorrow by phone.

There was a frown on Dr. Elias's face as he turned up the radio and sat back down in his chair. Nora's mother was dead. She had no family. Obviously the emergency was an excuse. Nora had panicked. She was breaking down and he had to find her.

It was only natural that the last few members of the group would try to leave town. Dr. Elias had prepared for this eventuality. He knew he could determine where Nora had gone. He had the advantage of knowing her response patterns. Nora had been honest and open in her therapy. Dr. Elias concentrated on remembering what she had revealed in her sessions.

The contralto was beginning the folk poetry lyrics in the fourth movement when Dr. Elias thought of it. Sarah Edwards, Nora's favorite drama teacher, was the key. She was the only person Nora had ever gone to for help. Dr. Elias got up from his chair and hurried to the office. He had the address in his files.

His records were cross-indexed and Dr. Elias found the information in minutes. Sarah Edwards lived in Chicago. If Nora had left by car, it would be difficult to intercept her.

Nora hated long cross-country drives and she had no patience in traffic. Dr. Elias was sure that she would not drive by herself. The first thing to do was to check the studio to see if Elena was still there.

Elena picked up the phone on the first ring. Dr. Elias recognized her voice. He apologized for reaching the wrong number and hung up quickly. Nora had not left town by car.

She would not take a plane. Dr. Elias knew that Nora was terrified of flying. A bus was too common.

Nora liked to travel in style. That left the train. Naturally she would reserve a compartment under an assumed name. Dr. Elias smiled as he dialed the Amtrak information number.

He was still smiling as he hung up the phone. There was only one train leaving for the East tonight, at eight forty-seven. He had over an hour to prepare. Union Station was in St. Paul, but the freeways provided an easy access. It was only a twenty-minute ride by cab. Nora couldn't have made things easier for him if she had tried.

Dr. Elias glanced at his watch. The gift shop downstairs was still open and they had precisely what he needed for Nora. He smiled as he walked down the hallway and pressed the button for the elevator. Human behavior was entirely predictable if one took the time to analyze the possibilities and narrow them down to an inevitable conclusion.

"Neat-o, Dad!" James grinned as he grabbed another slice of pizza and sprinkled it with crushed peppers. Mom called it garbage pizza because it had everything on it. Sausage, cheese, pepperoni, olives, tomatoes, Canadian bacon, onions, and a side order of anchovies for Dad. James took a big mouthful and chewed.

"It's just like this movie I saw on television last night. We'll be fugitives!"

"Not quite." Charles laughed. "We're just sneaking out of town for a couple of days, James. It's actually more like playing hooky. The governor does it all the time. Just make sure you don't tell anyone that we're going."

"My lips are sealed." James picked off a piece of pepperoni and threw it to Ralph. "I don't mind missing the hockey game as long as you pack my skis."

Trish looked disgruntled. She removed the slices of ripe olive from her pizza and arranged them neatly on the edge of her paper plate.

"Regina Cook'll be in seventh heaven. She'll throw herself at Darin while I'm gone. It'll be absolutely disgusting!"

"Let Regina make a fool of herself." Kay smiled at her. "Then Darin will appreciate you that much more when you get home."

"Oh, Mom!" Trish frowned. "Maybe that was true in the Dark Ages, but things are different today. Darin's a hunk. If I'm not here to keep him interested, he'll find someone else."

Trish was in the throes of her first love, a tall, gangly high school junior who tripped over his own feet unless he was on the basketball court. Kay failed to see the attraction, but Trish was only fifteen. There was still hope that she'd develop better taste in men as she got older.

"I've got it!" Trish smiled suddenly. "I'll call Darin right before we leave and tell him I have to go undercover for a while. He'll be so busy trying to figure out what's happening that he won't even notice Regina."

Charles shook his head as Kay offered him the last piece of pizza. James looked like a vulture, ready to swoop, and Kay passed it over to him.

"You kids wrap your presents as soon as you're through eating." Charles pushed his chair back from the table. "We'll load the car later tonight."

"What time are we leaving?" Trish set her paper

plate down on the floor for Ralph. There were seven slices of olive and a big piece of crust that she hadn't eaten. Kay sighed. Trish was dieting again. The anorexic look must still be popular with her peers.

"Your mother's got a fashion show she can't get out of, and I have to arrange some things at the office. We plan on leaving here about three in the afternoon."

"Will Grandma have a tree?"

Kay laughed at James's worried expression. "If she doesn't, we'll go out and cut one. Maybe you'd better box up some of those plastic ornaments, James. We don't want Ralph to ruin Grandma's tree."

"Oh, no!" Trish made a face. "I forgot about Ralph. I hope he doesn't get carsick again. Last time we took him along, he barfed all over my coat."

"That van just turned off, Mac." Nora shivered as she watched out the rear window. "I don't think there's anybody behind us now."

Mac nodded grimly. He had seen the van in the rearview mirror. It had been following them for the past ten blocks, but now it was gone.

"Where are you going?" Nora looked puzzled as they turned into the Kellogg Square parking ramp. "We're not going to walk from here, are we?"

"Of course not." Mac grinned at her as he took a ticket. "It's a trick I learned from the movies. We'll go up the ramp and come back down again. You keep an eye on any cars that pull in behind us and leave when we do."

Nora nodded. It made sense. A green Ford was behind them as they went up the ramp, but it turned off and parked on the second level. No one followed them to the top. A car pulled out as they started down the ramp, but two teenage girls were inside. Mac pulled off at the next level to let them pass.

"Mac! There's a red VW behind us!" Nora's voice was shaking. "I think it's the same one that followed us on the freeway!"

Mac almost told Nora not to worry, that there were thousands of red VW bugs in the Twin Cities. He caught himself just in time. Even though the probability was next to zero, it wouldn't hurt to check it out.

"See if you can get a look inside when I stop at the ticket booth."

Nora turned around on the seat to stare at the car behind them. "A man's driving. He's alone. Dark hair, glasses . . . oh, hell, Mac! There's a kid in the passenger seat. I can just see the top of his head."

"Okay. We're clear."

Mac drove to the post office and pulled into the lot. He shut off the engine and looked around before he opened the door.

"We'll walk over from here, Nora. We can get a good look at anyone who follows us across the street."

No one followed them. Nora stuck close to Mac as they walked across the street and entered the station. It was crowded with holiday travelers. Nora carefully examined every face, but no one was paying any attention to them. They stood in a long line to confirm her reservation.

As they neared the front, Nora tugged at Mac's arm. "The tickets are reserved under the name Christie, first initial A."

"Miss A. Christie." Mac nodded and then it sank in.

He started to grin. "Agatha, right? Nora . . . you really are incorrigible."

Finally they were done. Mac led her away from the ticket window and found a bench by the coffee machine.

"Do you want a bottle of water, or fruit juice? Or a cup of coffee? We've still got fifteen minutes before they call your train."

"Anything's fine as long as it doesn't have caffeine. I want to sleep all the way to Chicago."

Her nerves were still on edge. Nora felt her legs tremble as she sat down on the bench. It was no use trying to relax yet. When her train pulled out of the station, she'd finally be safe. Then she could lock the compartment door behind her and take two Valiums, just like Elena had told her to. It would be a tremendous relief to sleep.

Nora took a grateful sip of the orange juice that Mac brought for her. Her throat was dry and her hands were still shaking. The minute hand on the big clock over the doorway was stuck. It didn't move at all for five minutes, and then it jumped ahead to the next number. Nora watched the seconds sweep by on her watch. At least time was passing. Soon her ordeal would be over.

Just when she thought she'd scream from the waiting, the loudspeaker crackled with a burst of static. A man's voice said something about boarding at track six. Nora assumed it was her train. It was impossible to tell from the announcement. Either the transportation industry sent its employees to a special school to learn how to mumble, or the same speech-impaired voice was prerecorded for train stations, bus depots, and airports all over the country.

"Mac?" Nora held his arm tightly as he walked her to the track. "If . . . if anything happens . . . take care of Elena for me."

"Nothing's going to happen." Mac hugged her hard as they came out of the tunnel and walked to the train. It was noisy and he put his lips next to her ear. "You're safe now, Nora. Call me every night and I'll give you a progress report. We'll catch him. Don't worry."

Nora turned to wave as the conductor helped her up the steps. There were tears in her eyes. Even though she knew it was silly, she had the terrible premonition that she would never see Mac again.

CHAPTER 21

Mac got to the theater just as the third act was about to begin. He slipped into his seat on the aisle and grinned at Elena and Debbie.

"I stayed until the train pulled out of the station. Nora waved at me from the window."

"Oh, thank God!" Elena smiled weakly. "I'm so glad it's over!"

Elena sighed as the act began. April was very good, but it was impossible to compare her to Nora. She had faltered in a couple of spots, although the dance routine had gone well. Naturally tonight's performance was difficult for April. She ought to be thankful that she was here, and not in New York. The Minneapolis audience was always polite. They tended to give an actress the benefit of the doubt. The house was filled, despite Nora's absence, and there had been a burst of spontaneous applause after the dance number.

The New York audience was jaded. Half of them would have walked out before the play started, muttering angrily about the replacement and demanding a refund. In New York a play was a hit or a flop. There was nothing in between. April should consider herself fortunate that she had made her debut at the Guthrie.

Mac moved restlessly in his seat. Missing the first two acts was a definite handicap and he found it difficult to follow the play. Debbie was engrossed. She smiled as he took her hand, but she turned right back to the action on the stage. He found himself watching Debbie instead of the play, studying her face in the dim light from the stage.

She really looked gorgeous tonight. Mac thought she had done something different with her hair. It was pulled up in some sort of knot on top of her head and her neck looked long and graceful. Mac wanted to lean over and kiss the soft skin at the nape of her neck, but that was hardly appropriate now. He found himself wishing that the play would end so he could be alone with her.

The house lights came up at last. It was over. The audience had obviously enjoyed the performance. They gave April three curtain calls. If Nora had played the lead, Mac was sure she would have received a standing ovation.

They stayed in their seats until the crowd had thinned out. Then Elena led them backstage to meet the cast. Everyone was hugging and kissing. Someone passed around plastic glasses of champagne, and Mac and Debra hung back a bit, letting Elena field the questions about Nora. Finally most of the cast left for their dressing rooms.

"Are you sure you don't want to come to the opening night party?" Elena drew them away from the crowd. "My meeting won't last more than twenty minutes."

"Not this time." Mac gave Elena a hug. "We'll pick you up at noon tomorrow to go to the airport. Try to relax and get some sleep. You look exhausted."

Elena nodded, but the worried look stayed on her face. Mac doubted that she'd get much sleep tonight. Elena wouldn't relax until she was in Chicago with Nora.

"Let's stop for a steak on the way home." Mac held Debbie's arm as they left the theater. "I just realized I'm hungry. We haven't eaten since breakfast."

Debra pulled Nora's sealskin coat tightly around her. The wind was blowing and it was starting to snow again. Her high-heeled boots crunched against the snow as they followed the path to the parking lot.

"It's almost eleven, Mac. Nora must be halfway to Chicago by now. We really ought to do something to celebrate."

"We'll go to the Camelot." Mac opened the car door for Debbie. "I can't take you just anywhere in that coat. No more hash houses and hot dog stands for you. Nora was right. That fur coat is already changing your life."

The train was moving at last! Nora watched the lights of the city rush past her window. The danger was over. She was safe now.

She smiled as she walked to the table and sat down. The split of champagne icing in the silver bucket was her absolute favorite, Dom Pérignon. It had been waiting for her when the porter unlocked the door to her compartment. There'd been a package next to it, wrapped in gold paper. The porter had said it had been delivered before she'd boarded.

There was nothing like a surprise to make her feel better. Nora opened the present carefully. Inside was a small crystal box, handmade and delicate. She lifted the cut-glass cover and laughed. One perfect French truffle was nestled inside. There was no card, but Nora could guess who had sent it.

Only a few people knew her weakness for truffles. Elena, of course, and the members of the group. Nora had confessed that she was a chocoholic. Hershey's Kisses made her mouth water. Fanny Farmer candy shops drew her like a magnet with their clean white interiors and delectable aromas. Imported chocolates were even more dangerous. They sang the song of the sirens. Elena had standing instructions to pull her past all chocolate counters and show no mercy. Nora knew, from experience, that she could polish off a two-pound box of chocolates and go right back for more. It was a terrible affliction. But real French truffles, those creamy, rich, dark, exquisite confections, were the absolute epitome of decadence.

It was a plot. Nora laughed out loud. The truffle was calling to her. Thank God there was only one!

Kay wasn't part of the conspiracy. She didn't know that Nora was leaving town. That left Mac, Debra, and Elena. It was undoubtedly Elena's idea. They had probably pooled their money to buy her this wonderful bon voyage present.

Nora blinked back grateful tears. They had known she'd be nervous all alone on the train. It showed that they were thinking of her, that they loved her.

A single hollow-stemmed Tiffany glass sat next to the silver bucket. Nora smiled. There was no way she'd deprive herself of her favorite things even though the warning on her bottle of Valium said not to mix the drug with alcohol. She had been taking Valium for three years now. And she usually had a glass of wine at night to unwind. She had noticed no ill effects from the combination before.

Nora got up to put the PLEASE DO NOT DISTURB sign on the outside of the door. She undressed and slipped into her silk nightgown, hanging her clothes up carefully so they wouldn't wrinkle. She'd have to wear this same outfit tomorrow until Elena arrived at the airport with her suitcase.

The bottle of Dom Pérignon gave a soft, gentle pop as she opened it. The top always shot off like a rocket in plays or in movies. That was done entirely for dramatic effect. Nora knew that popping the cork forcefully bruised the wine. And even worse, most of it spilled out in the process. She had learned the proper way to open champagne very early in her life.

Nora poured the wine in her glass and studied the effect. It was lovely. The bubbles made a beautiful pattern in the Tiffany glass. She took a sip and smiled. This was pure luxury. Now she'd take her Valiums, eat the truffle as slowly as was humanly possible, and climb right into bed.

The train whistle blew as she opened the bottle of Valium and shook two blue pills out into her hand. It was a lonely sound, mournful but intrinsically exciting. There was something about train travel that captured the romance that was missing from airplanes or buses. If Elena were here, this would be an adventure. They could sip champagne and let the train carry them away into the night. She loved Elena so much, she might even share the truffle, although that was doubtful. There were some sacrifices that even a perfect lover had no right to expect.

Nora laughed as she swallowed the Valiums. She felt like a wealthy degenerate, washing down her pills with one of the most expensive champagnes in the world. She picked up the truffle and sighed happily.

Oh, it was marvelous! Nora took a small nibble and smiled as the dark, bitter chocolate melted on her tongue. She had intended to eat it slowly, savoring each tiny morsel, but her willpower vanished with the first heavenly taste. Nora popped the truffle into her mouth and moaned in ecstasy. It was divine, the best truffle she'd ever tasted.

In a moment it was gone. She was left with a memory of dissolving chocolate and a smudge of cocoa on her fingers. Nora licked them until not a trace of chocolate remained. Then she took another sip of champagne and sighed deeply. She would have to remember to ask Elena where she had gotten the truffle. She wanted a dozen more, just like it.

Her glass was almost empty and Nora filled it again. She would sit right here and drink it all. Two glasses would be perfect. Then she'd sleep like a baby, all the way to Chicago.

Nora lit a cigarette and smoked it down to the filter. She was beginning to feel a bit light-headed from the combination of the champagne and the Valiums. Perhaps it was time for bed.

She got up from the table and made her way to the berth, weaving slightly. The room was spinning a bit and it was difficult to focus her eyes. She wasn't sure if her unsteadiness was due to the Valiums, the champagne, or the rocking motion of the train, but it was definitely time to sleep. Her eyelids felt heavy and she sighed as she stretched out between the clean sheets and closed her eyes.

Her toes were cold and numb. Nora managed to pull up the blanket, even though her arms felt leaden. The cold numbness crept up to her legs and she shivered. *They really should keep these compartments warmer,* she thought. *Passengers could freeze in the winter.* Perhaps the porter had forgotten to turn up the heat.

Nora considered crawling out of bed and ringing for the porter, but it was just too much effort. She'd warm up in a minute. It was really a pity Elena wasn't there. Elena was always toasty warm. She was much better than an electric blanket on cold winter nights.

Elena. Nora's lips curved up in a smile. She had never loved anyone the way she loved Elena. The train whistle sounded again, but it was very faint in her ears. There was a small light on the dresser that was growing dimmer with each passing second. The rocking of the train had smoothed out and now it was perfectly steady. There was a rushing in her ears as the world went dark, and then all sound ceased.

Dr. Elias put the meerschaum back in its case. He took the last sip of port and glanced at his watch. It was past ten. Nora was dead.

The clerk had been helpful when Dr. Elias had explained that he was confirming his niece's reservation. Were they holding a compartment for her? The only reservation they had was for a Miss A. Christie. How strange. Perhaps he'd better call and check with his niece to make certain she was planning on leaving tonight.

Christie. Dr. Elias chuckled to himself. Nora was amazing. Her sense of humor would not be stifled, even by fear. And it had made things so very easy for him.

The delivery service had been delighted to take the package to the depot. A generous tip had ensured promptness. There would be no traces of the truffle left to analyze. Dr. Elias knew Nora would finish it all. She would take her prescribed Valium and crawl into her berth. Then the drug in the truffle would react with the Valium, causing a painless but fatal reaction that would resemble heart failure. It was neat and clean and quick.

Dr. Elias got up from his chair and walked painfully to his studio. It was impossible for Nora to resist her favorite vices. He had analyzed his plan again and there was no error. He knew it was time to paint in Nora's face, even though her body would not be discovered until the train pulled into the station in Chicago.

The group portrait was taking shape nicely. Dr. Elias smiled as he switched on the lights and examined his work. Father Marx looked relaxed. The lines of tension were gone from his face. Actually he looked much more handsome than he had ever looked in life. Tension was the great destroyer of beauty. He remembered touring a facility for the severely mentally retarded when he was an intern. He'd been amazed at how young the patients appeared to be, even though their median age was forty. A life without tension had certain compensations.

His hand was shaking as he squeezed paint on the pallet. Dr. Elias looked down and frowned. Could this be a guilt reaction?

The prospect was disquieting. Dr. Elias had never experienced feelings of misplaced or irrational guilt. He used logic to reach his decisions and fully accepted the consequences. He was much too stable to let his emotions rule his physical reactions. Could he possibly be suffering from the same problem that he had worked to cure in others?

It was extremely unlikely. Consciously, Dr. Elias knew that he was right. These systematic eliminations were necessary and unavoidable. He searched his thought processes carefully, but he could not identify any vestiges of guilt. Then why was his hand shaking as he prepared to paint Nora's face?

Of course! Dr. Elias gave a sigh of relief. It was after ten and he had delayed his regular injection. This was a purely physical reaction to the absence of the necessary drug in his system.

Earlier in the week, he had placed a packet containing his medication in every room of the penthouse. The disease was progressing and now he needed an injection every four hours to control the pain. Soon it would be necessary to increase the dosage as well.

Dr. Elias frowned as he mentally checked off his symptoms. Everything was proceeding according to the prognosis. It would be wise to gather his strength and escalate his work a bit. Soon his mobility would be severely curtailed and he would be confined to his penthouse, waiting for either the disease or the increased dosages of the narcotics he now had to take, to kill him. His time was running out and he had not yet finished his duty.

There was no time to waste on self-pity or personal concerns. Dr. Elias pulled out the drawer in his easel and removed the disposable syringe. In a few moments his hands would stop shaking and then he could finish Nora's portrait.

Dr. Elias smiled as he waited for the drug to take effect. He had closed Nora's case quite expeditiously. She was no longer a deadly menace. The terrors of her psychosis had ceased to plague her. Nora would look much younger without the ravages of fear on her face. It was possible that as much as ten years would be erased from her features. At last she would reach the age that she claimed. Yes, Nora would definitely approve if she could see her final portrait.

CHAPTER 22

By the time they got back to the house, it was past midnight, but Debra and Mac were too keyed up to sleep. It seemed as if Nora's escape had provided them with the energy they had been missing for the past few days. Debbie put her favorite collection of Christmas music on the stereo and turned on the Christmas tree lights.

"Let's have hot chocolate with brandy," she suggested. "I'll make it if you'll start a fire in the fireplace."

Mac grinned. He didn't see how Debbie could possibly swallow another thing after dinner at the Camelot. She had ordered prime rib with all the trimmings, Yorkshire pudding, creamed spinach, a baked potato with sour cream, chives, and butter. And amaretto mousse pie for dessert. Debbie looked small and fragile, but she ate like a truck driver. Mac had no idea where she could put all that food. She had even finished the last of his porterhouse and he was absolutely stuffed.

A moment later Debbie was rattling things in the kitchen. Mac carried a couple of logs over to the fireplace and put them on top of the kindling he had arranged on the grate. He crinkled up sheets of last Sunday's newspaper and tucked them in strategic places under the logs. Then he struck a match and hoped that he'd remembered to open the flue.

The paper caught fire immediately. It blazed and spread to the kindling. Flames licked up around the logs and they started to scorch. The smoke went straight up the chimney and Mac grinned. The flue was open.

As the fire began to crackle cheerfully, Mac found himself singing along with the Christmas music on the stereo. He grinned self-consciously. If anything could drive Debbie away, it was his singing. Mac had never been able to carry a tune. His grade-school music teacher, Mrs. Porter, had practically begged him not to sing at school Christmas programs. He had no musical talent at all, but Mac loved music as a nonperformer. He did his singing in the shower every morning. The sound of the water drowned out his voice and he pretended that he was Pavarotti, belting out Italian operas behind the pebble-textured sliding glass doors.

"That sounds nice, Mac." Debbie carried in cups of steaming hot cocoa and set them down on the table by the couch. "I like to hear you sing."

Mac shook his head. She must love him a lot. Or maybe she was tone deaf, too. Theirs was a match made in heaven. They could even sing duets in the shower.

"Let's build a snowman outside that window." Debbie perched on the arm of a chair and sipped her hot chocolate. "It's not really Christmas without Frosty the Snowman."

"Now?" Mac glanced at his watch. "It's almost one in the morning."

"That's a good time to build a snowman." Debbie

grinned at him. "You don't have anything better to do, do you?"

Mac could think of quite a few activities that appealed to him more, like nuzzling her left earlobe or kissing her neck. He almost told her it was a crazy idea, but she looked so eager, he hated to disappoint her. They'd be safe enough in the yard as long as they stayed together. They had a choice, the way Mac saw it. They could live in terror, huddled behind locked doors like animals in a trap. Or they could take reasonable precautions and keep on living as normally as possible. Building a snowman at one in the morning wasn't exactly normal, but it might be fun. It was certainly a switch from what he'd had in mind.

"You missed your calling, Debbie. You should have been a cruise director." Mac drained his cup and got up from his comfortable seat on the couch.

"We don't have lumps of coal for his eyes so we'll have to use onions." Debbie jumped up and headed for the kitchen. "I've got one carrot left for his nose. Find an old stocking cap or something for his head. And a broom for him to carry."

The wind had died down and the night was crystal clear. The light shining through the picture window reflected on the freshly fallen snow. It was beautiful outside, now that the snow had stopped falling. The cold, crisp air stung the inside of Mac's nose and his breath puffed out in frozen clouds as he made a snowball and rolled it in the unbroken snow by the fence.

Debbie started in the opposite corner of the yard. They met in the middle, pushing their growing balls of snow.

"That's enough, Debbie. Mine has to be bigger for the base."

Mac kept his voice down until he remembered that there was no one home at the Drevlows' next door. They had gone to visit their daughter in Florida. And Mrs. Urbanski was as deaf as a post when she took off her hearing aid at night. They could make as much noise as they liked and no one would complain.

Mac tried to lift his snowball, but it was too big. He ended up pushing it over to the spot in front of the window. Debbie's was smaller and he managed to lift it and place it on top.

"Now all we need is a small one for the head. Get the rest of that stuff together and hand it to me when I'm ready."

Mac made a snowball and rolled it around the base of the snowman. The snow was exactly the right consistency. It stuck to the ball and left empty paths where he rolled it. Blades of frozen grass stuck up in the bare spots. When the snowball was big enough, Mac lifted it into place.

"The eyes, please?"

Debbie handed him the onions, one at a time, and Mac dug little sockets for them. They looked ridiculous until he shoved in the carrot.

"Put on his cap and scarf. I'll get some twigs for his arms."

Mac snapped two long twigs off the lilac bush. He shoved them into the middle snowball and nodded. Frosty looked pretty good to him.

"What do you think?" He turned to see Debbie packing another snowball. "Hey, Debbie. We're finished. What's that for?"

Debbie grinned and drew back her arm. "For you!"

Mac ducked and the snowball sailed harmlessly past

his head. Debbie had been busy while he'd been getting the twigs. She had a stockpile of snowballs, all ready to throw.

She looked very fierce as she threw another one. Mac laughed. Debbie had bitten off more than she could chew. He'd been the undisputed snowball king of Whitney Elementary School.

"You can't win!" Mac shouted in warning. "Give up, Debbie. I'm an expert. You're insane if you take me on!"

A snowball flew past Mac's ear and Debbie laughed. "We dislike the use of that word. 'All people who behave strangely are not insane.'"

"Fritz Feld to Katherine Hepburn in *Bringing Up Baby*. Nineteen thirty-eight. All right, Debbie, but don't say I didn't warn you!"

She was getting closer. Debbie was throwing snowballs, one right after the other, the old shotgun approach. Mac ducked and packed his own pile of snowballs. If he had time, he'd build a fort, but Debbie's aim was definitely improving. He whizzed a couple over her head to keep her busy and laughed out loud as she scrambled for cover behind the blue spruce in the corner of the yard.

Mac ran a few feet and stopped to peg one right at the bottom of the tree. That would keep her in position. He zigzagged around the lilac bush and splattered another in the same spot. She was forced to lie low now, cut off from her ammunition. He could imagine her frantically packing more snowballs as she crouched behind the tree.

Only a few feet to go. Mac sprinted across the open space and came up behind her, a sneak attack from the rear. Debbie squealed and came up fighting, snowballs in both hands. "No fair!"

She tried to throw them, but he had her now. Mac pushed her back into the snowbank and fell full-length on top of her.

"Give up?"

"Never!"

The more Debbie struggled, the deeper they sank into the fluffy snowbank. The weight of his body pressed her down until they were both below the crust of the snow. Mac laughed as he pinned both of her hands with one arm and trickled snow down her collar with the other.

"Ready to quit now?"

He could tell she was considering it. Snow down the collar was a great persuader.

Debbie moved suddenly and he almost lost his balance. She was trying for an upset.

"Oh, no, you don't!"

Mac laughed as she twisted to the side and attempted to flip him over. Their legs were tangled together and he got his on top to pin her. She was amazingly strong for such a little girl. Then he found the zipper of her jacket and pulled it down.

Debbie gasped in shock as he pulled up her sweater. Mac knew he wasn't playing fair, but snowball fights called for ungentlemanly tactics.

"No! Mac . . . stop!"

Her body looked like it was carved of white marble in the cold, pale moonlight. Mac reached out to pick up a fistful of snow and grinned at her fiendishly.

"Oh, no! Mac! Don't you dare!"

"Say uncle?"

"I'll die first!"

The snow was starting to melt in his glove and it dripped down on Debbie's smooth warm skin. She sputtered and wiggled, trying to slide out from under him. Mac had never seen anything more beautiful than her breasts in the moonlight.

"Give up, Debbie?"

He heard his voice shake and he swallowed hard as he stared down at her.

Her eyes were enormous in the dim moonlight.

"No!" She gave a little smile and tossed her head. Her voice teased him a bit, she was so sure of herself. "You won't do it, Mac. I know you won't. You'll be a nice guy and let me go."

Mac grinned as he opened his glove and let the snow trickle down. There was an astonished expression on her face that was almost comical as he reached out for another handful and rubbed it deliberately all over her body.

"You . . . you rat!" Her squeal of betrayal was loud in his ears.

Mac laughed. "If you mean *dirty* rat, it's one of Cagney's lines." Mac pulled off his glove and covered her breast with his warm fingers. "Of course movie historians claim he never actually said it. There's some controversy about the whole thing. Evidently Cagney can't recall if he did or he didn't."

Debbie made a small sound as Mac's lips took the place of his fingers. The tension in her body changed as he kissed and nuzzled, warming her cold body with his mouth. Then she was straining toward him, crying out at the heat of his lips and tongue.

She threw her arms around his neck as he picked her

up and carried her toward the house. She wouldn't let go, even when he undressed her by the fire and laid her down on the soft rug in front of the hearth. The flickering heat of the fire matched the warmth in her eyes as he joined her, their skin still chilled from the cold night air.

They didn't speak. There was no need. Their bodies grew warm and then hot from the passion that blazed inside. She gave a glad cry as he entered her and then, when they were glowing and exhausted with love, she whispered softly in his ear.

"I give up, Mac. You won."

Mac grinned down at her and brushed his fingers across her toasty skin.

"No, honey. Let's call it a tie."

CHAPTER 23

"The National Weather Service reports a new arctic air mass moving in from Canada. Severe storm warnings go into effect at four P.M. in the Twin Cities and surrounding areas. The temperature is expected to drop well below zero tonight while winds from the north, gusting up to thirty miles per hour, will set the wind chill factor at minus fifty-six. Three to four inches of snow is predicted during the late afternoon and evening, so stock up for another bad spell and get your Christmas shopping done early. WCCO Radio countdown shows only three shopping days left before Christmas."

Debbie snapped off the radio by the bed and yawned. Sunlight streamed through the bedroom window and it looked deceptively warm outside. Not even the prospect of another winter storm could dampen her spirits today. She snuggled back down under the covers and hugged Mac tightly. She felt wonderful!

"Blizzard tonight?" Mac's voice sounded sleepy as he hugged her back. "We'd better stock up on some staples today."

"We don't have to get up this early, do we? It's only seven in the morning."

Their bodies fit together perfectly. Debbie snuggled so close that the hair on Mac's chest tickled her nose.

"I have to call the station for an update." Mac kissed the inside of her arm. "But that can wait until later."

"Would you believe I forgot all about it?" Debbie sighed happily. "I don't think anything can get me down today. Not even the mystery killer."

"Maybe we ought to help him out a little." Mac grinned and pulled her over on top of him. "We could save him the trouble and screw ourselves to death."

"Mom?" Trish ran into the kitchen. "You know the play we saw last night? The actress that got replaced is dead! I just heard it on the news."

Kay dropped the egg she was holding back into the carton and raced to the den behind Trish. Charles's breakfast could wait. Nora couldn't be dead!

A commercial was blaring from the television. Kay stood in front of the set and stared at the Pillsbury Doughboy doing his antics. "Nothing says lovin' like bakin' from the oven, and Pillsbury says it best." Her mind whirled. Trish must have heard the name wrong. Kay didn't want to consider what it would mean if Nora were dead.

Bill Moore's face filled the screen. His expression was somber.

"Nora Stanford, leading lady of the Guthrie Theater, died this morning at age thirty-six. Miss Stanford's body was discovered in her compartment when the Amtrak Express pulled into Chicago's Union Station early this morning. Preliminary reports indicate massive heart failure as the probable cause of death. Miss Stanford operated a theater workshop on Hennepin and is the veteran of more than fifty prize-winning productions, including—"

Kay snapped off the television. She couldn't bear to hear any more. Nora was dead. And it wasn't a heart failure, like Bill Moore said. Kay knew the truth. Nora had been murdered.

"Mom?" Trish took her arm. "Are you all right?"

"Oh . . . yes, dear." Kay swallowed hard. "Nora . . . Miss Stanford . . . was a good friend of mine. It's a shock, that's all. A terrible shock."

"Maybe you should sit down or something." Trish looked worried. "You're shaking."

"No, I . . . I have to call some people I know, honey." Kay took a deep breath. "Can you finish making Daddy's breakfast?"

"Sure, Mom." Trish started for the kitchen. When she reached the door she turned back and frowned. "Will we still go to Grandma's today? You don't have to stay for the funeral or anything, do you, Mom?"

"No. I can't stay!" Her voice was full of panic and Kay fought for control. She didn't want to scare Trish.

"We'll leave right after the fashion show, honey. No change of plans. Now hurry and make Daddy's breakfast. And, honey? Don't mention this to Daddy. I'll tell him later, when we're on the road."

Kay sat by the phone and fought down her panic. They should have gone to the police after all. Nora, Debra, and Mac had all tried to protect her. Their first concern was for her and for Charles's career, and now Nora was dead. Like Jerry. And Greg. And Father Marx.

It was her fault! Kay lowered her head and sobbed. Charles's political career seemed insignificant when it was weighed against Nora's life. She had been selfish and now Nora was dead. There was no way she'd ever forgive herself.

Kay's hands trembled as she dialed the phone. Nora had tried to run away, but somehow the killer had found out. Did he know about the plans she'd made with Charles? Would he try to murder her when they drove out of town?

She couldn't go. She was putting Charles and the kids in danger. Her heart beat so loudly in her chest, she thought she'd surely faint from the fear. She had to get control of herself or she wouldn't be able to talk to Mac.

The line was busy. Kay listened to the rhythmic beeping for a moment and then she dialed again. She had to catch Mac before he left the house. He would know what to do.

Kay tried to remember everything Mac had told her. The killer had a pattern. He only struck when the victim was alone. Nora had been alone on the train. If Elena had been with her, she might still be alive.

The panic lessened as Kay began to think clearly again. She was leaving with Charles and the kids. That would protect her. She'd make sure someone was with her every second until they left. Less than six hours from now, she'd be gone. Then she'd be safe at last!

* * *

"Debbie?" Mac turned from the phone and motioned to her. "Hurry and get ready. We'll leave for Kay's house in ten minutes."

Nora was dead! Debra's legs carried her toward the bedroom. She knew she should hurry because Kay needed them, but she couldn't seem to move any faster. She supposed she was in shock.

She stopped at the bedroom doorway. The room was washed with sunlight, but suddenly she was terrified to step over the threshold. She remembered feeling this way as a child, trembling as she went up the stairs to bed, dreading that moment of paralyzing fear before she snapped on the light in her dark bedroom.

This was ridiculous. It was broad daylight. She knew she didn't have time to panic now. She had to hurry and get ready.

Debra forced her trembling legs forward, away from Mac and safety. She could still hear his voice, comforting Kay on the phone. That helped a little. She glanced toward the shower and shuddered. The scene from *Psycho* flashed through her mind. Norman Bates with the knife, stabbing through the shower curtain. Blood mingling with the water that swirled down the drain.

She turned on the water and took a deep breath. At least Mac's shower had glass doors. The image from *Psycho* was not quite as vivid without the slashed shower curtain.

Debra shivered as she slipped off her robe. She closed the bathroom door and locked it. She wasn't sure if the locked door made her feel better or worse. She was either safe or trapped, depending on circumstances. She didn't have the time to think it out right now.

The water was hot, but nothing could warm her chilled body. Debra shivered under the steaming spray. She was numb with fear. The soap slipped out of her trembling fingers and she finally left it on the rack in the shower caddy. She'd rub the washcloth over the top of the bar. It would work almost as well.

She hurried through her shower as fast as she could and stepped out on the bath mat. Her face was very white in the steamy mirror as she dried off and wrapped herself in a towel. She had her hand on the doorknob when she realized she was afraid to leave the bathroom.

"Mac?"

Her voice was filled with terror as she called to him loudly. Someone was moving around in the bedroom. What would she do if it wasn't Mac?

"Hurry up, Debbie. We'll get coffee at Kay's."

It was Mac. Debra unlocked the bathroom door and rushed out. She threw herself into his arms.

"Psycho." Mac nodded. "I thought about it, too. Get dressed, honey. I've got another call to make before we can leave."

How could he be so calm? Debra's hands were still shaking as she dressed. She left her wet towel on the bedroom floor where it fell. She'd pick it up later. Right now all she wanted was to be close to Mac.

Mac was just hanging up the phone as she came into the kitchen. He slipped his arm around her and hugged her hard.

"There's a flight leaving for San Diego at noon. Call the paper, then call your cousin, honey. Tell her to meet you at the airport."

He wanted her to leave! Debra started to tremble again as the panic set in. He really wanted her to leave!

"I'm staying with you."

Her voice was shaking, but her mind was made up. There was no way she'd leave without him.

"Debbie . . . honey!" His arms folded around her. "Can't you see it's the best thing to do? You'll be safe in San Diego."

"As safe as Nora was in Chicago?"

Mac winced. Debbie had a point. He had done everything in his power to protect Nora, but it hadn't helped. He was positive that no one had followed them to the train station. And he'd checked every person boarding the train. Yet the killer had struck again and he didn't know how.

"Oh, God! I'm sorry, Mac." Debra put her arms around him. "I know you did your best, but the killer got Nora anyway. I . . . I don't want to go. The only place I feel safe is with you!"

"Debbie . . . don't cry." Mac pulled her even closer. Her whole body was trembling. Debbie was terrified. He had to protect her somehow.

Mac thought about it as he held her tightly. The tunnel at the station had been deserted when he'd taken Nora to the train. The killer had had the perfect chance to murder them both, but nothing had happened. It confirmed his theory that the killer struck only one victim at a time. That meant Debbie was relatively safe as long as they stuck together.

There must be a reason the killer had passed him by last night. There had been plenty of opportunities to hit him. Mac had stood alone on the platform as the train pulled out. And he had walked alone through the dark post office parking lot to his car. There had to be a reason why the killer hadn't taken advantage of the situation.

The killer might have known that he was a cop and assumed he was armed. Perhaps he was afraid of Mac's trained reactions to danger. It was a damn good thing no one knew about his problem with guns!

Whatever the reason, Debbie might be right in refusing to run. It was possible that she'd be safer sticking close to him.

Mac looked down at Debbie's face. God knows he didn't want her to go. There were so many selfish reasons to keep her here. His own personal safety could be threatened if she left. Then he'd be alone and the killer could decide to take a chance. If he got killed, the police might never solve the case. Mac knew he was the only one who had all the inside information. It would take poor Curt Holt months to put it all together, and by then it would be too late.

"Mac?" Debbie stood on her tiptoes and kissed him. "You don't really want me to go, do you?"

"No. I want you next to me every minute."

He bent his head to kiss the tip of her nose. It felt good holding Debbie in his arms. He wanted them to stay this way for the rest of their lives. Mac just hoped that would be longer than the killer intended.

Curtis Holt sat at his desk. There was a box of Kleenex man-size tissues next to his elbow and a thermos of hot lemonade in the bottom desk drawer. His winter cold was even worse today. Marge's vitamin C therapy hadn't worked worth a damn.

He still hadn't made any sense out of Mac's call this

morning. It had been a simple matter to get the report on Nora Stanford's death from the teletype and read it to Mac. But then Mac had dropped the bombshell. He'd asked Curt to call the Chicago police and tell them he'd received an anonymous tip that Miss Stanford's death was a homicide. And Mac hadn't been willing to tell him any more than that—just start the investigation rolling with the Chicago PD and keep his name out of it.

Of course he'd made the call. Even if it was a bad tip, Chicago had to be notified. Then he read over the dispatch again. Death from natural causes with no sign of foul play. The Chicago police listed Stanford DOA at Union Station with her compartment locked from the inside. Who had tipped Mac off and why?

Something told Curt there was a connection between Nora Stanford's death and the other murders. Assuming that Mac's tip was right, what tied Miss Stanford to the priest and the dentist?

Curt reached for a Kleenex and sneezed. He had read over all the paperwork again and the only known connection was Mac. Mac had known Feldman and he had discovered Marx's body at the church. And now he was interested in Nora Stanford.

He was missing something. Curt picked up the phone and dialed Mac at home. No answer. He'd keep trying every half hour until he got through. The key to this whole thing was Mac, and it was time for some answers.

Should he go to the captain? Curt sighed deeply. Sure, Mac was connected to all three deaths, but that didn't mean he was personally involved. If he went to the captain without giving Mac a chance to explain, he'd feel like a traitor. Mac was a good friend, and loyalty counted for a lot.

Curt wadded his Kleenex into a ball and lobbed it into the wastebasket. Two points. Then he sneezed again. The damn cold was getting him down. Somehow he had to stay on top of this whole thing. If he found a common thread linking Feldman, Marx, and Stanford and solved the case on his own, he'd be a cinch to make lieutenant.

"Where's your little automatic, Kay?"

"It's in my bedroom. I put it back in the drawer. Why?"

"Look, Kay . . . I don't want to scare you, but I think you'd better carry it in your purse today. Bring it down and I'll load it for you."

Kay frowned. "But, Mac! Don't you need a permit to carry a gun? I don't want to do anything illegal!"

Mac sighed. It was almost funny. Kay's life was in danger and she was worried about a lousy permit to carry her gun.

"Don't worry about it, Kay. I doubt if the killer's got a permit either. Just go up and get it and leave the legalities to me."

Debbie waited until Kay had gone upstairs. Her face was pale as she turned to Mac.

"Do you really think she'll need a gun?"

"It can't hurt. I've got a little Beretta I'll give you. Do you know how to shoot?"

Debbie nodded. "I took a 4-H course in gun safety. My dad insisted."

In a moment Kay was back. She held the gun gingerly as she handed it to Mac. Debbie and Kay watched as he cleaned and loaded it.

"This is the safety, Kay." Mac pointed. "All you have to do is click it off and pull the trigger."

"Charles made me practice when we got it." Kay's voice was shaking. "It makes me nervous to carry it, Mac. You know what happened the last time I had a gun in my purse."

"This time it's for real." Mac slipped the gun in her purse and snapped it closed. "I want you to carry it with you until you leave town. Then you can turn it over to Charles if you like."

"Thank you, Mac." Kay managed a smile. She was beginning to relax a bit. She was sure nothing would happen at the fashion show. Debra was staying with her in the dressing room and Mac would sit in the audience. The killer wouldn't dare to try anything in front of all those people.

She looked down at her purse and began to grin. Mac didn't know much about fashion shows. She was modeling a bathing suit and an evening gown and neither outfit called for a purse. The gun would have to stay in the dressing room the whole time, unless she used it as an accessory.

Kay almost laughed out loud as she imagined the sensation she'd cause if she appeared on the runway brandishing a pistol. *"Mrs. Charles Atchinson is wearing a George Stavropoulos classic evening gown, with side gathers and spaghetti straps, in a luxurious Crillon Blue satin. Her train is of matching chiffon. Diamond earrings and necklace by Van Cleef. Sidearm by Browning."*

CHAPTER 24

Dr. Elias snapped off the alarm clock and blinked in the morning light. Two pigeons were perched on the sill outside his window, regarding him with expressionless black eyes. They watched as he reached for the syringe by the bed and gave himself an injection.

He would be able to move comfortably in a moment. Dr. Elias leaned back against the pillows and waited for the drug to enter his system. One of the pigeons ruffled its feathers and hopped the length of the sill, head bobbing back and forth jerkily with each step. Its head seemed directly connected to the tendons in its feet. Pigeons reminded Dr. Elias of children's windup toys; they moved in such an awkward, mechanical manner. It was easy to imagine a series of springs and cogs controlling their actions.

The distress eased slightly and Dr. Elias sat up, sliding his legs over the side of the bed. He was still alive, muscles working normally, heart beating strongly in his chest. Perhaps he would live to see Christmas after all. It was only three days away.

There was still a little discomfort as he got to his feet and walked across the floor to the bathroom. The dosage of the injections would have to be increased very soon. He could not function with pain as a handicap while there was work left to be done.

Dr. Elias examined his face in the mirror over the sink. The jaundice was worse today. Even the whites of his eyes had a distinct yellow tinge. It made him look vaguely Asian, he thought.

He smiled at his reflection. Physical deterioration could be an advantage. His appearance had aged drastically since the onset of his disease. Lines had deepened in his face and the weight loss caused his cheekbones to protrude sharply. It seemed unlikely that any of his colleagues or former patients would recognize him. If he was spotted on the street today, he might be mistaken for an ancient Chinese gentleman.

Dr. Elias continued to smile as he conducted his daily regimen of tests. All vital signs were meticulously recorded. It was an accurate account of the progress of his disease. The results were as he expected. He had been correct in escalating his work schedule. There was no time to spare.

He closed the notebook and stepped into the shower. The hot water eased the stiffness in his joints and he felt remarkably agile as he dressed.

Kay had canceled her therapy appointment for the second time. She had promised to call her doctor after the holidays, but Dr. Elias knew she could not maintain without help for that length of time. There was no alternative. He must do his duty. Today's fashion show at Dayton's Sky Room would provide the perfect opportunity.

Dr. Elias prepared two sterile syringes and slipped

them into the leather briefcase he planned to carry. There was much to do today and he would certainly require his injections before he finished. He had researched every aspect, and the tools he needed to complete his task were already in the briefcase. There was no doubt in his mind that he would be successful. By the end of the day, his work would be finished.

Curt Holt put the phone down and sighed. Mrs. Feldman had not known Mac. The same was true for the priest's housekeeper. Father Marx had never mentioned Richard Macklin, and his name was not listed on any parish records. Curt had tried to contact Nora Stanford's partner, Elena Ribakoff, but she was heavily sedated in Fairview Southdale Hospital. He had struck out on all three counts and Mac was nowhere to be found. Curt had tried calling his house repeatedly, with no answer.

There was nothing to do but wait. Curt leaned back in his chair and popped another vitamin C chewable into his mouth. He stared at the institutional green paint on his office wall. Mac's office next door was beige. Green and beige. He remembered the same color scheme in the classrooms at South High. The city must have gotten a real buy on those two colors. Curt was willing to bet that Captain Meyers's living room was painted green and beige. The captain wasn't known for his originality.

At least Curt had a door to close. That was a step up from the little three-quarter-walled cubicle he'd used when he was Mac's assistant. And it would be even better once he made lieutenant. Along with the raise in pay, lieutenants got to pick their own color scheme if they paid for the paint. That was something to shoot for. These damn green walls brought back sickening memories of the South High cafeteria and the mushy macaroni and cheese they served on Fridays.

His mind was wandering again. Curt sat up straight in his chair and checked his city-issue appointment calendar. The janitor from St. Steven's was coming in at noon, but Curt doubted that he'd be able to shed any more light on Father Marx's death. The parish papers were already here, in a box by his desk. Fortunately Marx had been blessed with legible handwriting. He had gone over every scrap of paper last night.

Bazookas should be back from Feldman's office soon. Curt had sent her over to pick up the dental records. He took out his pen and jotted her name on a requisition form. Miss Carol Deluca. He'd ask for her as a temporary aide. Bazookas could help him go through Feldman's files this afternoon. And she could make the trek to the squad room to bring back his coffee.

Curt checked the list of notes that he had clipped to Feldman's folder. He had two men in the field doing legwork. Wednesday they had checked out the health clubs; Feldman belonged to three. They had shown Feldman's picture to members and personnel, but nothing had turned up. Everyone said he was a nice guy with no enemies.

They had spent Thursday morning interviewing Feldman's neighbors and friends. A total strikeout. And in the afternoon, they covered the personnel at the dental office. The girls said Feldman was the perfect boss—no quirks, no complaints, no mystery expenditures in the office ledger or checkbook. Curt had gone through the list of charges that came in from Feldman's credit cards. No motels in the middle of the day. No perfume or nightgowns for anyone other than his wife. No leads at all.

Yesterday he had concentrated on the priest. He'd sent his men to St. Steven's to interview parish members while he went to the archdiocese. Marx was a model priest.

Northwestern Bell had done a computer check of their recent telephone records this morning. He'd asked for a comparison of Feldman's, Marx's, and Stanford's calls. They had found no common numbers.

The Chicago police would be contacting him this afternoon. A Cook County coroner was doing an autopsy on Nora Stanford. Curt had a hunch it would turn out to be murder. Mac's tips were seldom wrong.

It was a quarter to twelve and all the bases were covered. Curt had exhausted every lead he could think of and he still didn't have any hard evidence that the murders were connected.

Curt remembered what Mac had told him when he was in training. A good cop opened his mind to every hunch, even if it seemed ridiculous. Murderers didn't play by regular rules. The best way to solve a crime was to suspect everyone until they were cleared.

By his own advice, Mac was a suspect. Curt couldn't see any way around it. He knew that Mac had mental problems. It was all there in his personnel file. As unlikely as it seemed, Mac could have killed off Feldman and Marx. And Stanford, too, if the autopsy came up murder.

There was no use fighting it. Curt picked up the phone and called Ma Bell's business office. He needed a complete record of Mac's calls. His hunch was probably wrong, but he'd feel a lot better if he checked it out.

Every instinct told Curt that Mac was innocent. Mac

was a nice guy, a moral man incapable of cold-blooded murder. Look how upset he'd been over shooting that kid. And that was a clear-cut accident.

Curt didn't like the way his mind was racing. His thoughts were disloyal to Mac, but he couldn't seem to stop them. What if Mac was having another mental breakdown? What if he had deliberately fed Curt the information to put it all together? What if Mac was crying out for Curt to stop him?

Maybe he'd seen too many movies. Curt rubbed his tired eyes. That theory was really far-fetched. When Mac came in to work tomorrow, they could have a good laugh over it in the squad room.

Unless he was right.

Mac chose a table for two in the center of the room for his vantage point. He could see anyone who came in the door and the models would walk directly past his table.

"Cream and sugar, sir?"

The waitress flashed a professional smile as she poured his coffee from a small silver pot. Mac watched her carefully. She seemed a bit nervous. Perhaps she was new at her job. Or there could be a more sinister reason for her anxiety. The black tea apron she wore had deep pockets. Along with her order pad, she could be concealing a weapon. No one was above suspicion. The killer could be anyone, man or woman, young or old.

"Could you leave the pot?" Mac returned her smile. "I hate to make you dash over here every time my cup's empty."

"Sure." She set the pot on the table behind the arrangement of fresh flowers. "Do me a favor and keep it out of sight, will you? It's against the rules and the manager's in a bad mood today."

Mac nodded. That explained her nervousness. He watched the doorway as she hurried off to cover her other tables. The Sky Room was filling up fast now. The storm predictions hadn't kept anyone away.

The killer would probably be alone. Mac concentrated on a man sitting near the front at a table for two. He looked agitated, and as Mac watched, he picked up his napkin to polish his glasses for the second time in the past ten minutes. Then he glanced at his watch and reached into his briefcase. Mac tensed until he saw what the man had in his hand. It was a small Instamatic camera. A teenage girl hurried to his table and slid in beside him. His daughter, no doubt. And his wife was probably a model.

A large woman sat alone at a table near the door. There was something just a little wrong about her mannerisms. Too feminine? Mac frowned. She crooked her little finger as she drank from her teacup. It was almost a parody of a society woman.

Mac sighed in relief as he saw a man take the seat next to her. It was Georgie Girl, the notorious gay hairdresser from St. Paul. The "lady" was obviously in drag, trying out a new outfit on the straight public.

The announcer was taking her place now. The fashion show was about to begin. Mac put his cup down on the saucer and leaned forward. He really didn't think that anything would happen in front of the audience, but he was ready, just in case.

"Isn't this ridiculous?" Kay turned from the mirror and shivered. "It's the middle of winter and they're showing bathing suits. Fur coats in July and bikinis in December. I'll never understand high fashion."

"They made the right choice this time." Debra smiled. "That white suit looks lovely on you."

"That's why I'm a model." Kay laughed self-consciously. "They needed someone who could stay in Minneapolis through the winter and still have a suntan."

Debra picked up the accessories, a floppy beach hat and a pair of high-tech sunglasses. She followed closely as Kay led the way down the carpeted hallway to the restaurant. Several women met them as they neared the Sky Room door.

"Knock them dead, darling!" A tall woman in a flower-print sundress kissed the air near Kay's cheek. "It's a full house and every woman there has a Dayton's Gold Card burning a hole through her handbag."

"Mrs. Wesley Ashton," Kay whispered to Debra as they walked on. "She cheats at bridge."

Kay felt better when she saw Mac sitting at a table in the center of the restaurant. One of the Dayton granddaughters was modeling a skimpy bikini, and Kay watched her pause and smile as she answered a question at one of the tables. There was something totally unreal about the scene, the potted palms, the beach hats, the mod sunglasses. It was schizophrenic to wear a bikini in the dead of winter while gusts of icy snow rattled against the windows. Nothing quite made sense. For the first time, Kay knew how Alice in Wonderland must have felt when she fell down the rabbit hole.

"You're next, Kay." Debra squeezed her hand. "Go ahead. It'll be fine."

Kay tried to step out into the room, but she couldn't move. Her feet seemed glued to the rug. Suddenly she was terrified. Someone out there might try to kill her as she walked the path between the tables. She wanted to turn and run back to the dressing room.

"Go, Kay!" Debra's voice was urgent. She gave a little push and Kay found herself moving forward, going through the motions of modeling without any conscious thought. She stopped at the artificial palms and turned around twice, exactly as she had done in rehearsal. Then she stepped down into the room, to follow the path that wound around the tables.

"Mrs. Charles Atchinson wears a white maillot suit especially designed for Dayton's by Lois Melin. A deep V neckline sports adjustable straps that cross in back. Detailed shirring at one side and a darling low-cut back are flattering to every figure. A matching three-quarter-length mesh knit cover-up makes this the perfect outfit on the beach or at poolside. Earrings and bracelet by Moira Adams of California are available in Dayton's Mod Shop."

Kay waited until the announcer had finished. Then she turned again and started down the path between the tables. She had to make a circuit of the entire room so the audience could ask questions about the outfit. A heavyset man with a beard sat at one of the front tables. He looked vaguely familiar. Kay shivered as he reached into his pocket. She had to use all her self-control to keep from whirling and running toward the exit. He could be reaching for a gun!

Her knees began to shake as she approached the table. Then she saw his name tag and almost laughed out loud in relief. Ralph Santiago. No wonder he looked familiar! She had met him at rehearsal. He was the publicist for Dayton's.

"You look good, Mrs. Atchinson." He drew a silver cigarette case from his pocket and returned her shaky smile. "Don't miss the paper tomorrow. They're doing a full-page review of the show."

A woman in the center of the room was staring at her. Kay forced a smile and tried to keep her pace unhurried. Anyone in the audience could hide a gun under the pink and burgundy tablecloths. She wanted to rush to the exit, but that wouldn't look right. A nice, slow, easy walk. "Show off the clothes, girls." That's what the fashion consultant had told them. Kay felt exposed under the woman's unblinking gaze. Her big leather purse was large enough to hold a gun. Could she be the killer?

"Does this suit come in extra long?" The woman reached out to touch Kay's shoulder. "My daughter's five eleven. You have no idea how hard it is to find clothes for her!"

"Yes, it does." Kay smiled. The woman no longer looked threatening. "All the clothes will be on display after the show. This particular suit comes in a full range of sizes."

"Hey, gorgeous lady!" Mac smiled at her as she came to his table. "I checked out the room. It's clean."

It was such a relief. Kay felt tears come to her eyes. She gave Mac a brilliant smile and passed his table with a much lighter step. Suddenly everything was fine. The room had lost its nightmarish quality. The killer wasn't there. She was safe!

The doors to the restaurant were closed. Mac relaxed a bit after Kay took her first turn. He had examined every face in the room and no one looked suspicious. And Dayton's management refused to let anyone enter while the show was in progress. He looked up as a red-head in a silver bikini brushed past his table. That suit would look nice on Debbie. Maybe he ought to buy it for her as a Christmas present.

Mac stopped listening as the announcer extolled the virtues of each bathing suit. He had learned to let his subconscious take over when he was assigned to his first stakeout. A man could go crazy watching an apartment door for ten hours straight. He'd perfected the trick of setting his eyes on a certain pattern and freeing his mind for other things. When the pattern changed, he was alerted to danger. The whole thing was difficult to explain, but Mac did it well. It made stakeouts bearable. Now he set his eyes to roam over the audience while his mind raced along other channels.

Mac had gone over everything before, but he knew he had missed something. The killer. The motive. He started with the obvious. Who knew about the group? He did. And Kay. And Debbie. They were the only survivors. Elena had known, but she had an alibi. The mayor knew, but he had been with Kay when Father Marx was killed. Had Dr. Elias told anyone else about his group?

Dr. Elias . . . Mac paused with his coffee cup halfway to his lips. They'd all assumed that Dr. Elias was dead, but what if he was still alive? Mac had to find out. Dr. Elias could help. He would go to his penthouse right after the fashion show was over. It was just across the street. The covered bridge ran from Dayton's second floor to the lobby of the IDS tower.

"Mrs. Charles Atchinson is wearing a George Stavropoulos classic evening gown, with side gathers and spaghetti straps, in a luxurious Crillon Blue satin."

Mac smiled as Kay appeared by the potted palms for the second time. He was elated now that he had a plan of action. Perhaps it wasn't right to bother a dying man, but Mac was sure Dr. Elias would understand.

"Her train is of matching chiffon. Diamond earrings and necklace by Van Cleef. This gown is an original, ladies, so hurry to the Oval Room after the show."

Mac took a sip of coffee and held up his thumb and forefinger in an *okay* signal as Kay approached his table. She looked lovely.

"I'll meet you outside the dressing room." Mac pretended a great interest in the material of the gown. "We'll leave early, before the rush."

As soon as the next model appeared on the runway, Mac finished his coffee and hurried toward the exit. The prospect of seeing Dr. Elias again made him feel tremendously relieved. Even though Dr. Elias was dying, he was still a brilliant analyst. Mac was positive that he was the one who could make sense out of this nightmare.

CHAPTER 25

"Yes, I'm fine, dear." Kay stood outside the dressing room with her right hand over her ear so she could block out the noise. Dayton's PA system was announcing a giant pre-Christmas sale in the toy department.

Debra and Mac stood behind Kay, blocking her from the customers rushing to the elevators. It seemed everyone in Minneapolis was doing their shopping today. If the storm hit as hard as predicted, this might be the last chance to buy gifts.

Mac gave Debbie's hand a squeeze. "Have you ever been in Dayton's toy department at Christmas? They've got a wonderful little train ride. Maybe we can borrow somebody's kid and get in."

Debra shuddered. She had "borrowed" a baby once. For a second she almost pulled away from Mac, but he was smiling at her guilelessly. She took a deep breath and smiled back. Mac had forgotten all about the kidnapping. He'd never try to hurt her by reminding her of the past.

"I'm leaving here now." Kay smiled at something Charles said. "I love you, too, honey."

Mac and Debra watched as Kay ended the call. "Charles wants me to come straight to his office. He says we'll leave my car in his spot and drive home together."

"I'll ride over with you, Kay," Debra offered. "Mac can follow us with his car."

"Oh, I'll be fine once I'm in the car." Kay smiled at her. "It's only six blocks from here. I'll lock the doors and drive straight there. Charles said he'd wait for me in the garage."

Kay's Datsun was parked in the VIP section on the sixth floor. Mac opened the door to the parking structure and motioned for them to follow. The fashion show was still in progress and the building was deserted. Cars gleamed in the fluorescent light from the overhead fixtures, but no one was backing in or out.

"Wait right here and I'll start it for you."

Mac took Kay's keys and left them standing by a post several feet away.

Although he had never seen a car blow up in all his years on the force, he remembered what Charles Bronson had done to Jan-Michael Vincent's car in the final scene from *The Mechanic*. The attendant in Dayton's parking structure was in the kiosk on the ground floor. There were several security officers who covered the building, but the killer could have easily slipped past them to sabotage Kay's car.

Kay's little Datsun was sandwiched in between a black Mercedes and a new red Chevrolet. She had backed in the space so she could leave quickly. Mac unlocked the door and pulled the hood release. He peered at the engine carefully. Perhaps he was paranoid, but he wouldn't feel secure until he checked it out. Everything looked normal under the hood.

Mac closed the hood and walked around to the back of the Datsun. He knelt down and checked under the car. Nothing was taped to the tailpipe or undercarriage.

Finally he got into the driver's seat. He felt around under the dash for extra wires taped to the ignition. Nothing was there. There was no evidence of tampering of any kind.

Mac's hand was shaking as he put the key in the ignition. He gave it a quick twist and hoped that he hadn't missed anything.

The Datsun started smoothly. Mac breathed a sigh of relief as the motor turned over and purred. There was nothing wrong. Mac toed the accelerator and let it idle as he got out of the car and motioned to Kay.

"All right, Kay. Go straight to City Hall. And give me a call tonight when you get to your mother's."

"Thanks for everything, Mac." Kay hugged him tightly. "You've been wonderful. You, too, Debra. I never could have made it through that fashion show without you."

There were tears in Kay's eyes as she kissed Debra on the cheek. She slid into the driver's seat and buckled her seat belt. Her purse went next to her on the passenger's seat. Kay patted it and grinned at Mac.

"Don't worry, Mac. I'll lock the doors, and if anyone comes near, I'll shoot them with my purse."

Kay waved as she put the car into gear and the Datsun moved forward. Mac and Debra watched Kay's car go around the far corner of the garage, heading for the ramp. Mac looked down at the space where the Datsun had been. There was a puddle of something on the concrete.

He reached down, dipped his finger in the puddle, and sniffed at it. Oil? No. Brake fluid!

Mac whirled and ran. He had to catch Kay before she entered the corkscrew ramp that led down to the ground floor!

"Kay! KAY!"

Mac waved his arms and shouted at the top of his lungs. Kay's car was almost at the entrance to the ramp. He saw Kay turn around to look at him. She gave him a smile and raised her hand in a wave. Then the Datsun turned sharply to the right and started the downhill spiral.

"Mac! What is it?"

Debra rushed up to his side. She clung to his arm as they stood at the top of the ramp and listened to the sound of the Datsun's engine.

Kay's knuckles turned white on the steering wheel as she pulled onto the ramp. She hated these things. The ramp was a silolike structure built on the outside of the building. It spiraled its way down, from the sixth floor to the ground. It was well designed and well built, but she never failed to get a little dizzy when she drove down it.

Charles said the ramp design was a good one. He had proved that it was possible to set the steering wheel in one position at the top of the ramp and not move it until he reached the bottom. Kay had tried, but she'd never managed to find exactly the right position. She always inched forward carefully, pumping her brakes, oversteering and overcorrecting all the way down.

Her tires hummed as she started to descend. Kay knew the grooves in the concrete were there to provide additional traction, but she hated the noise. It sounded like she was going much too fast, even though the speedometer read less than five miles an hour.

Kay jerked the wheel to the left. The curved concrete wall on the right side of the ramp was coming dangerously close to her right front fender. She passed the fifth floor level and touched the brakes.

Nothing happened! Kay pumped her foot on the pedal. It went all the way to the floorboard and nothing happened!

She couldn't panic now. Kay reached for the emergency brake and pulled the handle back sharply. The car was picking up speed and her brakes were gone!

For a moment she froze in terror. The speedometer was climbing. Ten, twelve, fifteen miles an hour!

She had to hit the wall. It was the only way to slow down. Kay twisted the wheel frantically to the right. The Datsun shuddered as it responded. There was a horrid screech and a violent impact as the Datsun bounced off the curved wall. Then another crash as the car skidded over and bounced into the opposite side. Kay's head snapped forward and hit the steering wheel hard. The Datsun straightened and picked up speed again. The ramp was too steep. She was going too fast. Nothing would stop her!

The ramp was a blur through her dazed eyes. Everything was growing dark. Kay reached up and felt her forehead. Wet. Sticky. She was bleeding. The blood dripped down and she blinked to clear her eyes. She had to try again before it was too late.

She had to scrape the wall with the side of the car. A sudden impact would not work. Slowly. Kay forced her hands to twist the wheel slowly. The wall loomed closer, closer . . .

Sparks flew as the Datsun careened off the cement and skidded sideways. For a moment it seemed the car would wedge itself sideways against the walls, but it was too small. The ramp was built for large American cars. Kay's little Datsun slammed into the opposite wall and bounced back to the center of the ramp.

Kay shut her eyes. There was a screaming noise in her ears. The car shuddered and squealed as it collided with the wall again. A hubcap flew off and clattered against the concrete. The side mirror was gone, sheared off with the force of the impact.

Suddenly Kay remembered Mac waving his arms at her. He had known something was wrong. Mac had been trying to stop her. The killer had struck after all. She was going to die!

How could Charles cope with all the details of running a household? His suit was at the new cleaners on LaSalle. Would Trish remember to tell him? What about James's referral to accelerated classes? And the school prom. Would Charles let Trish choose a dress that was totally unsuitable? No!

The Datsun fishtailed and slammed into the wall. The force of the impact snapped the steering wheel off and Kay felt the column hammer into her chest. She couldn't breathe. Her mouth was open. She was screaming. Blood was everywhere, on the windshield, spurting from the wound in her chest. The darkness was closing in and the horrible screech of metal faded to a dull whisper in her ears. It was too late. It was over.

CHAPTER 26

Mac and Debbie rushed through the street-level door from the stairwell to find that a crowd had already formed around the blazing wreck of the Datsun. Two security officers were trying to maintain order.

"Oh, Mac!" Debra took one look at the flames and hid her face against Mac's chest. There was nothing to say. Kay was dead. They were the only two left.

Mac held Debbie tightly and blinked back his own tears. The Datsun sent up plumes of black smoke, and the security officers herded the crowd back to a safer position. Mac pulled Debbie into the store's doorway, away from the crowd. Her slim body was shaking with grief.

The IDS Center was directly across the street. Mac stared at it and swallowed hard. Now it was even more important to try to find Dr. Elias. The killer had struck again, even though Mac had done his best to protect Kay.

He didn't want to leave Debbie for a second, but he couldn't take her with him to Dr. Elias's penthouse. He couldn't be sure of what he'd find. Dr. Elias might be lying dead in one of the rooms. It could be an awfully gruesome sight. Mac would have to find a safe place to stash her while he went to find the doctor.

A fire department truck pulled up outside the garage and men raced to the Datsun with chemical extinguishers. A black and white careened around the corner with its lights flashing and siren wailing. Suddenly Mac realized what it would mean if he were spotted here. Curt would put it all together. He was a top-notch detective. Mac had trained him. If Mac were found at the scene of another murder, Curt would have to pull him in for questioning. There wasn't enough circumstantial evidence to hold him for long, but valuable time would be lost.

"Inside, Debbie! Quick!"

Mac pulled her into the store and fought his way past the frenzied shoppers to an alcove by the winter scarves and gloves. "Call the paper, honey. Get someone to take your assignment this afternoon."

Debra blinked and nodded. She felt as if she were living in the middle of a nightmare. People in the store were laughing and Christmas music played over the loudspeakers. Didn't they know Kay was lying dead less than a block away in Dayton's garage?

"Go on, Debbie. Make the call."

Debra knew that Mac was right. She couldn't possibly cover her assignment at the new housing development.

Mac paced the floor behind her as Debra was connected to the right department. In a moment he heard her talking to someone.

"Oh, no. Well, I . . . I'm not sure. Hold on a second, Jackie. I'll check."

Debra turned from the phone and cupped her hand over the receiver. "Jackie's the only one available and she's got a babysitting problem."

"Tell her you'll babysit." Mac was firm. "You can't take that assignment. It's too dangerous."

Debra's face turned white. "I . . . I *can't* babysit! You know why. I just can't!"

"You can do it, Debbie." Mac folded his arms around her waist. "That's all in the past. Come on now, honey. Tell Jackie you'll take care of her baby."

Debra's voice shook as she arranged to pick up the baby. All her old fears were back. She had deliberately avoided babies since that night at the hospital. What if something terrible happened? Something that even Mac couldn't prevent?

Curt unfolded the printout that had just come in from Ma Bell. Mac had made a lot of calls last month. The phone company had listed them by order of frequency as he had asked, along with the names and street addresses of the numbers called.

Dr. Jerry Feldman—dental office. One call on the sixteenth. Feldman had been shot on the night of the seventeenth.

Greg Davenport. The sixteenth and seventeenth. Curt checked his records. Davenport had died in that fire on the eighteenth.

St. Steven's—rectory. Four calls from the sixteenth to the nineteenth. Father Marx was stabbed on the twentieth.

Nora Stanford. Six calls, the last call on the day she died, the twenty-first.

Mrs. Charles Atchinson—unlisted number. Curt stared at the paper in shock. Mac had called the mayor's wife a total of seven times in the past week! Why would Mac be calling the mayor's wife?

An affair? Curt frowned. That seemed highly improbable. Mrs. Atchinson was a really nice lady. He'd met her several times at fund-raisers. She certainly didn't seem the type to cheat on the mayor. And Mac wouldn't have an affair with someone else's wife. There had to be another reason for those seven calls.

"The mayor's wife is dead!" Bazookas rushed into his office.

"What?" Curt shuddered. "Jesus! What happened?"

"Her car went out of control on Dayton's ramp. Captain Meyers got the call and hightailed it out of here!"

"Run out to the desk, Carol, and see if you can find out any more." Curt waved at the door. "And tell Desk Sergeant Reinert that I want to see the captain the minute he gets back."

Curt winced. He didn't like the way this was stacking up. Mac was connected with all of them, and now the mayor's wife was dead! It might be circumstantial, but there was no way he could ignore this. Just as soon as the captain got back, he'd ask for permission to pull Mac in for questioning.

"You can't leave me all alone!" Debra stared up at Mac in terror.

"I won't be gone very long, honey. And I can't take you with me. Not with the baby. I may have to break and enter to get into the penthouse."

Debra nodded slowly. She knew Mac had to find Dr. Elias. He was their only hope. She glanced down at the sleeping baby and shivered. Mac said she was safe here. He had checked out the entire apartment before he'd allowed her to come in from the hall. Nothing had been touched. The killer had not been there. Everyone expected her to be on assignment at Riverside Estates. Even the paper didn't know that she'd switched places with Jackie. They were buying time, Mac had explained, sending the killer off in the wrong direction. By the time he discovered Debra was not there, Mac would be back from Dr. Elias's penthouse.

"I . . . I'll manage, Mac." Debra took a deep breath and smiled at him. "I've got that number you gave me. I'll call Curt Holt if you're not back in an hour."

Mac bent down and kissed her gently. She was dearer to him than anyone in the world and he had to protect her.

"Double lock the door when I leave. And don't let anyone in. I'll call you the minute I get through talking to Dr. Elias."

Debra kissed him back. She didn't want him to go. The thought of being alone in her apartment was frightening. Her arms tightened around his neck and she had to force herself to let go so he could leave.

"Please be careful, Mac. I love you so much."

Debra's hands trembled as she locked the door behind Mac. She watched from the window as he came out the doorway at the front of the apartment building and walked to his car. What if the killer was waiting somewhere out on the street? Mac was all alone!

He fumbled with the lock on the car door and Debra breathed a sigh of relief as he got it open at last and climbed inside. The Toyota looked small and fragile from her fourth-floor window. It reminded her of a child's Matchbox car as he pulled out of the parking spot and drove off.

She was alone. Debra stood at the window for a long time, staring at the bare branches of the trees surrounding the old apartment building. The wind whipped up snow and blew it against the pane. The storm was starting. Thank God Mac didn't have far to go.

The baby made a soft gurgling sound in his sleep and Debra whirled from the window in fright. Then she grinned self-consciously as she walked over to the car bed and peeked inside.

He was still sleeping soundly. Debra's smile widened as she stared down at him. The baby wiggled a little and one little bootie poked out of the bottom of his blanket. It was amazing that anything could be so small and still so perfect.

She tucked in his blanket again. He sighed, a soft tiny sound, and seemed to smile as he found his mouth with his thumb. He was a beautiful baby.

Debra picked up the car bed very carefully and moved it to the couch, where she could watch him. Something about his innocent, trusting sleep made her feel much less lonely.

At first she had been terrified. She had barely looked at the baby when Jackie had given her the diaper bag and the bottles of formula. She had hoped that he would sleep until Mac got back. Now she found herself wishing he'd wake. It would be fun to give him a bottle and rock him. Perhaps she had cheated herself by avoiding babies all those lonely years.

The baby sighed again and sucked at his thumb. The sound of his soft, even breathing was loud in the silent room. Debra went to put a bottle in the warmer, just in case. Then she came back and sat down in the chair by the phone to wait.

CHAPTER 27

Dr. Elias put down his brush with a satisfied sigh. He had saved Kay from her illness. She was no longer a time bomb, capable of exploding and injuring others. Her painted face looked tranquil, and he was glad. Kay's life had been frenzied, with schedules and commitments, but now she was free of anxiety and stress.

He had made his plans yesterday, after he'd seen the article in the paper about Dayton's charity fashion show. Kay was a featured model. Dr. Elias knew Kay would try to leave town, but her sense of civic duty would keep her there for the show.

The method practically dictated itself. The automobile was inherently a dangerous device. Several thousand pounds of hurtling metal was a formidable weapon in anyone's hands, especially someone like Kay, who knew nothing about cars. Dr. Elias knew Kay would not notice her Datsun's malfunction until it was much too late

One call to an auto parts store and the mechanic's manual had been delivered immediately, along with the tools he had ordered. He had reviewed the section on the braking system after he'd finished Nora's portrait last night.

Dr. Elias stepped back and smiled. It had been so easy. The faint wail of sirens outside his studio window told him that it was all over. Kay was no longer a problem. There were only two group members left to treat and he would be finished.

His smile twisted to a grimace of agony as he cleaned his brushes and set them out to dry. It had been barely two hours since his last injection, but he would need another before he left the building. First he would make his call to the newspaper and then he could reward himself by alleviating his pain.

The switchboard operator at the *Minneapolis Tribune* was most helpful. Most people were delighted to give out information if the query was worded effectively. Dr. Elias wrote the address in his memo book. Riverside Estates. It was out on Highway 169, on the way to Anoka. Another new housing development on West River Road, and Debra was covering the opening ceremony. It would be a forty-five-minute trip by taxi.

He wrapped himself in his warmest winter overcoat and slipped on his gloves. Snow pelted against the window as he waited for the cab to pull up outside. The weather ball was red. Storm warnings would go into effect in less than an hour, and that would work to his advantage. Not many people would be attending the opening. It would be much easier to catch Debra alone and terminate her therapy.

The taxi pulled up outside and Dr. Elias hurried to the elevator. The injection was working effectively on his nervous system. He felt strong and powerful, capable of completing his duty. First Debra. Then Mac. And then he could die in peace.

* * *

Mac parked on the lower level and took the elevator up to the penthouse. As the steel doors opened and he stepped out onto the thick gray carpet, he wondered how many times he had walked down this same hallway.

He remembered the first time, almost five years ago. He had been nervous, apprehensive. Then, as the weeks of therapy had passed, there'd been anticipation as the elevator carried him upward, a lightening of his burden as he walked down the hallway to Dr. Elias's office, a tremendous release of tension in the simple act of pulling open the office door. There was none of that now. Now Mac walked down the same corridor with dread.

Mac shivered as he approached the penthouse door. He hesitated a moment and then rang the bell. There was no answer. Dr. Elias might be in a hospital or clinic somewhere, but Mac doubted it. He figured the doctor was the type of man who would rather die in familiar surroundings, in his own home. There was a good chance he was lying in bed, too weak to answer the bell. Or worse.

Mac reached reluctantly in his pocket for his plastic. He knew he was committing an illegal act, but there was no choice. He had to get inside.

There was a slot for a dead bolt at the top of the lock, but it had not been thrown. Mac's hand was shaking slightly as he slipped his plastic strip into place and jiggled it expertly. The latch resisted at first, but at last it opened.

"Dr. Elias? It's me . . . Mac!" Mac called out loudly as he turned the doorknob. He didn't want Dr. Elias to mistake him for a burglar. "Are you home, Dr. Elias?"

The apartment was as silent as a tomb. Mac entered the foyer warily. He stopped every few steps and called out, but there was no answer.

Mac's trained eyes took in the living room at a glance. Christmas tree in the corner, lights off. Dr. Elias had been alive to order a tree. Mac checked the water in the stand. It was full. Someone had tended the tree recently.

An expensive stereo system sat next to the window. Mac glanced at the turntable. Mahler's Symphony no. 5 in C Sharp Minor. There was a book on top of the cabinet. *A Musical Analysis of Gustav Mahler.*

A huge glass case containing pipes hung on the wall. There were hundreds of briars inside. Mac recognized some of the brands. Dr. Elias had nothing but the best.

A Japanese hand-painted teacup with a matching cover sat on the table by a big leather chair. Mac lifted the lid. There was a half cup of coffee inside. Cold. There was no telling how long it had been there.

Mac glanced in the kitchen. It was empty, spotless. It told him nothing.

He walked down the hallway and stepped into the first bedroom. It had been converted into an exercise room, furnished with the best in bodybuilding equipment. Mac was shocked. Of course he'd noticed that Dr. Elias was in good physical shape, but he couldn't picture him pumping iron.

Suddenly Mac realized there was a lot he didn't know about Dr. Elias. The group had shared the most intimate details of their lives with him, but none of them had known anything personal about Dr. Elias in return. He had never invited any of them to these rooms. For all practical purposes, the man's personal life was a mystery.

The master bedroom was next. Mac found himself

tiptoeing as he pushed open the door and stepped inside. The bed was made neatly, with hospital corners. There was a pipe lying in an ashtray on the dresser. Mac felt the bowl. It was cold.

The bathroom was next. Towels hung neatly on the racks. Several were still moist. He pulled open the shower door. The floor was wet.

Mac didn't realize he was holding his breath until he released it in a grateful sigh. Dr. Elias was still alive. He had taken a shower this morning. Mac closed the shower door and hurried out of the apartment. Dr. Elias could be in his office.

There was no answer as he pushed the office buzzer. The door was locked and the lights were out. Mac used his plastic strip on the door.

He called out loudly as he stepped inside, but there was no answer. He didn't expect one. There was a cold feeling inside that Mac had learned to associate with vacant rooms. It was a kind of sixth sense that some cops developed after years of experience. The sound of human breathing was loud when the ear was trained to listen for it.

Two folders lay open on the huge wooden desk. Debra's. And his. Mac shivered. Why were their folders out, when the others were filed away? Was it because they were the only two group members left alive?

The conference room was deserted. Mac hurried down the carpeted hallway to the door at the end. He had always assumed it was another entrance to Dr.

Elias's living quarters.

This door was more difficult to open. There were two locks. Mac worked the plastic strip back and forth until the tumblers released at last. He stepped into what appeared to be a long corridor and snapped on the lights.

Portraits lined the walls. Each one was signed and dated. *Elias '57*, *Elias '64*. Mac glanced at several. He had not known that Dr. Elias was an artist!

This could have been a family gallery, but the paintings were too numerous and far too recent. Mac estimated there were over a hundred, painted from 1955 to 1980. He hurried past the staring eyes of the portraits and opened the door at the end of the corridor.

Inside was an immense studio with glass walls and a skylight. Dim gray light filtered in through the sheets of snow blowing against the glass. There was an easel in the center, and Mac gasped in shock as he caught sight of the painting in progress. The group. Their group! And all the faces were completed except Debra's and his. Suddenly Mac knew the truth!

He remembered sitting in Kay's living room, saying the killer had to be someone who knew the group and their habits. Who knew their habits better than Dr. Elias? No one had thought to suspect their trusted doctor!

Mac stared at the portrait and shuddered. Kay's face had a shiny cast that was different from the rest. He reached out and touched the canvas. Wet paint.

For a moment he was frozen with shock. Mac blinked and swayed slightly. Why was Dr. Elias killing off his own patients? Was he convinced they couldn't survive without him? Had the pain of his illness driven him mad?

Mac stood and stared at the painting for one awful moment, and then he ran for the door. He had to warn Debbie!

CHAPTER 28

Dr. Elias turned up his collar against the bitter cold and made his way painfully to the model home marked OFFICE. The red plastic flags flanking the sidewalk whipped in the wind. Several had torn loose and skittered across the snowy expanse of the front lawn.

The opening had not been canceled. Dr. Elias breathed a sigh of relief as he spotted a circle of people posing for pictures. A woman with her back to him was interviewing a man in a gray suit. Dr. Elias moved closer. The woman turned and he saw that it was not Debra.

Did she have an assistant? He waited until the woman had finished the interview and approached her.

Dr. Elias could barely contain his disappointment as the woman explained that she was filling in for Debra, a last-minute change of assignment. If he wanted to contact Debra he could call her at home. There was a phone in the next room that he could use.

* * *

"Oh, I'm so glad you called!" Debra hung on to the phone tightly. It was Dr. Elias. He was still alive!

"You've got to help us, Dr. Elias!" Debra tried to keep her voice calm. "Someone is killing off the group!"

That was the reason he'd called. Dr. Elias had been gone, but he'd come back when he'd heard about the murders. Even though he was very ill, he had gone to the housing development to warn her. She was in terrible danger. Was she alone?

"Yes, except for the baby." Debra glanced over at the car bed. The baby was beginning to wake up.

Something in his voice changed as he asked about the baby. Debra hurried to explain.

"Oh, I . . . I'm fine, Dr. Elias. Really." Debra gave a nervous little laugh. "It's not what you think. I'm just babysitting this afternoon as a favor for a friend."

Had she seen Mac? It was very important that Dr. Elias find him.

"Mac left here a few minutes ago. He went up to your penthouse to try to find you. We knew you were the only one who could help us."

He seemed very concerned about Mac. Was Debra sure Mac had gone to the penthouse? Was he alone? Or had he taken some of his friends from the police with him?

"He's alone. We haven't told the police about the group. Kay . . ." Debra choked back tears. "Kay was afraid for Charles's career. Mac tried to protect her, but . . ."

Dr. Elias's voice was soothing. Of course she was upset. It was terrible, what had happened to Kay. Now he wanted to know about Mac. There was something new in her voice when she talked about him. Was she involved with Mac?

"Yes." Debra smiled down at the phone. "I . . . I'm living with him, Dr. Elias. Mac's so wonderful! I never could have gotten through this without him. You were right. It was time to trust someone again."

There was a silence, and then Dr. Elias spoke again. He had some very bad news for her. About Mac. He wanted to be there in person to tell her, but there wasn't time. This was something she needed to know immediately, before Mac came back. Did she trust Dr. Elias enough to do as he said?

"Of course I do! What is it, Dr. Elias?"

At first the words didn't make sense. Dr. Elias went on to explain. Mac was the killer. He had suffered a setback, a terrible crisis in his therapy. Mac's illness had developed into an almost textbook case of schizophrenia. He was a very sick man. Obviously Debra knew the normal part of Mac's personality. The abnormal part was the killer. Debra and Dr. Elias had to help him.

Debra stared down at the phone. The little holes in the receiver were so small and symmetrical. It was a miracle how the human voice could carry over wires and transmitters to come out in such frightening words in her ear. Dr. Elias was talking to her again. She didn't want to listen. Mac was the killer. Dr. Elias had said so. The man she loved was a killer!

Mac's love for her might spare her, but Dr. Elias said they could take no chances. He had a cab waiting at Riverside Estates. As soon as he arrived at her apartment, they would go to the police together. She should stay right there in her apartment and wait for him. Would she promise not to let anyone in? Especially Mac?

Debra nodded. That was silly. He couldn't hear her nod. She remembered all that nonsense about view phones, the wave of the future. If the view phone had come to pass, Dr. Elias could have seen her nodding.

Mac needed psychiatric help. Dr. Elias would make sure he was treated fairly. Poor Mac might not remember anything about the murders. He could be totally unaware of his psychoneurosis.

Now Dr. Elias was trying to comfort her. Debra nodded again. No, she wouldn't let Mac in her apartment. Yes, she'd wait right there for Dr. Elias. Mac was the killer!

She listened to the dial tone for a long time after Dr. Elias had hung up. Debra felt the tears roll down her cheeks, but she couldn't seem to raise her hand to brush them away. It all seemed impossible, but she had to believe Dr. Elias. He was her doctor, the only one who had cared about her when she'd been in trouble. He had brought her out of her depression and helped her back to sanity. She trusted him.

But she loved Mac! Even now that she knew the truth, she still loved him. Debra tried to think, but a heavy fog seemed to have settled over her mind. Where had Mac been when Jerry was killed? She didn't know. And Greg? Mac had worked late that night. At least he'd said he was working late. How about Father Marx? Mac had no alibi. And Kay! Mac could have cut Kay's brake line while they were in the dressing room.

The phone was ringing. Debra stared at it for a long moment before she picked it up.

"Debbie! Thank God!"

It was Mac. Debra shivered as she gripped the receiver.

"Listen, honey. Don't let anyone in the apartment. I'm

on my way. Dr. Elias is the killer! I found the evidence in his apartment. Keep the doors locked. Do you hear me, Debbie? Dr. Elias is the killer!"

"Yes."

Mac hung up before she could think to ask any questions. Debra shivered as the dial tone buzzed in her ear. Nothing made sense. She had to trust the man she loved. She trusted Mac. And she trusted Dr. Elias. But one of them was lying. Which one should she believe?

She couldn't decide. It was too much to ask. Debra replaced the phone in the cradle and picked up the crying baby. She was late. She had a plane to catch. Steve would be worried if she wasn't on time. Now she had to call a cab and heat a bottle for her son. She could feed him in the taxi on the way to the airport.

Mac saw red lights flashing behind him as he turned at the corner of Grant and Nicollet. He pulled over to the curb and tried to remember if he had broken any traffic laws. Two officers got out of the cruiser and approached him politely. Mac didn't know either of them very well. He seemed to recall that the younger man's name was Perkins.

"Lieutenant Macklin? Sorry, sir. You'll have to come with us."

"Come with you?" Mac was shocked. "What is it, Perkins?"

"Orders from the captain, sir. He said to find you and bring you in right away. To Sergeant Holt's office."

"But I have to get to Lake Street! Jesus, Perkins! Can't this wait?"

"I'm sorry, Lieutenant." The older officer shook his

head. "We've got strict orders from the captain. Leave your car here and ride with us."

For all practical purposes, he was under arrest. Mac knew these two officers would go by the book. If the captain had signed an order to bring him in, they wouldn't cut him any slack.

A crazy impulse seized him as he reached for the key. What were his chances if he floored it and ran? He might get three blocks before another car picked him up. Then they'd cuff him and take him in anyway.

Mac shut off the engine and followed the officers to the squad car. He'd clear up this thing with Curt in a hurry. Thank God Debbie's apartment was secure. He'd checked it out himself. Debbie would be safe if she followed his instructions and refused to open the door.

"Which airline, lady?"

The taxi driver turned to look in the back. She must be meeting her husband or something. All she had was the baby. No luggage.

"Lady? Hey, lady! Which plane are you meeting?"

Debra stared at the driver in shock. What was she doing? The baby slept peacefully in her arms. She was holding a half-empty bottle of formula. A plane roared overhead and Debra blinked. She was at the entrance to the airport! With Jackie's baby!

"Oh. I . . . I'm sorry, driver. I've changed my mind. Please take me back to my apartment."

"It's your money, lady."

The driver turned around on the access road and headed back toward the freeway. Debra heard him grumble something about crazy passengers. Was she crazy? She must have been to bring Jackie's baby to the airport.

Suddenly Debra remembered and her face turned white. There had been the call from Dr. Elias. And then the call from Mac. One of them was the killer. Which one?

They were on the Crosstown Freeway. Debra saw the sign for Portland Avenue and made up her mind.

"Take Portland, please. I need to stop at Forty-sixth."

There was a panel truck in the driveway at Jackie's house. Debra told the driver to wait and ran inside with the baby. Jackie's husband was home. She told him she had a family emergency. Could he keep the baby?

"Hey, don't worry about a thing." He grinned at her and took the baby. "It's a lucky thing I got off work early. I'll call the paper and tell Jackie the kid's home with me."

A moment later she was back in the cab, heading for her apartment. She had slipped for a moment, but now she was thinking clearly again. Debra still didn't know which man was the killer, but running away wasn't the answer. She had to stay in her apartment and face it somehow.

"Mac, sit down a minute." Captain Meyers motioned to a chair. He'd never expected anything like this when Holt said he needed Mac picked up for questioning. A killer shrink and a therapy group that included the mayor's wife!

"I need two men to go with me to Debbie's apartment! He's going to kill her!"

"Hold on, Mac. Dr. Theodore Elias? Is that right?

And all the victims were members of his therapy group?"

"Right!"

Captain Meyers frowned. Mac was so agitated he could barely talk. It was pretty clear the man was going off the deep end. Meyers had just come from the scene of the accident and the mayor would be here any minute. He couldn't let Mayor Atchinson hear Mac's crazy talk about his wife!

"Look, Mac. Work it out with Curt. I have to meet with the mayor. We'll pick up this Dr. Elias for questioning if you've got something to back up your story. You stay right here until I'm through with the mayor!"

"But, Captain! You don't understand! I . . ."

Captain Meyers hurried out of Holt's office and shut the door behind him. Poor Mac was having another breakdown. It was sad to see a good cop go down the tubes.

"This whole thing has gone far enough!" Mac slammed his fist down on Curt's desk. "I'm going out that door, Curt. If you try to stop me, I'll deck you."

"Mac . . . wait!" Curt put his arm on Mac's arm. "Captain Meyers ordered you to stay here until he got back."

"Forget Captain Meyers!" Mac got to his feet.

Curt swallowed hard. If he didn't keep Mac here, he could kiss his promotion good-bye. Captain Meyers thought Mac was crazy, but the captain didn't know Mac as well as he did. Curt made up his mind. If Mac said there was a crazy killer shrink, Curt believed him.

"I'll drive." Curt stood up and buckled on his service revolver. "Come on, Mac. Let's go!"

CHAPTER 29

She was all alone in the apartment now that the baby was gone. Debra paced the floor and listened to the storm raging outside her living-room window. She was scared. And she still hadn't come to a decision. Should she believe Dr. Elias? Or Mac?

Dr. Elias had saved their lives, in a sense. Why would he kill them now after helping them for so long? It wasn't logical, but Mac had claimed he'd found evidence that Dr. Elias was the killer.

And Dr. Elias had said it was Mac. After five years as Mac's psychiatrist, Dr. Elias would surely know if Mac was in crisis. Debra tried to imagine Mac as a Dr. Jekyll and Mr. Hyde. It was possible. She had been living with him for almost a week and she had never seen the killer side of his personality. There had been so many opportunities to kill her. Mac could have slipped poison in her coffee that first night at his house, stabbed her with a knife as she'd prepared dinner in his kitchen, strangled her as she'd slept so trustingly in his arms. But he hadn't. He wouldn't. Mac loved her. He was no killer. Mac couldn't kill anyone! Unless he were truly insane . . .

Debra shivered and reached for her sweater. The thermometer on the wall registered seventy-five degrees, but she was cold with fear. Which man should she trust? Who was telling the truth?

Gusts of wind blew so hard they rattled her windowpane. The old brick building seemed to shudder under the force of the storm. Snow whipped in icy sheets against the glass as Debra peered out anxiously. She could barely see the street.

Who would arrive first—Dr. Elias or Mac? And which one would she let into the apartment? She had to make up her mind soon. One of them could pull up at any second.

A Yellow Cab came around the corner and slowed to a stop outside her apartment building. Debra's breath caught in her throat as the driver got out and opened the rear door. Dr. Elias was here!

He looked old and frail as he got out of the cab. Debra's heart went out to him. She had placed her life in his hands four years ago and today was no different. Of course she trusted him.

His steps faltered a bit as he walked up the sidewalk. Tears came to Debra's eyes. Dr. Elias was dying. How could she have doubted him?

Debra swallowed past the lump in her throat. She heard the elevator rising. In a moment he would be knocking at her door. She had to let him in.

The elevator doors opened. Slow footsteps came down the carpeted hallway. Debra pictured him standing there, alone and desperately ill, outside her door.

The buzzer rang and she jumped, even though she was expecting it. Her heart pounded loudly in her chest as she hurried to the door and put her hand on the safety chain to release it.

Debra hesitated, her fingers on the chain. She remembered the love in Mac's eyes, the gentle way he had brushed back her hair and kissed her. He *couldn't* be the killer!

She left the chain in place and opened the door a crack. "Debra? It's Dr. Elias. Let me in, dear."

His words had the same authority as always. He expected her to open the door. It was very difficult for her to resist.

"I . . . I can't, Dr. Elias. Mac called. He'll be here any minute. I promised him I wouldn't unlock the door for anyone."

There was a long silence. When Dr. Elias spoke again his voice was filled with sympathy. "I understand, dear. It's only natural that Mac would try to trick you. Did he attempt to convince you that I was the killer?"

"Yes."

Debra could feel her resolve start to weaken. His voice was so kind, so understanding. She felt like a child, denying her father. Dr. Elias loved her. It was there in his voice.

"Debra, dear. Poor Mac is very ill. He can't consciously accept the responsibility for what he's done, so he's built up a highly systematized pattern of delusions. Now let me in, Debra. We must help Mac while there's still time."

Debra reached for the chain again. It all made perfect sense. She wanted to do what was best for Mac. She loved him.

Something more powerful than logic stopped her hand. She had promised Mac. It didn't matter whether

Dr. Elias was right or wrong. She would not let him into her apartment.

"No!"

Debra jumped back as the door rattled on the end of the chain. He was trying to break in. Mac was right! Dr. Elias was here to kill her!

She whirled and ran to the bedroom. There was no lock on the bedroom door and Debra tugged at the heavy dresser against the wall. Her desperation lent her strength and she managed to shove it over in front of the door. If Dr. Elias tried to get in the bedroom, she'd shoot him.

Debra's knees turned weak as she realized that she had left her purse on the table in the living room. The gun Mac had given her was inside. What if Dr. Elias got past her barricade?

The fire escape! Debra ran to the window and shoved with all her might. It was stuck! There was the sound of wood splintering from the living room. Dr. Elias was breaking in. She had to get out the window!

She shoved again desperately and the window flew up. Debra grasped the icy sill with her bare hands and climbed out on the slatted metal stairs. She knew she couldn't look down. Heights terrified her. Debra stared at her feet, at the pink fuzzy toes of the slippers she wore in the apartment, and climbed down as fast as she could.

The fire escape was narrow and Debra hung on to the metal railing with both hands. Eighteen steps down to the landing on the third floor. Another eighteen steps and she was on the second-floor landing. She had to be very careful not to slip. Her feet were already so numb from the cold that she could not feel her toes. Only one flight to go. The wind whipped at her fiercely and needles of icy snow stung her face as she climbed down to the first-floor landing.

She knelt on the cold metal slats to tug at the ladder designed to drop down to the ground. Her fingers were so cold she could barely grip the handle. Debra pulled and shoved until her knuckles were bleeding, but the ladder was frozen solid. She was trapped!

Debra stared down at the ground and shuddered. It was too far to jump. She turned and climbed back up. There was a bedroom window on each landing. She pounded her fists against the glass on the first floor. Someone had to be home.

She hammered at the window so hard she thought it would surely break, but the double-paned glass resisted her blows. Why didn't Mrs. Chambers hear her?

Mrs. Chambers was gone. Debra gave a sob as she remembered her landlady's bridge club. She had to try the window on the second floor. There was nowhere to go but up.

Debra scrambled up the metal stairs again. Her fingers were burning from the cold. She reached the second-floor landing and shuddered as she looked in the window. There were dust covers on the bedroom furniture. The Nelsons had left town for the holidays.

The third floor. It was her last chance. Debra stumbled as she ran up the stairs. She caught herself awkwardly and rushed on.

The third-floor window was thick with ice. Debra's hands were numb as she pounded frantically. No one was home. She was alone on the fire escape and no one was home!

Debra shivered as the wind whipped past her. The roof. She could hide on the roof, but first she had to pass her floor. Dr. Elias could be waiting for her just inside the open window. She had to take the chance. She couldn't stay on the fire escape, trapped between floors.

Her legs were so numb they felt like blocks of ice. Debra drew in her breath sharply as she climbed past her window. The dresser was moving! Dr. Elias was coming!

Thank God the fire escape went all the way to the roof! Debra scrambled up onto the asphalt and sobbed as the wind blew gusts of icy snow against her face. She had to find a protected place to hide. It was bitter cold and she would freeze to death up here in the open.

There was a small shed on one side of the flat roof that housed the building's physical plant. Debra stumbled toward it and tried the door. Locked. She huddled against the side away from the wind and pulled her sweater tightly around her shoulders. Her teeth chattered with the cold.

Perhaps Dr. Elias would think she'd jumped to the ground. The blowing snow would cover her tracks on the fire escape. She had to be very quiet and hide until Mac found her. He should be here any minute. Debra closed her eyes against the bitter wind and prayed for Mac to save her.

CHAPTER 30

Dr. Elias took in the open window at a glance. Debra had gone out on the fire escape. He crossed the room to the window and leaned out. The ladder at the base of the fire escape was still in the storage position. He had the advantage of knowing his patient's fears, and Dr. Elias was certain that Debra's acrophobia would render her incapable of jumping the last fifteen feet to the ground.

That left one simple conclusion. Debra had gone up to the roof. Dr. Elias shook his head sadly. She was making this very difficult. Because of Debra's resistance, he was forced to climb the fire escape and trap her on the roof. Dr. Elias removed the handgun from his briefcase and slipped it in his coat pocket. No one would hear the shot in the storm.

He hesitated a moment and then took the one remaining syringe out of his briefcase. The trip to Riverside Estates and the effort of breaking into Debra's apartment had exhausted him. He needed another injection. It would be disastrous if he faltered now.

After he had injected the narcotic, he sat on the windowsill and swung his legs out the window. A moment later he was standing on the fire escape landing. There was a smile on his face as he climbed up the metal stairs. Debra was waiting for him on the roof and the drug flowed through his veins, giving him the necessary relief he needed to finish her therapy.

"Where are you, Debra? Come out in the open, dear. I know what's best for you." Debra shuddered as the wind blew his words to her ears. Dr. Elias was coming up the fire escape! "Come here, Debra."

His voice was closer. He was on the roof. Debra bit her lip so hard she tasted blood. Where was Mac?

Then she heard it, the thin high wail of a siren turning on her street. The sound cut off abruptly below her. Mac was coming!

Debra held her breath until she heard the car door slam. She had to let Mac know where she was.

"MAC!" She screamed at the top of her lungs. "THE ROOF! MAC!"

Strong arms clamped around her as she struggled to rise. Dr. Elias had found her. Debra trembled in fear as she saw the gun in his hand. There was cold madness in his eyes.

"That was perfect, my dear." Dr. Elias's lips turned up in a bitter smile. "Now all we have to do is wait for the last member of our group."

Debra twisted frantically, but Dr. Elias's arm was like a steel vise around her waist. Mac was coming. She could hear his heavy steps on the fire escape. She had to warn him! Mac was climbing to a certain death!

"GO BACK! HE'S GOT A GUN!"

Dr. Elias's hand clamped over her mouth. Debra tried to break free, but his hold was too tight. It seemed impossible that a dying man could have so much strength. If only Mac had heard her!

"Come up alone, Mac! I've got Debra!" Dr. Elias's voice carried clearly through the sound of the howling wind.

Debra's legs would no longer support her as Dr. Elias pulled her out into the open to face the fire escape. She sobbed in fear and he turned to look at her coldly. Then he smiled. It was the arrogant, condescending smile of a madman. Debra shuddered in horror as they stared out at the blowing snow and waited for Mac.

"Drop it, Dr. Elias!"

Debra screamed. It was Mac! He had circled around the ledge at the top of the building to come up behind them.

Dr. Elias smiled as he whirled her around to face Mac. It was a smile of derision, of triumph. He knew Mac's weaknesses.

"There's no need to pretend with me, Mac. I know you can't use a gun."

Mac shivered at the cold judgment in Dr. Elias's voice. It brought back memories of countless therapy sessions where he had been the hotheaded, emotional one and Dr. Elias had been the voice of pure reason. Dr. Elias must be right. He had always been right. It took every ounce of courage Mac had to continue the bluff.

"You're making a mistake, Dr. Elias." Mac moved a step closer.

"All right then, Mac. Let's put it to the test."

Dr. Elias was smiling as he raised his gun and pointed it directly at Debra's head.

"In ten seconds I will fire this gun. You can stop me

by shooting me first. Perhaps that would be better for all of us. A quick, easy death for me, and life for the woman you love. That's quite a reward for one simple act, don't you think?"

Dr. Elias's smile vanished as quickly as it had appeared. He stared at Mac with cold, calculating eyes.

"Then there's the alternative. If you fail, you will watch Debra die. And then I'll kill you, of course. It's a simple equation, Mac. Two lives for one. All you have to do is pull that trigger!"

Mac felt his resolve falter as he faced his former therapist. Dr. Elias was so sure. Then he saw Debra's frightened face and everything changed.

"Well, Mac?"

The expression on Dr. Elias's face altered slightly as Mac's hand steadied. There was a hint of uncertainty that grew to shocked realization as Mac's finger tightened on the trigger.

Mac aimed carefully. Then he took a deep breath and pulled the trigger. For Debra. For himself. For the group.

EPILOGUE

One Year Later

Mac sat in the leather recliner Debbie had given him for his birthday and a peaceful look settled over his face. He was content. Actually, he was more than content. There was a cheerful blaze in the fireplace, soft strains of Christmas music were playing on the stereo, and he could hear Debbie in the kitchen, singing along with *Silent Night*. She missed the high note, but that was okay. The important thing was that she sounded just as happy and content as he was.

An incredibly delicious aroma was coming from the kitchen and Mac got up to track it down like Winnie the Pooh on the trail of a honey pot. He found Debbie, looking completely adorable in the chef's apron he'd given her, taking a large roasting pan out of the oven.

"That roast looks incredible, Debbie!" Mac started to salivate as he eyed the beautifully browned piece of meat.

Debbie set the roast on top of the stove and turned around to smile at him. "Thanks. It's a standing rib roast. I wanted to make something special tonight. Jackie and Roy don't get out much now that the baby is starting to walk. Jackie says Chrissie needs constant watching or she gets into things."

"But Jackie's still working at the paper, isn't she?"

"Yes, but only part time. Roy's mother comes over to watch Chrissie when Jackie has an assignment."

Mac watched while Debbie basted the roast and slid it back into the oven. "I don't know if I can wait until dinner. My stomach's growling."

"There's a bowl of mixed nuts on the end table by your chair. Have some of those, but don't spoil your dinner. Jackie's bringing an appetizer, something with shrimp, and Marge is bringing a vegetable casserole. I'm making mixed rice with mushrooms and the roast, but just wait until Barb gets here with the dessert."

"Knowing Barb it'll be something spectacular. Which country did she use this time?"

"France. She said it was something with three kinds of chocolate."

Mac grinned. This was the first real dinner party they'd hosted, but Debbie didn't seem that nervous even though she was cooking for eight. He liked the way Debbie had become fast friends with Barbara Gunderson. Every once in a while the two women would drag them off to a concert or the opening of an art gallery, and every so often Mac and Fritz would drag them off to a sports event. "Is there anything I can do to help you?" Mac asked.

"Not really, but thanks for offering. I had today off, remember? I didn't want to just sit here and think, so I got almost everything done ahead of time."

For a moment Mac was puzzled. Then he remembered. It was exactly one year ago to the day that Dr.

Elias had tried to kill them. "You didn't want to think about him," he said and then he wished that he could call the words back.

"That's right. I was afraid that if I thought about him, it would depress me. But the funny thing is . . . it didn't depress me at all. I remembered how he tried to kill us, but I also remembered how you saved me. And then I thought about how much I love you and how happy I am." Debbie paused and frowned slightly. "How about you? Did you think about Dr. Elias?"

"Yes, but it didn't depress me, either. He *was* a good therapist before he went off the deep end. And I never would have met you if I hadn't joined the group."

"That's true."

Debbie gave him a loving smile and Mac knew that this was the moment. He'd been carrying the ring around for almost a week, trying to decide when to give it to her. He'd almost decided on Christmas Eve, but now would be better. Now would be perfect.

"Debbie?" he said, pulling the ring box out of his pocket.

"Yes?"

She turned to look at him and he knelt down next to her and opened the velvet box. "I love you, Debbie. Will you marry me?"

"Yes!"

There was no hesitation on Debbie's part and Mac wore a happy smile as he rose to his feet to slip the ring on her finger. "Merry Christmas, darling," he said, kissing her deeply.

"And many more just like this," Debbie answered, pulling him down for another kiss.

Please turn the page for an exciting sneak peek of

Joanne Fluke's

FATAL IDENTITY

coming soon from Kensington Publishing!

PROLOGUE

He knew he'd lived in a house once, but it hadn't been as big as this mansion in Mandeville Canyon. Although he couldn't remember it, he'd had a mother and a father, and maybe even a dog. The Red Lady had told him that once, when she was having one of her good days.

He remembered that day very clearly. It had been the best day of his life. Miss Razel had given him a box of new pencils for his birthday, with his name stamped on them in gold letters. There were twelve pencils in pretty bright colors. Three orange, three green, three blue, and three yellow. He'd counted them out for Miss Razel and she'd said, *Very good, Jimmy.* And then she'd hugged him and told him that he was a very good student, the best she'd ever had in kindergarten.

The flat box of pencils had rattled under his shirt, and there had been an unaccustomed smile on his face as he'd run all the way back to the apartment building. He'd pulled open the door to the dark, cramped little lobby with its row of broken mailboxes, and his smile had abruptly disappeared. The Red Lady was waiting for him upstairs, and he had to be very careful. He never knew which one she'd be. The one who slept on the rumpled bed in the red room with her mouth slightly open to let out the snores, the one who sat at the table and smiled and told him how much she loved him, or the one who grabbed him roughly and made him do nasty things with one of the Uncles because he was a bad boy who needed to be punished.

As he tiptoed up the creaky wooden steps that led to the fourth floor, he put on the mask he wore for her. It was a good mask, and it had saved him from her punishment several times in the past. He wore it so she wouldn't learn how much she hurt him.

His eyes were downcast, so she couldn't read his expression and call him a rude little bastard. His head was bowed in an attitude of respect. His expression was carefully blank, like the glass-eyed face of the teddy bear Miss Razel had on the shelf in their classroom. It was a look of impassive surrender to the things over which he had no control.

It was a lot like the reading contents in school. If you could read the word, Miss Razel let you go out for recess early. But if you missed your word, Miss Razel gave you another and another, until you got one right. It wasn't fair to compare her to Miss Razel, but he'd learned the whole thing was very similar. If he got the mask right, the Red Lady hit him once or twice, and then she gave up and let him go. But if he whimpered or started to cry, she hit him again and again, until he was perfectly quiet.

When he reached the second-floor landing, he stepped around an old drunk sleeping off the effects of the bottle in the brown paper bag he still clutched in his hand. The landing smelled bad, a combination of human waste and breath wheezing past rotten teeth. As he started up the stairs, they creaked loudly. The drunk woke up and reached out for him, but he was young and fast and he scrambled up the stairs as fast as he could.

There was garbage on the stairs, and he held his breath as he hurried past. Flies crawling over something that looked like dog food. The Red Lady had told him that some of the people who lived here ate dog food. It was cheap and it kept them alive.

As he came to the top of the stairs, he bent down to pick up a piece of ripped cloth that was caught on the bannister. Then he took out his pencil box and stuffed in the cloth, so his pencils wouldn't rattle. If the Red Lady was having a bad day, she might break them all, especially if she guessed that he liked them. The first chance he got, he'd hide them under the loose board in the closet. The rats might find them, but that was better than watching her destroy the present Miss Razel had given him.

He stopped and felt his face to make sure his mask was in place. Then he took off the key he wore on a string around his neck, and opened the door very cautiously. She was up, sitting at the table, her back to him. Before he could say anything at all, she turned. There was a smile on her face, and she looked almost happy, but he still kept the mask in place. He'd seen her smile turn into a frown in the blink of an eye.

"Happy birthday!" Her smile was still in place. "Come over here, sweetie. I've got a present for you."

It still wasn't safe, so he approached very quietly in case she was having one of her bad days. But she hugged him and patted the chair next to her.

"Open it, sweetie." She handed him a heavy box

wrapped in silver paper with a big blue bow on top. "Uncle Bob picked out this present for you."

He couldn't help it. He started to smile. Uncle Bob was his favorite Uncle. He was older than the rest, and when he did the nasty thing in the red bedroom, he was always very gentle.

She held out her hand, and he took off the blue ribbon and handed it to her. She liked ribbons and she kept them. Then he loosened the tape and took off the paper, so she could use it again. There was a white box under the paper, and he was almost afraid to open it.

"Go ahead." She urged him. "Take off the cover."

The lid of the box was taped shut, and he slit the tape with his fingernail so it wouldn't tear. Then he lifted off the cover. His smile spread all the way across his face as he saw what was inside.

"Books!" He turned to her, almost afraid she'd say it was all a mistake and they weren't for him. But she just smiled.

"Uncle Bob thought you'd like them. They must be pretty old, because he said he read them all when he was a boy, and Uncle Bob's no spring chicken. Now listen to me, sweetie. You keep these books right here on the table. I want Uncle Bob to see you reading them."

He nodded. "I will. I promise."

"All right then." She smiled and opened one of the books. Her eyebrows lifted, and she started to frown as she handed him the open book. "These words are hard. Can you read them?"

"Sure." The moment he said it, he knew he'd made a big mistake, especially since she'd dropped out of school in the sixth grade, and she'd never learned to read very well. Now there was a frown on her face.

"Oh yeah, Mr. Smarty Pants? You'd better watch it, because I'm starting to see red!"

He looked up at her with a worried frown on his face. He had to eat his words fast, or she'd start having a bad day and punish him.

"These really *are* big words!" He looked properly contrite. "Could I ask Uncle Bob if I don't know some? That way he'll know I'm reading his books."

It took her a minute, and then she clapped her hands and smiled again. "You're a smart little boy! Every time Uncle Bob is here, you ask him about a word. He used to be a teacher, you know. If he thinks he's helping you, he'll come to see us more often. And that'll mean more money for us."

"Okay." He nodded. "Shall I pick out a word right now?"

She shook her head. "No hurry. Uncle Bob isn't coming back until later, and then we're gonna have us a little party. Now open this."

He tore his eyes away from the box of wonderful books and took the small envelope she handed him. "What is it?"

"It came with you, and I saved it for you. I think it belonged to your mother."

His hands were shaking as he opened the envelope. Inside was a picture of a young woman, all dressed up in a long white dress. She had a halo of beautiful blond hair around her face, and her lips were curved up in a gentle smile. She was standing in front of a white house with green trim around the windows, and she was holding a bouquet of flowers. There was a dog at her feet, a small dog with a happy face, and he could see the shadow of the man taking the picture. His father?

"Is that . . . her?" His breath caught in a painful sob.

She looked like an angel, and he wished she were here right now. His mother looked kind and sweet, almost like Miss Razel, except much prettier.

She shrugged. "I guess so. I told you, it came with you, so it's gotta be her. I bet you think she's pretty, huh?"

Something in the way she said it, made the hair on the back of his neck bristle a warning. Careful. He had to be very careful. A line from a cop show he'd seen on Miss Gladys's television flew through his mind. *Anything you say can and will be used against you.*

"Her hair's white." He looked down at the picture again. "Was she real old?"

That made her laugh, and he breathed a sigh of relief. He'd done the right thing. He didn't know why, but she was jealous of that picture.

"No, she's young. Her hair's just bleached out real white. And see those flowers she's carrying? That must have been her wedding picture. And you see the shadow in front of her?"

He looked down at the picture again and nodded. "I see it."

"It's a man's shadow, so maybe it's your father. Somebody had to take the picture, right?"

He nodded and did his best to look impressed. "That's right! I never thought of that!"

"I'd make a pretty good detective, huh?" She grinned at him as he nodded. "I think that was their house. You can almost make out the name on the mailbox. It's kind of fuzzy, but their last name starts with a B, and it's got seven letters, just like yours."

This time he was really impressed. "You really know a lot, Aunt Neecie! I wish I could be as smart as you."

A quick smile spread over her face, and for just a

moment, she looked almost pretty. She reached out to ruffle his hair, and he was careful not to flinch. This was a good day, not a bad day, and he wanted to keep it that way.

"Okay. So now you've got the picture. And don't go asking me questions. All I know is they found you in a basket in front of the place, and that picture was tucked inside your blanket. Now, why don't you—" She stopped suddenly, and reached in her pocket to pull out a flat, tissue-wrapped packet. "I almost forgot. Here's my present. It's old, but I can't afford to buy you new."

"Thank you, Aunt Neecie." He took the packet and unfolded the tissue paper. Inside was a thick silver chain. Why would she give him a silver chain? His mind sifted through the possibilities, but he couldn't come up with a thing.

"Well?" She was frowning slightly, and he put on a delighted smile. "Wow! It's . . . it's wonderful, Aunt Neecie!"

"You bet it is!" She smiled. "Old Roy gave that to me, when we got married. 'Course you don't remember your Uncle Roy, do you? He died when you were just a baby."

"I think I remember him." The truth was, he didn't remember Uncle Roy at all, but he said what she wanted to hear. According to her, Uncle Roy had been a saint. And since he'd lost a leg in a train accident, they'd had his disability check every month. When Uncle Roy died, the checks had stopped coming, and she'd sold everything to pay the bills. That was when they'd gone on welfare and moved to this old apartment building.

"You can keep your key on that chain." She smiled at him. "Then you can't lose it. Now you go pick out a couple of big words and write them down, so you can ask Uncle Bob. He's bringing Chink food for our party.

And after we eat, you'll make him feel real good about that present he gave you, won't you?"

He nodded. It was what she expected, and it wouldn't do any good to tell her that he didn't want to do the nasty thing in the red bedroom anymore.

"You like to help me with the Uncles, don't you, sweetie?"

He'd nodded again, because he'd learned that it was the smart choice. If he told her that he hated what the Uncles did to him, she'd beat him. And then she'd tie him to the bed in the red room, so Uncle Bob could do it anyway. But if he wore the mask and agreed with everything she said, he could avoid the beating. Of course, there was no way to prevent what the Uncles did to him. It was a part of his life, like breathing.

"I'm going out for a pack of smokes." She picked up her purse and headed for the door. "You stay right here and don't you make any noise, you hear?"

The moment she was gone, he picked up one of the books and started to read. It was all about two boys who lived in an orphanage. Orphanage was a good word to ask Uncle Bob. It was nine letters long, and no one would expect him to know it.

There was a smile on his face as his eyes skimmed the words, following the story. These books were old, but they were still good. He would be able to live in a wonderful, storybook world for as long as they lasted. And then he could start reading them all over again. It was very good of Uncle Bob to give him these books. Now he'd have something interesting to think about when he was alone in the red bedroom with the Uncles.

* * *

He came back to the present with a jolt, as he heard the glass door to the patio slide open. He parted some of the dense leaves in the hedge bordering the side of the pool, and peered out anxiously. It was only the housekeeper. She had a broom in her hand and she was going to sweep off the patio, as she did every night.

He liked the housekeeper. She was always friendly, and she took good care of the children. She thought she knew him, but all she really knew was the mask. They thought they were locking him out with the new security system, but he could get inside the gates anytime he wished. And they'd never guessed that most of the time he was here already. It was like the Red Lady used to say, there was always a way around everything, if you used your head. Of course, she wasn't saying anything now. Now her mouth was closed forever.

He could feel the red mist threaten as he thought of that night, and he pushed it away. Not now. He had to be alert. The housekeeper was sweeping back and forth with hard, even strokes of the broom. It reminded him of something that made him shiver, but he pushed that out of his mind, too.

He felt the hair on the back of his neck prickle, as a voice called out from the house. Not one of her children. And not the husband, either. This was a different voice, a voice that made him ache inside with its hauntingly familiar tone.

And then he saw her, and his breath caught in his throat. She was wearing a white bathing suit, and she looked like a swan, all sleek and glossy and graceful. Or perhaps she was an angel. Her beauty was pure and immaculate. He felt his hands began to tremble uncontrollably, as she stepped into the light by the pool.

She was going to swim, and he loved to watch her swim.

The warm feeling rushed through him as she slipped into the water. Ah! How beautiful! How lovely her arms were as they rose up and down in the water, stark white columns of curving beauty that cut through the dark surface to reemerge again for the next stroke. Her long, shapely neck arched out of the water, and her glorious blond hair gleamed in the moonlight, even though she'd piled it high on her head in a shining knot. She was supple and strong, like a young sapling, but as delicate as a piece of fine lace. She was Homer's Helen of Troy, and Poe's Lenore, and Sir Lancelot's Lady of the Lake. She was the only woman he had ever loved. She was Jimmy's lost mother, and he wouldn't let her leave him again.

But there was something wrong, a hateful red color spilling out from the garden just beyond the pool. Red blossoms like the blood that had bubbled and bloomed from Aunt Neecie's mouth. He had to stop it before it spilled out and covered him.

The red mist began to swirl around his feet, rising, rising. He had to move quickly, before it was too late. He stepped out very softly, very quietly, to do what had to be done. Around the pool, behind the hedge of lush green boxwoods without a rustle. Like a cat in the dead of night, he moved without hesitation. And then he dropped to his knees on the soft earth by the bubbling blossoms. And he whimpered as he plucked them off one by one, crushing the petals between his fingers and feeling them die.

Her head turned in his direction. It seemed as if she were looking directly at him with her beautiful green eyes. But he knew that was only an illusion. She saw only a shadow, heard only a faint rustle. A neighbor's cat in the garden, a fierce night prowler stalking his blood prey. Her head rose out of the water, watching, listening. But he was as still as death.

And then she began to swim again, her fears laid to rest. As well they should be. He was here. And he would always protect her from the red.

Tears fell from his eyes, like warm spring rain. How he loved her! He had broken the rule to warn her, broken his vow of silence. He had chosen the words to tell her, cut them out of paper and pasted them to the letter he'd sent to her. *Red is the color of blood.*

He knew he had frightened her, and he was ashamed. But his words had done their work, and she had been wise enough to listen. She had changed her hateful red bedroom to a sea green place of beautiful peace.

The red mist was rising now, rising up to claim him. In a few moments it would reach his mind, and then there would be a merciful darkness. But there was work to be done before he could rest.

He dropped to the ground, shredding the petals into thin strips that blew away in the winter wind. They would shrivel and fade, buffeted by the air until they turned to a harmless brown. Earth, air, fire, and water. They were the ancient elements. They had the power to destroy the red, to send it away forever.

At last he was finished, and he smiled as he got to his feet. It was his job to keep her safe. He was her guardian, her lover, her unseen protector. Only he knew how to save her from the certain destruction of the red.

CHAPTER 1

Even though she'd had a grueling day, Mercedes Calder flashed the driver one of her famous, million-watt smiles, as he helped her out of the studio limo. Her smile was totally genuine. Mercedes liked the new driver the studio had assigned to her. George never tried to make idle conversation on the twenty-minute trip to the studio, when she had lines to learn; he didn't mind stopping at the school to pick up her twins on the days she finished shooting early; and he was unfailingly prompt. Even though George was well paid by the studio, Mercedes planned to give him a generous bonus when they wrapped her film.

"Six-thirty tomorrow morning, George? I have an early call."

"No problem, Miss Calder. I'll be here. Do you want me to check out the house for you?"

Mercedes shook her head. "That's not necessary, George. They finally finished installing the security system. But thanks for asking. That was very thoughtful."

George tipped his hat and slid back in, behind the wheel. He was a retired policeman who looked like a fullback, over six feet tall with the muscular body and lightning reflexes of a professional athlete. He'd told Mercedes he'd taken his early retirement option when he'd been shot chasing down a murder suspect. He'd known they were planning to kick him upstairs, and he hadn't liked the idea of sitting behind a desk all day. Early retirement pay wasn't all that much, and George had done private detective work for a year or two. Then he'd landed this job with the studio as a combination bodyguard and driver.

Although the studio had dismissed Mercedes's threatening letters as a crazy prank by an unstable fan, they'd immediately assigned George to be her driver. And it had worked, as far as Mercedes was concerned. She never worried when George was around. He was more than capable of defending her, and when she was with him, she felt safe. At least there hadn't been any threatening letters today. Mercedes had checked the mailbox at the end of the driveway, when they'd stopped at the gates. She hoped that her ordeal was over, that her crazy fan was locked up tight in some mental hospital or jail.

Mercedes still shivered when she thought about the letters that had come in the mail. The words had been cut out of magazines, and pasted on pieces of plain notebook paper. The whole thing had sounded like something you'd see in a bad B-movie, but the message had been chilling.

Most stars got an occasional letter from a crazy fan. It was so common, it was almost normal. Ashley Thorpe, her costar in *Summer Heat,* had told Mercedes about the proposal he'd received from a seventy-year-old widow, who'd offered her life savings if he'd spend the night with her. And Sandra Shepard, the character actress who played her mother in the movie, had mentioned a letter she'd received last year from a high school student in Iowa, inviting her to be his date for the Senior Prom.

Mercedes had been in the "biz" for over fifteen years, and she'd shrugged off plenty of proposals and propositions from crazy fans before. But the letters she'd received two months ago were very different. They'd come to her home, instead of the studio.

The first letter had arrived on a Saturday, and Mercedes had been alone in the house. She'd been out at the pool, enjoying the warm rays of the sun, when she'd heard the distinctive squeaking brakes of the mailman's jeep. Since she usually got a letter from Marcie on Saturdays, she'd hopped into her car and driven down the long, winding driveway to pick up the mail.

Marcie's letter was there, and Mercedes had taken the time to read it. Then she'd noticed another letter marked "personal," with no return address, and she'd opened that as well.

I am watching you. I will always be near. Do not try to hide. You can keep nothing from me. I am with you at night when you swim in the pool. I am with you when you go to bed in the red room. Please do not sleep in the red room. Red is the color of blood.

The others will tell you lies about me, but I am not what they say. Do not try to escape me. I will not let you leave me again. You will be with me always, even in death.

Jimmy

Mercedes's hands had been shaking as she'd finished reading the letter. He knew her bedroom was red! He really *was* watching her! She'd jumped back into her car, locked all the doors, and peered out of the window in fright. The grounds seemed peaceful enough, but was he was out there somewhere, taking vicious pleasure in her fear? Her instinct had been to race for the house, but she'd left it unlocked, and he could be waiting for her inside!

Pure panic had propelled her as she'd turned on the ignition and put her car in gear. She had to get away! But where should she go? What should she do? She'd made a quick V-turn, tires sliding on the gravel, and headed down Mandeville Canyon Road.

She'd glanced nervously in the rearview mirror, but no one had seemed to be following her. She was safe. For now. As she'd turned on Sunset Boulevard, she'd suddenly remembered the interview she'd done for a popular fan magazine. It had mentioned her exercise regime, twenty laps in the pool every night, and there had been several photos of her in her newly redecorated bedroom. If he'd seen a copy of that article, he would have known about the swimming and the color scheme of her bedroom. Perhaps he wasn't watching her after all.

With each mile Mercedes traveled away from the house, she'd felt a little calmer. She knew that most people who wrote threatening letters never dreamed of actually carrying out their threats. This man was probably nothing more than a harmless neurotic, who got his kicks by scaring people. Still, it couldn't hurt to take a few precautions, like buying a hand gun and learning how to use it. And while she was at it, she'd order a new security system. The one she had was over ten years old.

It turned out that buying a handgun in California was a frustrating experience. Although her life had been threatened, and she had a legitimate reason for wanting to arm herself, there was still a mandatory fifteen-day waiting period before she could take her new Lady Smith revolver home. Rules were rules in California, where the anti-gun lobby was strong. Crooks could buy guns immediately through illegal means, but honest citizens had to wait and hope that they'd still be alive at the end of the waiting period.

Mercedes had walked away from the gun store shaking her head. She was probably overreacting, but she had to take precautions, just in case. She'd stopped to call a home security service, and she'd hired an armed guard to patrol the grounds, until her new state-of-the-art security system was installed. Then she'd arranged to have her room redecorated in a lovely shade of sea green. That would please Brad. Green was his favorite color. Brad hadn't liked her red bedroom. He said it was like sleeping inside a catsup bottle, and she'd been planning on changing the color scheme anyway.

That night, when Brad had come home and found the security guard, he'd told her he thought she'd done exactly the right thing. The letter *was* scary. And while it was true that Mercedes probably wouldn't hear from this particular man again, she was a big star, and there were lots of crazy fans out there. Then he'd hugged her and told her he wished he could always be home to protect her. Unfortunately, his investment business demanded a lot of traveling. He'd certainly rest much easier after the new security system was installed. It would give him peace of mind, knowing that Mercedes and the twins were safe, behind locked gates.

The second threatening letter had arrived a week later. Luckily, the security guard was on duty when Mercedes had taken it out of the envelope, and she hadn't panicked. Her crazy fan was still out there, but at least she now knew what he wanted.

I am still with you, watching and waiting. No one can protect you. You must do exactly as I say.

Give your husband twenty thousand dollars in a backpack. Tell him to go to the phone booth on the corner of Sunset and Gower at noon tomorrow. I will call him and tell him where to leave the money.

I love you. You belong to me. I have no wish to cause you pain.

Jimmy

When Brad had read the letter, he'd urged her to call the police. Naturally, Mercedes had refused. The police could do nothing, and there were bound to be leaks to the press. The studio wouldn't like that kind of publicity, and this whole thing was probably just a crazy prank.

Exactly a week later, the third letter had arrived. It was almost identical to the second, except that the sum of money had doubled, and there was one additional postscript after the signature. *Your security guard cannot protect you. If you continue to ignore me, perhaps your death will not be as merciful as I planned.*

When Brad read the letter, he was convinced that they had to take action. While he agreed that he didn't believe in giving way to threats, he'd suggested that perhaps they should pretend to do what the crazy fan wanted. He'd go to the phone booth, get the instructions, and deliver the money himself. And then he'd stake out the area and catch the nut case, when he came to pick it up.

Mercedes had vetoed that idea immediately. There was no way she'd let him do something that dangerous. But Brad was insistent. He was her husband, and he wanted to protect her. There was no way he'd let a crazy fan get away with threatening his wife!

They'd argued about it long into the night, but Mercedes had been firm. She wouldn't let Brad put himself in danger, and she wouldn't even pretend to give way to blackmail. Brad knew how blackmail worked. If the crazy fan actually succeeded in getting the money, he'd keep right on sending threatening letters, demanding more and more cash. It was best to take a strong stand in the beginning, and not give in to this type of extortion.

Even though Mercedes had shrugged off the threats, she was concerned enough to take the letters with her to the studio the next morning. The studio hired experts to deal with crank letters from crazy fans, and Mercedes had asked their advice. They'd agreed that she had done all the right things to protect herself. They'd said not to worry, that they'd dealt with hundreds of extortion letters, and nothing had ever happened. It would have been an entirely different matter if someone had come up to her face-to-face and made these kinds of demands. But no one had, and chances were her crazy fan was already back in a mental institution or a jail cell.

Mercedes felt much better after she'd talked to the studio experts, especially since they'd assigned George to be her driver. George was armed and he was formidable. There was no way anyone would bother her, while she was under his protection.

After she'd finished work for the day, Mercedes had asked George to drive her to the gun store. She'd picked up her handgun, and bought a gun safe that only opened if she pressed a series of coded buttons. George had installed it for her, and that weekend he'd driven her to a firearms safety class, where she'd learned how to use her Lady Smith with deadly accuracy.

Of course, Mercedes hadn't mentioned any of this to Brad. And she'd decided not to tell him if she got another threatening letter. Brad might do something brave and foolish, like trying to catch the blackmailer himself.

The letters had definitely changed Mercedes's life. Opening the mail had always been fun for her, but now she dreaded it. She held her breath every time she picked up the neat stack of letters her postman slipped in the box. It had been almost a month since the last threatening letter, and she was almost convinced that her crazy fan had given up. But even though their new security system was up and running, George had told her to carry her handgun from room to room, whenever she was alone in the house.

"Are you sure you're all right, Miss Calder?"

George looked concerned, and Mercedes nodded. "I'm fine. See you in the morning, George."

Mercedes waved as the limo drove off. The moment the gates had opened and closed again, she reactivated the alarm system. There was no way anyone could open the gates without the code. And if anyone tried to climb over the bars or force his way in, a patrol of armed security guards would be on the grounds in less than five minutes.

The alarm on the front door was set, and Mercedes punched in the code on the numbered panel. The advisor from the security company had cautioned her against using her birthday as a code. That was a matter of public record. Brad had suggested they use their anniversary instead, and he'd joked that it was one way to make sure she never forgot the date. As if she could!

As she opened the door and walked across the tile foyer, Mercedes caught sight of her reflection in the gold-framed, oval mirror on the wall. She'd never considered herself beautiful, although everyone else seemed to think she was. Green-eyed blondes weren't all that unusual in her home state of Minnesota.

When Mercedes had landed her first movie role, the studio publicity department had called her a cross between Doris Day and Marilyn Monroe. The comparison had made Mercedes laugh. Doris had been bubbly and innocent, while Marilyn had exuded sex from every pore. Mercedes knew she wasn't bubbly and innocent, or super sexy. She was just an ordinary actress, who worked hard to learn to play any role she was offered.

At first Mercedes had played the fun-loving teenager, the cheerleader who fell in love with the quarterback on the football team. Then she'd graduated to college roles, playing the young freshman coed who fell in love the professor. From there she'd played the young professional who fell in love with her boss. She was always falling in love and ending up happy, the essence of the female romantic lead. Finally, she was mature enough to play other, more demanding parts, but her latest role in *Summer Heat* was the biggest challenge she'd ever faced.

Summer Heat was a story of deception, of a marriage gone awry. Mercedes played the victim, a wife whose husband was slowly poisoning her, so that he could be free to marry his mistress. She had to be naively trusting and totally unsuspecting in the early part of the movie, a woman who was so in love with her new husband that she was completely blind to his faults. As the movie progressed, her character deepened and matured. The wife began to doubt her husband, and finally realized, in horror, that he was trying to kill her. At the end, Mercedes had to play a woman so crazed by her husband's duplicity, she exacted a terrible revenge.

Her role in *Summer Heat* wouldn't have been all that difficult, if it had been a play. Most plays were chronological, starting at the beginning and progressing in a straight line to their conclusion. But movies weren't like plays, although most people who weren't in the industry didn't realize that. Almost all of Mercedes's scenes were shot out of sequence.

The scene they'd done today had been near the end of the movie. Mercedes had played the vengeful wife, preparing to kill her husband and his mistress. Tomorrow they would shoot the park wedding at the very beginning of the movie, and that meant Mercedes had to jump back in time to play the trusting bride, meeting her husband's mistress for the first time, and being completely unaware of their relationship. It took mental preparation to jump back and forth like that, but it was more cost effective. Scenes that took place in the same setting were shot on the same day, regardless of where they occurred in the movie. Mercedes reread the script every night, starting at the beginning and stopping at the scene they'd shoot the next day. That helped her to get into the right frame of mind for the morning's work.

"Rosa? I'm home!" Mercedes walked down the hall and peeked into the immaculately clean kitchen. Her housekeeper wasn't there. She walked through the beautifully decorated rooms on the ground floor, but Rosa and the children were nowhere to be found.

Since she was still uneasy when she was alone in the house, Mercedes got her Lady Smith from the gun safe and carried it upstairs to her pretty sea green bedroom, where she undressed and slipped into a robe. She loved the new color she'd picked for her bedroom. It was very calming and restful. Then she sat down at her white wicker dressing table, and peered into the mirror to assess the damage after her long day of shooting. There were tiny lines at the corners of her eyes, but that wasn't surprising. She'd waited up for Brad to come home last night, despite her early call. Her green eyes were clear and bright, thanks to the eyedrops her makeup artist had applied, but her pale blond hair was wet with perspiration.

Mercedes walked to the huge mirrored bathroom and turned on the shower. She'd feel much better once she washed her hair and used some conditioner. She took off her robe and surveyed her body critically. Her skin was still tight, and her breasts were high and firm with no signs of sagging. Another week of dieting, and she'd be in better shape than she'd ever been in before. And she needed to be in perfect shape, since she would wear a bikini in the honeymoon beach scene.

As she stepped under the hot stream of water, Mercedes gave a weary sigh. She really didn't feel like swimming laps tonight but she knew she should. Physical fitness and a proper diet had kept her looking like she was in her twenties, when she was actually thirty-four.

When Mercedes emerged from the shower, fifteen minutes later, she felt refreshed. She changed to a warm-up suit that had been especially designed for her. Then she towel-dried her hair—the ends were beginning to split from having it blow-dried too often—and carried her Lady Smith downstairs with her. Perhaps she was being a little too paranoid, since the new security system was armed, but it did make her feel much safer.

Her first stop was the den, where she poured herself a glass of perfectly chilled chardonnay from her husband's new wine cooler. Brad was a wine connoisseur, and he had over two hundred labels in his temperature-controlled Euro-Cave. At least this hobby of his was useful, not like the racehorses that never won, or the antique cars that were stored in their specially designed warehouse garage.

The wine was delicious, a light, fruity vintage, and Mercedes smiled. A hundred and ten calories, she'd have to skimp on dinner, but it was worth it. Then she flopped down in the leather massage chair behind her husband's desk, and called the florist to order flowers for her hairdresser, who had just given birth to her first baby.

After five minutes in the massage chair, Mercedes felt rejuvenated. She took another sip of wine, picked up the phone again, and called the number for her voice mail.

The first message was from Brad. He wouldn't be home until late. There were harness races at the track tonight, and he wanted to check out some of their competition. By the time she got this message, he'd be at the stables with their horse trainer. Metro Golden Mare was having some problems, and they might have to scratch her in Sunday's race.

Mercedes frowned and tapped her pen on the message pad. Thoroughbreds were an expensive investment, and they weren't paying off. She'd wanted Brad to minimize their losses and sell out, but he'd convinced her to hang on for one more season. And now their prize racehorse was going to be scratched! When she'd married Brad two years ago, she'd thought that he was a shrewd businessman. But instead of increasing her capital, he'd reduced it considerably. It was a damn good thing she'd met with Sam Abrams, her lawyer, on the set today. She knew Brad would be upset at first, but he'd understand when she explained exactly why she'd hired another investment firm to handle the bulk of her assets. If he continued to funnel her money into risky ventures, there'd be nothing left for her twins!

When Mercedes pressed the button for her next message, her hand was shaking. She took another sip of wine and got ready for more bad news. But this message was from her housekeeper, and Rosa always made her smile. Rosamunda Szechenyi Kossuth was a welcome addition to the family. Mercedes knew she'd always be grateful to her first husband, for hiring Rosa to help out when the twins were born.

When Rosa had first come to work for them, there had been a language problem. Rosa spoke perfect English, but she had just emigrated from Hungary. Her accent was so thick, Mercedes had been unable to understand her. They'd solved the problem by calling in a friend, who made his living as a dialogue coach. After two months of speech lessons, three times a week, Rosa's accent had faded to only a faint trace.

Rosa had given Mercedes a worry-free decade. Mercedes's children were her children, and Rosa was a Super Mom. The twins would be ten years old next week, and Mercedes had planned a big party. What Rosa didn't know, was that the twins had a surprise for her. Mercedes had taken Trish and Rick to an expensive jewelry store, and they'd picked out a beautiful watch to give to Rosa. Mercedes had assured them that Rosa would love it. Of course, Rosa would love anything "her babies" gave her. Rosa's room was decorated in what Mercedes called Early Twin, with crayon drawings, framed finger-paint handprints, and dried flowers they'd picked for her in the garden.

Mercedes laughed as she played Rosa's message. She

could hear the twins in the background, urging her to please hurry. Rosa had left a message to say that she was taking the kids to an early movie, and they'd stop for a hamburger on the way home. Mr. Brad had insisted the kids needed a night out, and he'd given her money to spend. She'd prepared a chicken salad for Mercedes. It was in the refrigerator, along with a big pitcher of iced tea.

Mercedes sighed. Salad, again. A thinly sliced, skinless chicken breast on a bed of mixed greens with diet dressing. Three-hundred-and-fifty boring calories, but she had to lose another four pounds before they shot the bikini scene.

Thirty-four was a rotten age for an actress, too old to play the ingenue, and too young for "mature woman" roles. There weren't many parts written for actresses in their mid-thirties, and the competition was fierce. Her best hope for continued success was to stay in perfect shape.

Even though she tried not to think of it, Mercedes pictured Rosa and the twins in a green leather booth at Hamburger Hamlet, munching on thick, juicy burgers with crispy french fries. The twins would talk Rosa into ordering huge slices of chocolate cake with fudge sauce and ice cream for dessert. They always did. And Mercedes was stuck here with chicken salad! Or course, she couldn't have gone along, even if they'd waited for her to get home. She had script changes to memorize before tomorrow morning, and she couldn't afford to blow her diet.

Mercedes swallowed—her mouth was watering—and punched the button for her next message. It was a polite reminder from her dry cleaners, asking her to pay her last month's bill. She jotted down the information on a yellow sticky and placed it on the top of Brad's desk. Since she was so busy with her career, Brad handled the bills for all of their household expenses.

The fourth message was also about an overdue bill, the landscaping service, this time. Mercedes wrote out another yellow sticky and placed it next to the first. Brad had mentioned that they were having a slight cash-flow problem, but this was ridiculous! Perhaps he just hadn't gotten around to writing the checks yet.

The next message was a typical call from her sister. *"This is your twin sister, Marcie Calder, in Minnesota."*

Mercedes put the message on pause and laughed out loud. She only had one twin sister, and she knew where Marcie lived. But Marcie was shy, and she felt so uncomfortable about leaving a recorded message, that she always identified herself that way.

"I called to tell you that cousin Betty is getting married on Saturday. She's Aunt Bernice and Uncle Al's youngest daughter . . . the one who used to wet the bed when they came to visit? I'm not going, it's way up in Hibbing, and they're predicting snow for the weekend, but I'm sending a gift. I called to ask whether you want me to include your name on the card."

Mercedes frowned. She vaguely remembered cousin Betty, and knew that anything that Marcie picked out would be fine. Her sister was an art teacher, and she'd always had impeccable taste.

"I bought a beautiful pottery bowl at the college art sale, cerulean blue with pink and lavender blossoms that remind me of the ones in Cezanne's 'Vase of Flowers.' It was fifty-four dollars, which is a lot, but since it was the last day, the artist took ten dollars off. If I don't hear from you by tomorrow, I'll just add your name to the card and send it off."

Mercedes grinned. Thank goodness one of them was organized! She remembered receiving Betty's wedding invitation last week, but she'd tossed it aside and forgotten all about it. How could twin sisters be so different? They looked alike, tall with blond hair, green eyes, and light complexions. If they dressed alike, no one would be able to tell them apart. But they had totally different temperaments. Marcie was solid, dependable, and sweetly naive, while Mercedes was exactly the opposite. The only thing they had in common was their disappointing luck with men.

Mercedes had married Mike Lang, the producer of her first picture, the year after she'd arrived in California. It was a May-December marriage, Mike was thirty years her senior, but both of them had wanted children. Mercedes bad gotten pregnant almost immediately and delivered twin babies, a boy and a girl. They'd named them Patrick and Patricia, and they'd called them Rick and Trish. Both Mercedes and Mike had been delighted with their happy, healthy babies. But Mike had been a workaholic, and the stress of producing hit after hit had taken its toll. He died of a massive heart attack, when the twins were only two years old.

At first, Mercedes had thought she'd never love again. Then she'd hired Brad James as her investment counselor, and everything had changed. She'd married him at the high point of their whirlwind Hollywood courtship, and she was beginning to wonder if the old adage was true. She'd married in haste, and she was worried that she might repent in leisure. It seemed as if all the romance had gone out of their marriage. Brad was gone more often than he was home, and although she had no proof, she suspected that he was involved with someone else.

Marcie had suffered through a bout with a fickle lover, too. She'd fallen in love with a fellow art student, when she was in college. Mercedes had met him, he was handsome and very talented, but she had been worried that he was only using Marcie until someone else came along. As it turned out, she'd been right. The day after their graduation ceremony, Marcie's boyfriend had flown off to France with a wealthy widow, leaving Marcie with nothing but a note and a couple of his paintings.

"Oh, yes. I got the airplane tickets in the mail today, and I'll be there for the twin's birthday party. I can't believe they're ten years old already! But really, Mercy, I absolutely insist on reimbursing you. It makes me feel like a charity case when you pay for everything."

Mercedes grinned. Marcie was the only person who used her nickname. The Calder twins had been Mercy and Marcie all through high school, and Mercedes had hated it. Every time she'd complained, Marcie had told her she ought to be grateful their parents hadn't named them something even worse. They'd compiled a long list of names that made them shudder, like Patrice and Caprice, Mabel and Sable, Clarissa and Marissa, Edwina and Bettina, and the very worst, the one that had made them collapse in gales of laughter, Drusilla and Ludmilla.

"Guess I don't have any other news. Curtis Benson spilled green poster paint all over the tan leather shoes you gave me, but it came right out with a little saddle soap.

Give the twins a kiss for me and keep one for yourself. 'Bye."

Mercedes was still grinning as she wrote another yellow sticky for Brad, telling him to send Marcie a check for twenty-two dollars, her half of the wedding gift. A call from Marcie always cheered her up, and having her here for the birthday party would be wonderful.

The last message made Mercedes frown. Her agent and business manager, Jerry Palmer, wanted to discuss her next project over lunch tomorrow. But there wouldn't be a next project for Jerry. She'd already talked to someone else, and she was planning to switch to them right after *Summer Heat* was completed.

When she'd broken the news to Brad last night, they'd had a nasty fight. Jerry was Brad's friend, and she'd hired him on Brad's recommendation. They'd argued for hours, but finally Brad had agreed that she needed to go with someone who had more clout with the big boys. And that brought up another problem, one she needed to solve immediately.

Mercedes picked up the telephone and called Sam Abrams. He'd been her lawyer for almost a dozen years, and he was practically a member of the family. That gave her certain privileges other clients didn't enjoy, like access to his home telephone number.

It took only a moment to make sure that all her future earnings would go directly to Sam's office, and Mercedes was smiling as she hung up. By this time it was almost seven in the evening, and she was beginning to think much more kindly of Rosa's chicken salad. She'd swim twenty laps, treat herself to another glass of wine, and eat in the poolside cabana.

Since she'd already lost a total of ten pounds, none of her old bathing suits fit her new, svelte figure. She'd ordered more, twelve lovely, white suits that had been especially designed for her, but when she opened the drawer in the cabana, she found that the designer had made them in the wrong color. There were twelve new suits, but all of them were red.

Mercedes frowned as she remembered a line from the first threatening letter. *Red is the color of blood.* Her fingers trembled as she held up the suit, but she forced herself to remain calm. The crazy fan was long gone. And even if he wasn't gone, there was no way he could get past the sophisticated security system. She took another sip of wine to fortify herself, and slipped into the red bathing suit. She wasn't about to give up her exercise regime, because some looney objected to the color of her bathing suit!

There was a sound, and Mercedes froze. It sounded like the security gates were opening. Were they home already? She waited a moment, expecting to hear Rosa's station wagon, but there was no crunch of tires on the crushed rock driveway.

It took no more than a second for Mercedes to pick up her handgun. The solid weight of the tempered steel was comforting, and she held it tightly as she listened for any other alarming sounds. But everything was perfectly quiet.

Since her security system was new, and she wasn't quite used to relying on it, it took Mercedes a moment to remember to check the closed-circuit monitor. There was one in every room, including the cabana. When she switched it on, the camera showed that the gates were fully closed. The sound she'd heard must have come from the pool equipment, or perhaps her neighbor's gate had opened. Sound sometimes carried quite far in the canyon.

Mercedes felt a little prickle of fear as she stepped out of the cabana. Of course, there was no reason to be nervous. Her security system was armed. If anyone tried to get into the house, bells would clang, sirens would blare, and the police would be notified immediately. She was perfectly safe from any intruder.

She put her Lady Smith down at the side of the pool, and tested the water with her toe. The pool was warm, just the way she liked it, and Mercedes slid into the water. She'd learned to swim at an early age, like most kids who grew up in Minnesota. The Land of Ten Thousand Lakes had several within biking distance, and Mercedes and Marcie had spent practically the whole summer in the water. But the swimming season was short in Minnesota, barely two months long, Mercedes was glad she lived in California, where she could use the pool year round.

Mercedes used the Australian crawl for her first two laps. She was an excellent swimmer, and when they were teenagers, both she and Marcie had qualified as Red-Cross-certified Life Savers. When she'd moved to California, she'd actually taken a job as a lifeguard at Santa Monica Beach. It had paid for her acting lessons, and given her a great opportunity to get a tan. Then Mike had discovered her, and her dream had come true. She'd gone from her one-room, ramshackle apartment in Venice, to this gorgeous, twenty-room mansion in Mandeville Canyon.

She pushed off at the deep end and swam another lap, using the butterfly stroke. It was physically exhausting, lifting herself out of the water with her arms, and Mercedes was puffing by the time she finished. Time to change to something less rigorous, like the breast stroke. Two laps of that, and she switched to the side stroke for another three laps.

Free style was next, and Mercedes alternated between her favorite strokes for five more laps. She was